Lawful Lies

Book One
Justice For All Series

By
JL Redington

©JL Redington 2015

No part of this publication may be reproduced, or stored in a retrieval system, or transmitted in any form or by any means, electronic, mechanical, photocopying, recording or otherwise without written permission of the author.

Table Of Contents

Chapter One
Chapter Two
Chapter Three
Chapter Four
Chapter Five
Chapter Six
Chapter Seven
Chapter Eight
Chapter Nine
Chapter Ten
Chapter Eleven
Chapter Twelve
Chapter Thirteen
Chapter Fourteen
Chapter Fifteen
Chapter Sixteen
Chapter Seventeen
Chapter Eighteen
Chapter Nineteen
Chapter Twenty
Chapter Twenty-One
Chapter Twenty-Two
Chapter Twenty-Three
Chapter Twenty-Four
Chapter Twenty-Five
Chapter Twenty-Six
Chapter Twenty-Seven

Chapter Twenty-Eight
Chapter Twenty-Nine
Chapter Thirty

I wish to dedicate this book to my friend Bea. We lost Bea recently and she will be sorely missed among those of us who were her Facebook friends. She was kind, and funny and loved a good adventure. My heart is heavy as I write these words, hoping she has found her rest and is healed from life's wounds. I will miss you every day, Bea. We all will. Sleep well.

Chapter One

Sawyer watched with wanting eyes as Jillian made her way seductively around his kitchen. She didn't have to try to be seductive, and he was certain she was clueless to the effect she was having on him. Just by virtue of being who she was, her every movement made him sweat. He was supposed to be helping her with dinner, but he couldn't seem to take his eyes off of her. Actually, he didn't need her to cook for him; he could do that himself. It wasn't about that. It was more about the fact that if *he* was busy doing stuff, he couldn't watch *her* do stuff, which limited his ability to actually 'help.'

Unable to contain himself, he moved across to where she stood stirring her delicious spaghetti sauce and cuddled in behind her, placing his arms gently around her waist. He softly kissed her neck and felt her stiffen. Jillian hated cuddling and shook him off gently without turning.

"You're missing out, you know," he said, flashing his most charming smile, not deterred in the least by her chill.

"Yeah?" she said, totally immersed in the recipe she was following and whether or not the sauce was looking as it should. "And what do you think it is I'm missing?"

Sawyer stepped back and held his hands out to either side of a fit 6'2" body and said, "*This.*" He began motioning with his hands, displaying the muscles in his arms and bringing them around to flex his chest. He flipped back short sandy brown locks and stood before her, proudly displaying himself. She ignored him and he sighed, returning to the chopping he was supposed to be doing in the first place.

"We're going to have gorgeous kids, you know," he said. "They're going to look just like me." He grinned a perfectly white smile and batted his large green eyes at her.

"We're not having kids," she said flatly. At first he thought she was teasing him, but her look never changed.

"Who says we're not having kids?" he said, leaning on the counter with one arm and crossing one leg over the other, trying to look casual.

"I say. It's my body and I'm not ruining it with a slimy, pooping, ungrateful little brat who ruins my shape and makes me crazy for lack of sleep. Are those onions done yet?" she asked.

"Almost."

They were to be married in a month. Thirty days. One twelfth of a year. He shook his head and returned to the onions. Was she serious? Why hadn't this subject come up before? It was just assumed they'd have children because that's what married couples did, at least where he'd come from. It seemed so stupid that the subject hadn't come up, that he'd been so wrapped up in the here and now that future plans were never discussed. But this was a serious snag. How could anyone not want kids? This was going to have to be discussed further, and soon.

Jillian always seemed distant in the relationship, detached, but he just figured that was the lawyer in her. She never slept over, never put the flowers he bought her in a vase, they went straight into the garbage. Every time. *What was that about?* He wasn't sure they'd really had any magic between the two of them. He questioned whether or not he'd been given the *chance* to show her his magic. So, if that were the case, if she didn't want children, if she was moving away from him emotionally...why, again, were they getting married? He glanced at the stove once more. Jillian's back was still toward him, and he quietly laid down his knife.

He proceeded to move himself around his end of the kitchen with a small shuffle-type belly dance, wiggling his hips and thrusting every once in a while, emphasized with a grunt. He was beginning to crack himself up with his gyrations. The fact that she was trying so hard to ignore him made it all the funnier in his eyes.

"I see you, you know."

"That's the *point*," he said, continuing his not-so-erotic dance. "You know, some male animals in the wild have to do a fancy dance to attract their females."

"Yeah, and some just jump on and take their turn."

"I could make that happen if you prefer," he said, stopping abruptly and leaning innocently against the counter top next to the stove.

"Very funny." Her head turned and she looked at him for the first time that evening. Her eyes were large and deep, chocolate brown with lashes that seemed to fall all the way to the end of her nose. Her skin was creamy and smooth, and she wore it really, really well. "You trying to be funny again?"

"I don't *try* to be funny. I *am* funny."

"So you say."

He returned to cutting the onions and in his most pathetic voice said, "Oh, look. Now you've just upset me. I'm crying like a baby."

"If you don't cut the roots off the end of the onion, that won't happen."

In his best whimper, he teased, "It's not about the onions."

Apparently at a good stopping point, she laid down the spatula she was using to stir and reduced the temperature on the stove. She turned, facing where Sawyer stood, and folded her arms across her chest. "Poor baby," she cooed. "Nobody loves it."

Jillian had a difficult time showing any kind of compassion. He knew this about her, and he loved her anyway. When she was at her warmest, she would use 'it' as a term of endearment, and he loved when she did. Her usage of the term was as warm as he would ever see her, and that made him appreciate it all the more. Sawyer hid his smile as he continued.

"Only my mother," he said, feigning a childish sadness.

Jillian laughed this time and returned to the stove. "Your mother has no idea what she's created." Her moments of warmth were brief and Sawyer appreciated her attempt.

"Yes, she does. And she's totally okay with it...I mean me."

"Well, you do have your moments, I guess." She was once again immersed in the cookbook, dipping her finger into the hot contents of the pan for a taste. She stuck the sauce-covered fingertip in her mouth and slowly pulled it out from between her full, delicious lips.

Jillian Carter wasn't *just* beautiful. She was the prosecuting attorney for the DA's office, and on her way up with each passing case, which made her very smart, as well. She'd prosecuted several of Sawyer's cases, and done so with professionalism and ease. He loved watching her in the courtroom, in her snuggly fitted dress suit and large, dark rimmed glasses. She was a sight. He wouldn't be surprised if criminals broke the law just for a chance to be prosecuted by her. He would, if he had to.

Sawyer brushed the back of his hand across his forehead, removing a small portion of the sweat forming there, partly from the heat in the kitchen and partly from the heat he felt watching Jillian. He finished with the onions and set the knife on the counter. Sawyer then strolled across the kitchen with flair and placed the small cutting board over the pan, slowly and sensuously scraping the finely cut onions into the sauce. He'd barely started when Jillian let out an anguished cry.

"WAIT!"

Her voice was so loud he dropped the cutting board into the sauce, splashing the contents of the pan all down the front of her. Quickly grabbing the board, he removed it from the pan, but not before all the onions landed in the sauce.

"You're supposed to *sauté* those in butter before they go in the sauce!"

Jillian took two things very seriously. One was the courtroom, the second was her spaghetti sauce…and he'd just ruined it. At least the part that was still in the pan, which was now down by half, the other half displayed loudly on the apron and blouse she wore. Glancing at Jillian he grabbed a dishcloth and began running it over the front of her to clean off the sauce. The sauce moved, the red glaring stain left on her clothing and apron did not. Still, he'd enjoyed wiping her down.

He stood there with a silly grin on his face before he realized she wasn't smiling. She was furious, and the previous playful mood in the room, however small, was really, really gone.

She slowly and deliberately removed the sauce soaked apron, revealing a nice, clean, square area on her white blouse where the apron had protected her. She glanced at the ruined blouse and sighed, tossed the apron on the counter and turned toward the door. Before she reached the exit, she pulled the roses Sawyer had brought her from the vase and tossed them into the garbage.

"You keep buying me flowers and I keep throwing them away. What part of this picture don't you understand? I hate flowers. Stop buying them."

She proceeded to the front door of the apartment, opened it and stepped into the hallway, slamming the door behind her.

Sawyer stood in the silence of the kitchen for a moment before tossing the towel disgustedly on the counter. Shaking his head, he turned off the stove and went into the living room, dropping into his easy chair. There seriously was no pleasing that woman.

He knew he wasn't the easiest person to live with, and being a cop made him unavailable much of the time. He often felt a little detached from Jillian, and sometimes thought it better if he didn't see her when he was working a difficult investigation. He had to be careful what he said in front of her, he couldn't talk about the details of any case and she knew it. Still, there were times it felt like she was trying to pry information out of him. He'd had to tell her on several occasions to basically butt out and drop the subject. That didn't go over well with her, or with him. But he certainly wasn't going to start out a relationship with Jillian thinking she had the 'inside' track on cases she would eventually prosecute. He'd lose his job, and too many times it felt like she didn't care about that.

This newest revelation of no children in their home truly shook him. He'd been the football stud in high school, and during college dated a lot before Jillian came along. In all that time he'd never once even thought about having kids. But now, with the concept staring him in the face, he found a sense of surprised disappointment somewhere in the center of his gut. Part of that surprise was the fact that the discussion hadn't happened in the nearly two years they'd dated. Add to that the uncomfortable feeling he got in that same area of his stomach when he realized there was a *lot* they'd never talked about. In fact, they didn't really talk much at all. Not about the things that impacted their upcoming marriage.

As Sawyer sat in his chair reviewing their conversations over the last two years, he was surprised at the picture that now formed in his head. Their discussions were either about their day, their work, their cases (the parts that *could* be discussed) or the people they worked with. Sawyer was always happy with the people he worked with. His partner, Jack Baker, felt more like a brother to him than a partner. As for the rest of the department, they were fun people with integrity and a good sense of humor that generally helped them through the rough cases. According to Jillian, the people she worked with were all self-absorbed, filthy mouthed pigs that only talked about sex and who was or was not having any. It made him wonder, after their discussion today, whether or not *she* was the problem in their office. Aloof and condescending, Jillian was cold and distant on her warmest of days. So, why was he hanging in there with her? His only thought was there was no accounting for loving someone. He'd seen her good days and he knew her heart and how she covered her feelings with her intelligence. Those feelings that she kept stored away and covered up most of the time were the main reason he couldn't let her go. No one else would understand her like he did. He could live with the cold and distant because he'd seen the up close and personal.

Talking to Jillian wasn't easy, especially when it came to a subject like children, where she'd rather forcefully put her foot down. He had feet as well, and the topic of children in their home *would* be discussed further, she could count on that, along with several other topics he could think of.

Chapter Two

Blakely, Iowa was a nice medium sized town of about 75,000. Amongst the farmers and business owners, there were ordinary people trying very hard to raise responsible children who obeyed the law. However, just like most towns the size of Blakely, there was an ugly underbelly that made a living on the misery of others. When times are tough even the best of people can be driven to the back doors of unscrupulous businesses and end up in trouble. Blakely's underbelly consisted mostly of drug dealers, escort services, bookies and loan sharks. Most of the good people of Blakely steered clear of these businesses and worked through the hard times legally. Overall it was a good town to live in and a good town to grow up in.

Jack Baker loved living in Blakely. He'd lived there his whole life and was never tempted to leave, which made him a rarity for sure. Most of the kids he'd gone to school with those twenty plus years ago were long gone, but Jack just couldn't bring himself to follow them. He'd joined the force because he wanted to keep his town clean, and free of the influence of some of the bigger towns in the state. There wasn't a college in Blakely, or a casino, which, from the outside looking in, would make one think the quiet hamlet would remain fairly trouble free. However, in the past few years, gangs had moved into the area, and he'd seen the changes; harder, more dangerous drugs, graffiti, prostitution, gun trafficking, and gunfights that started and ended quickly. Sometimes the shootings brought tragedy that left the whole community in mourning. The previous year, a three-year-old girl playing in her front yard, was hit by a stray bullet from several blocks away as two gangs raced through the streets, shooting at each other. She'd died instantly, leaving the town to grieve with the broken-hearted parents.

Jack shook his head sadly as he pulled into the police station. He'd gotten a call to come in early, but nothing more had been said. That was never a good sign. He'd done his best to protect the innocent and serve his community, but there were days every now and again when he felt like it didn't matter what he did. He worried this would be one of those days. The bad blood of the bigger cities was making its way to Blakely, and it seemed nothing could stop it.

Pulling the station door open, he walked from sunshine and springtime into chaos. Jack hurried up the stairs to his office and found his partner, Sawyer Kingsley, speaking softly to the captain. Jack approached the two of them.

"The kids are in interrogation," the captain was saying. "They're pretty shook up."

"What's going on?" Jack looked at the long faces.

The captain shot him a sad glance then stared at the floor.

In his mid-fifties, Captain Amerson demanded and received the respect of his department. He was well liked by the officers and staff, known for being fair but strict. With black hair, now more salt than pepper, his hawk-like eyes missed very little and often the officers felt his hearing was more like a wolf than that of a human. He was a good man, kind and compassionate, and though he tried to hide it, everyone knew. He had an image and he wore it well.

"There was a shooting early this morning. A family was killed; dad, mom and three teens, high school age. They were found by friends of the kids who were getting a ride to the last day of school festivities. Had to have happened sometime during the night or early morning, and it looks professional. All of them shot execution style, even the kids."

Jack regarded his partner with interest. There was determination on his face mixed with pain. Jack felt like he was looking in a mirror.

"What's the plan, Captain?" Jack needed to get on this; he needed to be doing something. He was an investigator and he needed to investigate.

Sawyer cast that same determined gaze at Jack and then to the captain. "We'll go get the investigation started. Is CSI out there now?"

"Yeah," sighed Amerson. "They should be out there for a while. Just be prepared. It's a hard one to deal with."

Sawyer nodded and motioned for Jack to follow him. They got into Jack's car and headed to the scene, bracing for the worst they'd seen in a long time, if ever.

"Are you thinking what I'm thinking?" Jack glanced sideways at his friend.

"What?"

"I have to wonder," he began, "if this is connected to the murder reported in Smithville last year. It's close enough, and the killing there was execution style. Nothing was found at the crime scene, not a single fingerprint or footprint. It's been six months and there are no leads. I'm betting forensics will find the same thing at this crime scene, which begs the question...has the killer made his way to Blakely? Wouldn't be that big of a move."

"Yeah," sighed Sawyer. "I was wondering that myself. I guess we'll have to see when we get there. How long has CSI been out here?"

"The family was found about six this morning, and it's almost seven, so about an hour. I'll be interested to hear when they died. Makes me wonder what kind of a jump the killer has as far as miles."

"Makes *me* wonder if the killer has left the area."

Jack shrugged and stared at the road ahead. "Hard to know anything for sure until we get a look at the crime scene."

Sawyer agreed with a nod, staring at the road ahead.

The family farmed property about ten miles outside of Blakely. Jack and Sawyer would need to investigate whether or not there were property line disputes and with whom, if there was family that disputed ownership and who the neighbors were. Also, they would ask if there were bad feelings between the family and anyone in proximity of their home, including whether or not a stranger had been seen or any new people had been hired. All these questions would be part of an investigation that was going to take time. Jack wished the combing and searching through belongings and lost lives was done and behind them by now. Searching a home like this was painful and strongly disliked among investigators, yet necessary. Jack thought it was easier to interview neighbors than to go through personal effects.

The Franz family property fronted the highway and was well kept with cattle grazing in the field. There were five family members, Victor, the father, Marylisa, the mother, and kids, Janssen, seventeen, and the twins, Skylar and Samantha, both fifteen.

Once the outbuildings were checked and the okay given by the police, the neighbors had come in and milked the few cows the Franz family had, fed the livestock, but stayed clear of the house. Farms don't stop needing to be kept, even if the keepers are stolen away in the night. It didn't seem likely, right off the top, there would be bad feelings amongst neighbors who would willingly jump in and help like these neighbors had. Still, each one would have to be questioned as to their whereabouts at the time of the murders (as soon as forensics gave them a time of death) and what their relationship with the dead family was like.

Jack turned the car up the long drive that ran along fenced fields and up to a large, well kept farmhouse. CSI was still busily coming and going from the house with cases of evidence. All decked out in their white one-piece suits and blue exam gloves, they seemed like white ants, busily doing their work. It turned Jack's stomach.

The two men got out of the car and each slipped into a white jumpsuit, struggling into the gloves. They walked up the front porch and entered the home. The bodies laid face down in the living room, almost as if they'd been placed perfectly together. Jack and Sawyer stayed clear of the living room until CSI could finish taking all the evidence and samples they needed. It wasn't that hard to stay away, though there was a part of each man that needed to know what had happened and what CSI had found. Still, they checked the rest of the house to see if there was anything out of place. If there'd been a struggle, there was no sign of it. Had the intruder been someone they knew?

    Both men entered the kitchen and found meal preparations suddenly interrupted. Jack could almost hear the cheerful conversation amongst the family members as they gathered around the table for their breakfast. He shook his head. He couldn't let his own emotions mess with his head. He had to think clearly. The monster who'd done this must be found before he could do it again, and emotions only got in the way of the hunt.

    "Over here," called Sawyer. Pointing to the kitchen sink he said. "That look like blood to you?"

    "Yes, but it could be from a chicken egg or hamburger. May not even be blood at all.
Better check with CSI and make sure they got a sample of it. I'd be surprised if they didn't."

    Sawyer left and Jack continued searching the kitchen. Not so much as a grain of salt anywhere. *What kind of a cook doesn't spill a little salt when she's cooking?*

    Jack heard the noise of pots banging together and turned, heading to the pantry. "Kingsley! In here!" Sawyer was on his way back to the kitchen when he heard Jack's call and began running in his direction. Jack had his sidearm out and was creeping toward the pantry. Sawyer unzipped his jumpsuit and pulled his gun as well. Jack nodded to his partner and held up three fingers, mouthing silently, *"On three...One, two, THREE!"*

Sawyer pulled the door open with one swift movement and Jack pointed his gun into the small room. Someone had been there, but they were gone. There was a window that was open and Jack hurried over to look out. No one was there. Sawyer was already sprinting to the front door and around to the side of the house. Had anyone really been there? Were they imagining things? Highly doubtful. Someone had been in that pantry. Jack came quickly up behind him and pointed to the barn. "Call for backup. I'm going in."

Sawyer grabbed his arm and stopped him. "What are you doing? You can't go in there alone. I'll call for backup on the way, but you're not going in by yourself."

"Fine. We're wasting time! Get moving!"

Sawyer put in the call over the radio as he ran. Several police cruisers arrived shortly after Jack and Sawyer and the officers had been searching the area around the front of the house. Six officers answered the call for back up, running around to the back of the house and joining them at the barn. Jack motioned for two of the officers, to cover the back exit and for two others to stay on either side of the front end of the barn. Jack and Sawyer moved slowly inside the barn, one moving left, the other right. Two officers, Will Lansing and Joe Miston, followed them inside and they all fanned out, creeping slowly through the barn with guns drawn.

As each group called out the 'all clear,' Jack, Sawyer, and the two officers with them, began to search stalls and piles of hay. Lansing and Miston searched the loft but found nothing.

Disappointed, they left the barn and headed to the front of the house just as Sam Golding, head CSI, was putting the last of his equipment into the van. Forensics was ready to take the bodies to autopsy. Jack asked them to hold for a minute; he wanted a look at the crime scene before the bodies were moved. The two partners put new covers over their shoes and walked into the living room. Jack squatted down beside the body of Victor. The wound was clean, through the back of the head at a short distance. As he inspected each body, he found the same type of wound and hurried back out the door to speak with Sam.

"Hey Sam," Jack called out. "Hold up."

Sam was just opening the van door and turned to watch Jack approach.

"Sam, what kind of evidence did you find in there?"

Frustration lined the CSI's face. "We found a few hairs. Most likely they'll belong to the family, but we took them anyway. It was all we could find. There wasn't even a fingerprint from the family. The scene had been wiped clean. Everything. Every doorknob, every molding, even the wood pieces of the furniture were wiped off. The killer took his time and cleaned the house. At least the area he was in. I don't know if I'm going to have anything more than time of death for you. This killer knew what he was doing."

Sam turned and climbed into the van. He rolled down his window and offered one last concession. "We can hope he made a mistake somewhere, and if he did, I guarantee you, we'll find it. These were good people. They didn't deserve this."

The van engine started and it slowly pulled away, tires crunching on the gravel drive. Sawyer and Jack stood staring at the van, both thinking they were dealing with a killer who had killed before and would kill again if they didn't find him. Neither man knew how true their thoughts were, or how close to home that truth would hit.

Chapter Three

Although there had been two divorces in Jack Baker's life, he was a happy guy. He'd escaped both marriages with only alimony payments, which were now finished. After the hassle, heartbreak and hurts of the second round of marriage, he realized he was better off single. The fact that his partner and best friend, Sawyer, was getting married bothered him only minimally. He was happy Sawyer felt he'd found the right woman, but Jack was far from agreeing with him on that. Jillian seemed way too obsessive/compulsive for his friend, and far too…he couldn't think of the word, but it had to do with the phrase "stick up her butt." Though she was gorgeous, and smart, she was just too stiff for the likes of Jack Baker.

Sawyer's life was his own, and he'd either learn his lessons through divorce as Jack had done, or he'd learn them living in misery. Didn't sound like a life to Jack, but still, it was Sawyer's life.

He was scowling, now, which meant his friend's wedding was bothering him more than he'd thought it would. He'd meet up with Sawyer this evening for dinner and a few drinks at the Rank and File tavern as planned, and maybe they'd talk a little about the upcoming nuptials then. He wasn't sure if that made him feel better or not, but he was happy to have some time with Sawyer alone, without the constant interruptions and irritated sighs from Jillian.

In the meantime, there were questions to be asked on the Franz murders and he was on his way to pick up Sawyer and get started on those. Several individuals had been asked to come to the station for interviews. Those that couldn't or wouldn't come were interviewed on site at their homes. The two men felt much more in control if the visits were conducted at the station, where outside interruptions didn't interfere with the flow of questions.

Jack pulled up in front of Sawyer's home and waited. It didn't take long for Sawyer to emerge, but he wasn't very happy. The frown pretty much said it all.

"Hey," called Jack, as Sawyer approached the car. "What's up? You look like you just swallowed a barrel of grandma's pickle juice."

Sawyer scoffed and paused, but then continued around the car and got in. "How does anyone ever learn to deal with women?" he said as he sat back in the seat. "I mean, if they're not hormonal they're in a 'mood' and if they're not hormonal or in a mood they're just...." His voice trailed off in frustration.

"That about sums it up, I'm afraid. I've never been able to figure them out, but I'm not sure any man has." Jack paused before voicing his shock. "She actually stayed over?"

"No. Phone call. Incredibly irritating phone call. What's the plan today?" Clearly his partner didn't want to discuss it.

"Interviews with three of the Franz's neighbors. These are the three who mentioned the newly hired hand at the Franz farm."

Sawyer shook his shoulders as if trying to rid himself of the bad vibes he felt. He clapped his hands then rubbed them together vigorously.

"What are you doing?" Jack said, chuckling.

"I'm freeing myself of all negativity so I can focus my brain where it needs to be. You should try it. It really helps."

"Yeah, I can see that. You're just a bundle of positive energy now."

"You laugh," smiled Sawyer, "but just wait. I'll bet I get further with the neighbors than you do."

"Right."

They pulled into the station and headed to the interviews. The first couple, Michael and Jessica Whittley, was already there and waiting.

The two men introduced themselves, and the four of them entered the interview room and sat down at the table.

"My name is Jack Baker, and this is my partner, Sawyer Kingsley. We're investigating the Franz murders, as you know."

"Nice to meet you," mumbled Mr. Whittley. "This is all very…disturbing. All the neighbors are wondering if we need to be worried. We're afraid to let our children and neighbors out of our sight."

"Yes, I know it can be unnerving. We're so sorry to have to bother you with these questions, but we have to find out if anyone knows anything at all that could help us. You may have seen something you feel was unimportant but for us it could be that one missing piece that may crack the case. We'll be as brief as possible."

The Whittleys both nodded, wide-eyed, and Jack continued.

"What can you tell us about this new employee the Franz's had?" asked Jack.

Michael Whittley spoke first. "We never actually met him. We just heard Victor talk about him. Said he was a good worker and it was working out well."

"Have you seen him around the area since the incident?" asked Sawyer. "Seen him in town or anywhere you've been?"

"Nope."

Sawyer turned to Jessica. "Did any of the Franz family ever say how they found this person? A want ad maybe, or through someone they knew?"

Jessica thought for a moment. "No, not that I recall. It just seemed like one day he showed up and started working for them. There was never any time they were thinking about hiring someone, at least that they mentioned to me. They just up and hired this boy."

"Do you have any idea how old he was?" asked Sawyer.

Michael looked at his wife, questioning, and then back at the detectives. "I saw him from a distance once and he looked to be in his mid or maybe late twenties. But that would just be a guess. Like I said, I never met him."

"And you, Mrs. Whittley? Did you ever meet him?"

"No, he was always working out on the farm somewhere whenever I stopped by."

"Do you remember what his name was?" Jack asked.

The couple stared at each other for a minute, trying to remember. Michael finally spoke.

"It was Jason, or Jamison...I just don't remember. Something like that."

"No last name?" asked Sawyer.

Jessica spoke this time. "I think Marylisa said it was Adams, or Adamson maybe."

"How long had he worked for the Franz's?" Jack studied the couple as they tried to figure out a timeline.

"Well..." began Michael, once again turning to his wife. "It was after we bought the tractor, right?"

She nodded back at him. "Yes, so it was at least a couple of weeks ago. But there's really no way to know how long he'd been there by that time. Victor stopped by to see the new tractor and mentioned he'd hired someone."

After a few more brief questions, Jack dismissed the couple with several minutes to spare before the second husband and wife team were scheduled to arrive.

"Whaddaya think?" he stared at his partner as they sat back down.

"Well, the thought occurred to me during that interview, if we could get a lead on where they found the kid, maybe we could find him that way."

"Unless he just showed up at the farm one day, out of the blue, asking for work. Let's see what we get with the other two couples."

The remaining interviews went much the same as the first one. However, the last couple, the Sealy's, seemed to know a little more. They'd actually met the young man and gave them a name, Justin McAdam, but there was no way of knowing if the name was real or fake. As with the Whittleys, they'd not seen him around since the murders.

The next several days were spent scouring not just the city, but also the county, for the name McAdam. There were several McAdams spread throughout the area, but none of them had a friend or relative of that age and with the description given them. It was a definite dead end and even more frustrating, it was definitely suspicious. His disappearance left a lot of questions.

By the time they finished with their day, it was nearly seven p.m. They headed to the Rank and File and found a seat by the window, per Sawyer's request.

The evening was relaxing and after dinner and a few drinks, Jack left to go use the men's room. He left Sawyer staring out the window. It was staying light much later now and the streetlights were only just beginning to come on.

As Jack entered the bathroom, he heard voices further down the row of stalls. He could hear the conversation and was zipping his jeans as the voices became louder, more agitated. *Great. Who was the genius that labeled these places 'restrooms?'* He grinned at his own sarcasm as he opened the stall door and stepped into the main area. The voices were louder, but the words sounded garbled, hard to understand. It was difficult to tell if there was an argument brewing or if someone was sick; but it definitely sounded like two individuals, at *least* two. Wondering if he should go get Sawyer, he shrugged and headed in the direction of the voices. It couldn't be *that* bad. They didn't sound like they were coming to blows yet. Best to stop it before they did.

"Hey, you fellas need some help?" Jack continued toward the voices and paused outside one of the stalls. The door was open just a tiny bit and, he pushed it slowly open. "Everything alright in h--?"

Jack saw the recorder on the back of the toilet at the same time he felt the knife go into his back. He tried to turn, but before he could, the knife went in again, and again, and again, as the room slowly went dark.

***

Sawyer checked his watch, wondering what could be keeping Jack. When twenty minutes had passed he made his way to the men's room, opened the door and saw blood. Lots of blood. It was streaked from one end of the men's room to the other. He pulled out his cell phone and hurriedly called for backup, trying his best to ignore the massive amount of blood.

"I have a possible officer down at the Rank and File. Need back up and search party. NOW!"

Sawyer ran frantically from stall to stall, each stall door slamming loudly against the wall.

"Jack! JACK!"

Jack was nowhere to be found, but the blood trail in the men's room looked like a body had literally been drug into and out of each stall in the room. That was impossible. Who would do that? This had to be another one of Jack's sick jokes. But this was over the top, even for Jack.

"Jack!" He followed the trail of blood up the wall and out an open window. "Jack!"

Sawyer could feel his heart racing. He sprinted out of the tavern and into the alley that bordered the building. "Jack! Ja--!"

His voice caught mid-call when he saw the lifeless body of his friend lying with his feet and legs over an overturned garbage can, his torso twisted, his head and back lying on the cold brick floor, vacant eyes staring up into the darkened sky, arms wide, hands open.

He dropped quickly down beside Jack's body, ripped his shirt open and listened frantically for a heartbeat. He heard nothing but started chest compressions anyway. "Come on, Jack. Come on! BREATHE!" He stopped and listened for any sign of life and heard nothing. "Jack! Don't do this. Don't you do this. Come back, dammit! JACK!!!"

Sawyer pummeled himself with guilt as he pushed on Jack's chest, each compression accenting the anguish he felt. *Why did I wait so long? I should have checked on him after five minutes. I could have stopped this. What was I thinking? I should have been there for him. I'm his partner. He counted on me to watch his back. That's what partners do. Why did I wait so long?*

Several cruisers roared up the road with lights flashing and sirens blaring. Police swarmed the alleyway, guns drawn, flashlights blinding as they searched for any sign of the perp. The usually deafening noise of a hurried search was unheard by Sawyer. The chaos was nothing but a buzz in the background as he continued chest compressions; sure his efforts would produce the desired result.

It happened all the time, right? He'd seen it himself. People came back when everyone else gave up and thought they were dead. They came back, didn't they?

His arms ached and his lungs burned. Still he called to his friend, ordering him back to life. "Come on Jack! Come on! I know you're in there. *Get up, damn you!*"

Softly and quietly, a gentle hand rested on Sawyer's shoulder and a voice, above the din said, "He's gone, Kingsley. Let it go. He's gone." Captain Amerson stood over him, never taking his hand off Sawyer's shoulder.

Captain was right. His partner was dead, and Sawyer felt like his gut has been torn open. In a single instant he wanted to scream, to kill, to shoot anything in his line of sight. His anger forced his blood through him at an accelerated rate while closing his ears to everything but his Captain's words, feeling only the devastation that pulsed through him.

He stopped the compressions and placed his hands on the cold brick floor beside the body of his partner, dropped his head in defeat and leaned limply forward. He whispered to his friend, "Jack, Jack…who did this to you?"

Sawyer wished for all he was worth his partner would cough or sputter, then roll on his side and begin breathing. But that wasn't going to happen. Jack Baker was dead.

Chapter Four

Jillian sat down on the bed beside her fiancé. Like a soldier sitting at attention, she placed her arm stiffly around his shoulder.

"Sawyer," she began, with forced patience. "It's been two months since Jack died. You need to get some kind of hold on this. It's time to get moving again, Sawyer." Then as an afterthought she added, "You know Jack wouldn't have wanted to see you like this."

Sawyer looked at her with cold, angry eyes.

"Cut it out, Jillian. You're lousy at condolences and your empathy is even worse. He was *my* partner, not yours. I'll mourn this loss any way I see fit."

Jillian stood and adjusted her suit jacket. "You're not just pitiful, you know. You're rude."

Sawyer stood and faced her. "Really? Well just how does that feel, huh? Because you've been just like that since the day we got engaged. See how irritating it is?"

Jillian marched out of the bedroom with Sawyer right behind her.

"I'm outta here. Let me know when you grow up and I'll be over. Until then, don't bother me with your pity party. I don't have time for it." She continued to the front door and left without looking back.

These confrontations were getting worse with each passing week, right along with Sawyer's need for sleep and booze. He couldn't help wondering what was happening to him. Captain Amerson had that worried look on his face every time they spoke. Sawyer *hated* that look. He felt like it was somewhere between disappointment and pity, neither of which was good.

Sawyer felt like he'd lost an arm or leg. There was no way to perform his duties without Jack. He may as well quit and find something else to do, but every time that thought reared its ugly head, there was this tiny voice inside him that screamed out from somewhere beyond the anger and fury. For as small as the voice was, it was insistent, and repeatedly told him not to stop, to hang in there and find Jack's killer, and the killer of the Franz family.

Were the two connected? Both crime scenes were wiped clean, not so much as a print. No murder weapon at either site. It was as if the investigators saw exactly what the killer wanted them to see and *no more*. How could that be? There was always a hair or a partial print, *something* that came up and blew a stalled investigation wide open, but not on these two killings. There was nothing, literally nothing, to go on and alcohol seemed to be the only comfort he could find to quell his frustration. He had to numb himself from the bitterness that made him want to yell at suspects, pummel them with his fists, and dismiss stupid people with rudeness and foul language. None of these things was Sawyer, and yet here he was.

He'd been dismissed from Jack's investigation because he was "too close to be objective." That left him the Franz case, and he was slowly going nowhere, unable to focus for the alcohol, and when there was no alcohol, unable to focus for the anger and the frustration. Sawyer felt like one giant raw, open wound, never allowed healing, and he had no idea how to fix it. Jack was gone. There was no fixing that. There was no changing the fact that Sawyer had let his partner down, hadn't checked on him soon enough, didn't watch his back like he should've. There was no fixing any of it.

The wedding had been postponed for who knows how long; he couldn't even bring himself to think about it. The relationship was now strained almost beyond repair anyway. And yet, he knew he loved Jillian. He hated being so rude to her, hated hiding from her, hiding from loving her. Things had to change, but he had no idea how that was going to happen.

He was ordered into Captain Amerson's office that morning and once he was ready, meaning appropriately sober, he headed down to the station. He dreaded what he was about to hear, but removing Sawyer from the department was really the only option Captain had at this point. Would he really lose his job? Was this really the end? Or had the end happened the night his partner died?

Sawyer pulled into the station and headed up the stairs to the captain's office with leaded feet.

Captain Amerson had obviously cleared his calendar for this meeting, which would be standard procedure for a termination. The man was like a father to Sawyer, he'd been the one to encourage him to join the force, even trained him for the detective position. Letting him down was the worst part of this whole ordeal. He hated how he'd become a disappointment to a man he respected as much as his own birth father. Entering the captain's office, the shame hit him, harder than before.

"Sit," commanded the captain. Captain Amerson sighed and leaned back in his large office chair, considering Sawyer before speaking.

"You're a mess, Kingsley," he began, "and I'm a bit surprised."

Sawyer kept his dark eyes on the floor, too filled with regret to look him in the face.

"This whole thing you're doing to yourself," he said, motioning flat handed in the direction of Sawyer. "This isn't you. I *know* you, Detective Kingsley, and this is not you."

He sat in silence waiting for a response.

"What do you want me to say?" Sawyer's voice was harder than he'd wanted it to be, but he continued. "Jack's death hit me hard. I feel like I've lost a part of me I can't replace. We were more than partners, we were family."

"Most partners are," said Amerson, softly.

In spite of the captain's kindness, or maybe because of it, Sawyer could feel his anger rising. He could feel the familiar heat creeping up his neck and covering his face. He didn't want kindness and compassion from his captain; he wanted Amerson to fire him so he could justify his need to hurt someone, to make the world pay for his loss, even if they weren't responsible. He wanted to let the chaos and pain inside him loose on anyone standing in front of him.

Sawyer sprang from his chair and began pacing, his arms flinging wildly as he spoke far too loudly. "What do you want from me, Captain? What am I supposed to tell you? That I'm perfectly content with life? That my expectations have been met? I'M ANGRY! I want answers, and it doesn't matter where we look there are none! NOTHING! How can that be? It doesn't make sense, and yet I'm supposed to act like it does. Is that what you want me to say?"

"Sit down." The captain nodded toward the chair Sawyer had vacated.

"I don't want to sit down. I want to figure out what happened to my partner. I want in on that investigation. I want to *work* and *think* and function again like I-"

"I SAID SIT DOWN!"

Sawyer froze, staring at his boss. He shuffled to the chair and collapsed into it, anger and defiance blanketed his face.

"As I see it," began the captain, patiently, "you have a choice to make. You can continue to cry like a baby over what has happened in your life, or you can pull your head out of your butt and do something about it. You are the best investigator this department has, and you're wasting valuable time in the new pity pool you've constructed. I hope the water's warm in there, because out here where the real work is being done, it's cold, and it's real, and it hurts sometimes. You didn't just walk away from the pain and anger you felt, Sawyer. You walked away from this town. You walked away from the department and left us all to fend for ourselves. You weren't the only one that lost Jack. We *all* lost Jack."

The room went silent as Captain Amerson let his words sink in. When he spoke again, it was not the words Sawyer was certain he'd hear.

"At eight tomorrow morning you have your first session with the department counselor."

Sawyer started to protest and the captain raised his palm and kept talking.

"You'll continue with these sessions every week until I have a report from the counselor that tells me you're cleared for duty." He dropped his hand back into his lap and continued. "Until I hear that 'all clear,' you're on desk duty. I don't want to hear any belly aching about it, I want you sitting out there *every day* completing supplies orders, prisoner transfer orders, whatever's on that desk, that's what you'll do."

"But you just said yourself I'm an investigator," began Sawyer. "I can't sit at a desk all day. It'll drive me crazy."

"From this side of the desk that looks like a pretty short putt. This change of venue will give you a chance to clear your head, focus on something else, and figure out what you're going to do. If I see you late or absent from that desk even one time, you're done. If you miss even *one* counseling appointment, you're done. Do I make myself clear? Done."

"Yes, *sir*," said Sawyer between clenched teeth. "Clear. Are we finished here?"

"That totally depends on you. Stay out of the investigations, both Jack's and the Franz family. I don't want you anywhere near any of that evidence. You've got a new assignment starting today. Now get to work."

Thin walls being what they were at the station, all eyes were on the captain's door when Sawyer emerged. They were quickly diverted and each individual hurried to look busy as the former detective made his way to his new desk.

There were stacks of invoices, orders for new equipment, and fleet inspections. Every form he'd never wanted to see. Yes, the captain was right. He had a decision to make and he needed to force himself to look at what he'd done to his career. He dropped wearily into his chair.

The captain's words rang in his ear. "...you walked away from the department...we *all* lost Jack." He was exactly right. They needed him as much as he needed them. Somehow, he had to do as the captain asked him. If he wanted to keep his job, if he wanted to crack these two cases, he would do as he'd been ordered. However, the part about staying out of the investigations, that wasn't happening.

Sawyer had copies of every shred of evidence from both crime scenes at his home. He *would* investigate. This would be his new evening activity, replacing the booze and ensuing need for sleep. He had everything he needed to try and piece a picture together that made some sense. Sawyer felt bad going against what the captain said he was to do, but the department needed his help, and he would help. He would help, even if he had to break a few rules to do it.

***

The next morning Sawyer was at the station right at eight, shaved, showered and headed to the counselor's office. He'd heard a lot about the department's therapist and none of it was good, but he'd do what he was supposed to do. Somehow, he had to get back into the investigation that would find Jack's killer. He had a gut feeling this killer would turn out to be the same one who killed the Franz family.

Maizy Trakerson was a motherly sort, bulky, but kind and soft-spoken. Though he'd heard it was best not to cross her, she seemed quite nice. Having never been to a counselor before, he wasn't sure what to expect.

"Good morning...Detective Kingsley, is it?" she reached out to shake his hand.

"Yes, call me Sawyer," he said, shaking her hand.

She motioned for him to be seated and she took a seat across from him.

"Now, start at the beginning and tell me what's going on in your life."

Surprisingly, he did start at the beginning. He unloaded everything that had happened over the past two months onto Maizy. Even more surprising was how good it felt to get it out. He was shocked at how easily the words rolled from his mouth, how his brain appeared to let go without a fight, and how wonderful it felt to talk to someone who really *wanted* to listen to him and heard every word he said. Sawyer couldn't believe the relief he felt once he was finished. He was certain she would tell him that's all he needed to do. She had to see the effect getting this out had on him, and he was sure he'd be cleared for duty right away. But that wasn't the case.

The visits with Miss M, as he affectionately began to refer to her, would continue on after that initial visit, and he'd return to his desk after each session, disappointed at not having that written release in hand, but feeling somehow stronger than he had before the visit. It didn't seem to matter what he'd say, he never got the clearance he so desperately sought. But slowly, over time, the trust and friendship between them grew, and Sawyer felt like he'd found his grandmother again.

After the first visit with Maizy, Sawyer went home feeling more hope than he'd had in a long time. He kicked himself for taking so long to get his act together. If he were being totally honest, had he cleaned up his act in the beginning, he would've been investigating all along and probably found the killer by now. Even if he hadn't, at least he'd have been working toward that end instead of drinking and sleeping the pain away.

The fog that had surrounded his brain for so long was beginning to lift. He was itching to get into the newspaper clippings and notes he'd saved from the investigation with Jack. The more he thought about the Franz case and Jack's case, the more he was convinced it was the same killer. But why? What was the connection between the two? That was the big question. The killings appeared random and just to be sure, Sawyer had driven to Smithville to see if there was any connection between those two murders. There wasn't, that he could find in a preliminary look, with the exception of the killer's MO. In both the Smithville and Franz murders everything was wiped clean and the bodies laid out as if by a contract killer. Jacks murder was so different from the two, and yet...something connected the two and he wasn't sure what that something was. Maybe it was Sawyer, himself, but that made no sense.

That night, when he returned home from the station, certain he had a new perspective, he dove into the box of evidence he'd kept hidden deep in his closet. These were copies of evidence, something he wasn't supposed to look at, let alone have in his possession. Prior to Jack's death, Sawyer liked to review evidence before he turned in for the night, and the only way to do that was to make copies of everything he could, which he did. Jack knew he had this information and said nothing to Amerson about it. In fact, Jack often used it when they were knee deep in an investigation.

Sawyer heard the key turn in the lock on the front door and hurriedly shut the bedroom door, hiding the box of evidence inside the room.

Jillian walked through the front door, gorgeous, but not happy.

"Hey, Beautiful," he said as he put his arms around her to give her a kiss. It felt strained and awkward, but he knew if he was going to fix the damage, he had to start somewhere.

She pulled away softly, the look on her face feigning sadness. "I'm leaving, Sawyer," she said as she collapsed into the sofa. "I'm taking the job in Baltimore."

Chapter Five

Jillian's words were not just a kick in the gut for him...they made him angry. For the first time in their relationship, Sawyer let it all out.

"You know, you never had any compassion in you from the start of this relationship, and Jack's death really brought that home. That you could up and leave at this time proves that to me. So look as sad as you like, you're not fooling me. Go back to Baltimore. Have a nice life."

Jillian's mouth twitched, her eyes were wild with fury.

"You're seriously going to throw that in my face? Really? It's been months since Jack's death and now I hear you're sitting at a desk at the station. What's that about? You've been telling me for weeks now that you're moving on, and yet, here you are...at a *desk* because you can't seem to step back into life. Nice. Do you have *any* idea what that makes me look like?"

The realization of what she was saying slowly made its way across his face in the form of a soft, sarcastic smile. "Ah, so *that's* it. It's always been about Jillian and how to make Jillian look good, how to make her look *successful*." Sawyer's smile disappeared and was replaced by a cold scowl. "Silly me. How could I ever have thought you were thinking my partner's death was about the loss *I* felt? I've been so blind in this relationship, but I can sure see clearly now. It never was about us. It was always about *you*. Well, good luck in Baltimore, Ms. Carter. I'm sure you'll do just fine on your own."

Jillian stood and pulled the engagement ring from her finger. She tossed it onto the carpet and watched it settle in place next to the chair leg. "We're done here. Keep the ring. I never wanted it in the first place." With that she stomped to the door, letting herself out, and slamming it behind her.

Sawyer stood in the living room, frozen in place, trying to wrap his mind around what Jillian had just said. He sat down on the sofa, sinking into the soft cushions, and stared at the ring lying on the carpet across from him. Her words stung somewhere inside him. He considered the life behind him, the life with Jillian, and found it difficult to reconcile it with the life ahead of him. He didn't really feel like he'd be alone, and as he thought through the last year and a half, he had to ask himself a very important question. *Had he ever really been in a relationship?* Clearly there was a person there, in his life, taking up space, but had she given anything to the relationship?

He continued to stare at the ring, slowly coming to the realization that the ring on the floor was the only downside to Jillian's leaving, and he could always sell it if he wanted to. So...no downside? He smiled sardonically and shook his head. She'd never wanted to be engaged in the first place? He'd known that all along, hadn't he?

"Yes," he said to the empty room. "Yes, I knew that, and I was moving ahead anyway. What kind of an idiot does that? Apparently...my kind of idiot." Sawyer chuckled to himself and headed back to the bedroom, leaving the ring right where it landed. He had more important things to do.

Shaking off the conversation with Jillian, Sawyer poured himself into the box of evidence from the two murders, and began arranging the contents on his bed. This format wasn't working, though. He'd have to start sleeping on the couch so as not to disturb his "story board," and that would never do. He had to get himself a board, a large board that would allow him to put up the information he had and leave it up. He smiled as he realized he didn't have to worry about Jillian seeing it now, so he could leave it wherever he wanted. His bedroom would do nicely.

It was 7:30 p.m. and he still had time to make it to the building supply store. Driving to the store gave him some time to digest the things Jillian had said. Her words made clear what he'd been thinking for a long time now. They weren't meant for each other. Jack had told him that a hundred times. Jack. He was like the big brother Sawyer never had, and blatantly honest. Jack didn't like Jillian, not one bit. He'd said she was a...how had he put that? *"She's a self-centered climber who will do whatever it takes to get whatever she wants."* That's why Jillian didn't go with him whenever he met up with Jack.

And what was this? He felt a new realization forming at the pit of his stomach, one that totally surprised him. He'd actually liked his visits with Jack much better when Jillian *wasn't* a part of them. Wow. How blind had he been, anyway?

Sawyer turned into the parking lot, parked, and entered the store. He knew exactly what he wanted; he grabbed a flat cart and began pulling and placing the items he needed on it. Once he had all the necessary materials, he hurried to the checkout, paid for the purchases, and transported everything to his car just as the store was closing.

He was nearly running to his SUV, his excitement pushing him to move faster. Once at home, he set his board on the easel he'd purchased and placed the evidence, one piece at a time on the board, in an order that made sense only to him. There was some adjusting to do; moving this article here, that article there, inserting written notes, then moving a few more clippings. When he finished getting everything posted, he stood back and looked at the board. It was a thing of beauty.

The exhaustion he felt made him look at his watch. He was shocked to see it was three in the morning; he had to be at his desk in five hours. No wonder he was so bleary-eyed. Not bothering to remove his clothes, he set his alarm before turning off the lights and closed his eyes as his head sank into the pillow. He was out almost immediately.

He woke the next morning to the annoying buzz of his alarm. It had apparently been buzzing for a while because it was now at its loudest, which meant he was late getting out of bed. He hurried through a shave and shower, paused briefly to consider his work from the previous evening (and early morning) and left for the day.

Pushing through the large glass doors of the station, Sawyer hurried up the stairs to his desk and collapsed into his chair with two minutes to spare. Not only could he not afford to lose this job, he loved his job. Now that the cobwebs were clearing, he was remembering the good parts of the job, the parts he'd buried somewhere behind the sleep and the booze. He loved the feeling of solving a case, of going to the Rank and File with Jack and toasting to their success. It wasn't showy, no one knew what the two of them were doing, and that was fine with Sawyer. The important piece was Jack, and beyond that, the satisfaction of a job well done. He was determined to work his way back to where he was before Jack's death.

There it was, that sick feeling in the pit of his stomach when he thought about the loss of his friend. Would it ever stop? What made him feel like this when he thought of Jack? Was there something he was missing? There was something that made him uneasy each time he thought about Jack. Sometimes, when he was alone, he would talk to his partner, asking for his help, asking if he'd seen his attacker, asking, asking, asking. There were never any answers, but somehow he felt better asking all the questions. That sickness, or uneasiness, or whatever he decided to call it usually made him lose his appetite. Today, it reminded him he'd not had breakfast. That was new.

This morning, as he viewed the stack of forms before him, Sawyer was determined to do what he'd been ordered to do. However, it was fairly mind-numbing, and so as he worked he pictured his board at home in his mind and reviewed the facts, making notes when he made a mental discovery or had a question only the board could answer. He gazed at the stack of forms and started in with the first one, completing it as he mentally worked out details of the Franz and Baker murders. He was getting very good at the forms and requests and had most of his work done by mid-afternoon.

Once a week, after lunch, he'd have his visits with Miss M and return disappointed to his desk with another stack of forms to complete and no end of counseling in sight. He sighed. It was what it was.

One evening, about a month into his desk assignment and mandatory therapy, he stood in front of his evidence board, musing. Jack's body was moved from the bathroom to the alley through the bathroom window. Of course forensics would've cleared the window, taking any samples that were there. Yes?

Sawyer froze. He hadn't seen any evidence from the window. He returned to his nearly empty box, searching what was left to try and find 'window frame' evidence.

"They wouldn't have missed that," he said, quickly removing items and placing them on the bed. "Would they have gone back and gotten that later, and I didn't get a copy of it? I would never let them get away with-"

But you weren't paying attention were you?

There was nothing in the remaining evidence that showed the window frame and sill had ever been checked. This was a problem. He didn't have any way to collect the evidence himself, which meant ingratiating himself with the forensics people and hoping he'd not ticked any of them off in the past few months. He had to know if the window seal had been checked.

The next day, he noticed an order for supplies for the Forensics department on his desk. How fortuitous. He smiled as he picked up the form and headed to Forensics.

"Hey Joe," smiled Sawyer as he entered the lab. "I have a form here, just wanted to verify it was correct before I sent it over to supplies."

"Sure," smiled Joe Branoff, taking the form. His dark eyes scanned the information. Joe's laughter was infectious, his dark hair, strong jaw and good build were considered eye candy for the ladies, which made him the life of any party. Sawyer felt like he had a pretty good rapport with Joe. "Looks good to me," he said, handing it back to Sawyer.

Sawyer took the form and started for the door, stopping abruptly. "Hey Joe," he said, offering his most likeable smile. "Can you check something for me?"

"Sure, what you need?"

"I was just wondering, on the Baker case, if you could check and make sure the window was checked for trace."

Joe smiled knowingly. "Smooth, Kingsley. Really smooth, but Amerson has already told us you're not to be given any information on that case. You know that."

"Yeah, yeah, I'm not asking for the info to be given to me. I just wanted to know if anyone checked the bathroom windowsill and frame. You don't even have to tell me what was found, just if it was checked and tested."

Joe shrugged. "I guess there's no harm in that. I'm sure it *was* checked, but give me a minute. We're still working on that one, so the evidence hasn't been removed yet. Hold on."

As soon as Joe was out of sight, Sawyer scanned the room and found the shelf with the DNA packets and fingerprint kits. He grabbed one of each and stuffed them into his inside jacket pocket, then returned to the counter.

Joe came around the corner with confusion on his face. "I don't understand. There's nothing in the evidence box that says bathroom window, sill or frame. It's really unusual something that obvious would be missed. I'll get someone over there as soon as I can. Thanks for asking, you saved me a tongue-lashing down the road."

Sawyer smiled. "Happy to help. I was just curious. Thanks!"

He left the lab and, after dropping the form off at his desk, he hurried to his car. He was going to go have a look at that bathroom window.

***

Mocking eyes watched him unlock his car and get in. Ears in hiding listened to the roar of the engine as he drove away. Lips smiled with satisfaction at the driver's hurry. This was fun. This was what life was all about.

Chapter Six

It was all Sawyer could do to make himself walk calmly into the Rank and File. He went immediately into the men's room, quickly opened the door and froze in place. He hadn't been in there since the night of Jack's murder. He was in the middle of it again, watching himself run from stall to bloody stall, screaming Jack's name. He could still see the blood on the floor; its smell permeating his nostrils, though in reality, it was long since cleaned away. He stepped back out the door and leaned against the wall in the hallway, sweat beaded on his forehead. He was breathing heavily as if he'd just run a marathon, unable to calm down and think clearly.

Softly at first, he heard the voice of Miss M float into his head, calming him, explaining to him in their last session how to relax and think his way through just such a situation. Taking deep breaths, Sawyer closed his eyes and felt the panic slowly leave him. He turned toward the men's room door and with another deep breath in and out, opened the door and entered. This time, the room was as it should be. He found the window in question and pulled the DNA kit from his jacket.

The window was about four feet off the ground and easily opened. Sawyer leaned over the open window and caught his breath as a voice whispered to him, "*It's here. Look closely. It's all here.*"

Thinking someone was behind him, he gasped and turned expecting to see one of the Forensics team enter the bathroom. Sawyer was ready to give them grief for sneaking up on him, but no one was there. Sawyer turned back to the window and his arm hair bristled with goose bumps.

The sill on the window was filled with dirt, having never been cleaned out. He found traces of blood, and a fairly large bunch of hair clinging to the window lock. Was it Jack's? Had it caught on the lock as he was forced through? Or was Jack still alive when he went through the window and pulled the hair from his killer?

Sawyer picked up the strands of hair with the tweezers from the DNA kit. He pulled out one of the vials and wiped at the blood with a cotton tip, placing it carefully into the vial when he was finished. He looked further at the window and found a crushed button inside the windowsill. It was broken in five pieces and he collected those with the tweezers as well, placing them in a small plastic evidence bag. The button didn't look like it'd been there very long.

Before he closed the window, something in the alley below caught his eye. Something he'd not seen the night of the murder. He leaned out the window, and looked straight down to the alley floor. Right between the wall below the window and several wooden boxes stacked just in front of the wall, he saw it. How could they have missed *that?*

Nearly buried under some bricks between the wall and the boxes, lay a bloody knife. Sawyer quickly closed the window and locked it. He ran from the men's room, out the tavern door and into the alley. He found it immediately but didn't touch it. He pulled his cell phone from his jeans pocket and called the department.

This was too important to keep to himself. He realized by calling the department now, he'd have to turn in all of the evidence he'd found, but he couldn't keep the murder weapon to himself. He'd planned to turn the windowsill evidence in anyway, quietly to Joe, hoping Joe wouldn't make a big deal of it. That wasn't the hard part. The *hard* part was going to be explaining to the captain what he was doing in the alley in the first place.

***

"Sit."

Captain Amerson stared at his hands clasped together on his desk. Sawyer sat down. He squirmed in his seat and tried to explain.

"Captain, I-"

Immediately the captain raised one hand, palm toward Sawyer, and the detective's mouth clamped shut. The captain's eyes never left the hand remaining on the desk as he brought the other down and, once again, clasped the two together. Sawyer could see he was struggling to keep his composure.

When he finally spoke, Captain Amerson's words were spoken slowly, carefully.

"I thought I'd made myself perfectly clear about your involvement with these investigations. I was fairly certain you understood you were no longer an active detective, but were confined to desk duty. Funny word...confined. I believe the dictionary will tell you it means 'unable to leave a place because of illness, imprisonment, etc.' What part of desk duty were you unclear of, Mr. Kingsley?"

Sawyer shifted his position in the chair and swallowed.

"I understood it, Captain, but the windowsill hadn't been inspected for evidence and I-"

"And you knew this, how?"

"Well, I was just wondering, I'd been thinking about it and thought maybe I should make sure. I was very sure when, I asked Joe in the lab, if the windowsill had been checked, that-"

Captain Amerson cleared his throat. "You asked Joe in Forensics?"

"Yes, and at first he told me he couldn't discuss the case, but I assured him I didn't want to do that. I only wanted him to check and see if the window area had been cleared."

"And so he obliged and told you what?"

"He was very surprised, and said that it hadn't been and that..."

Captain Amerson's voice rose significantly as he finished Sawyer's sentence for him. "...and that *he* would get a team on it right away. Yes?"

"Something like that, yes."

"And so you decided to have a go at it first, gather some evidence and then what were you going to do with the evidence?"

"I was going to turn it in! That's why I wanted to check out the window. I wanted to make sure if there was any evidence there, it was found. Captain, I found the murder weapon, didn't I?"

Amerson had picked up a pencil and was fiddling with it in his hands, which were still resting on top of his desk. He sighed heavily and tossed the pencil onto the desktop.

"Yes. Yes Kingsley, you did. And there's the rub."

The captain shoved his chair back and stood, walking to the window. He stared out at the town for a moment and turned toward Sawyer.

"You're forcing me to do something I do not wish to do. I told you your career would be over if I caught you meddling in either of these cases. You've just used the only 'get out of jail free card' you had. From this point on, if I find that you've been involved in either of these murder cases before I give you the go ahead, I'll fire you. You'll be done with police work, I'll see to that. I'll make sure any department you apply to knows you were let go for an inability to follow orders, and that will be the end of your career."

He turned back to the window. "Dismissed."

Sawyer stood, trying to think of something to say, but when he opened his mouth nothing came out. His jaw snapped closed and he left the captain's office.

His work desk was covered with paperwork, due in part to his foray into the field. He collapsed dejectedly into his chair and began to organize the work into stacks. Sawyer hoped if he worked hard enough and focused on what he was assigned to do, he could forget what an idiot he'd been.

An idiot? Really? He wondered if the Forensics team would've seen that knife. It was only because of the time of day that he'd found it. The sunlight from the street was just where it needed to be at that moment to cast the glint off the steel blade. He'd seen that flash of light and that's how he'd found the knife. Would the team have found it if they'd been there even an hour later?

Sawyer wanted to return to Amerson's office and read him the riot act. What if Forensics didn't get there in time? What if the knife hadn't been found? How could the captain possibly be upset with him for helping the investigation? He knew exactly why the captain was upset with him, but he felt finding the knife justified his actions. Amerson didn't even acknowledge how important this new evidence could be.

Just then, Miss M entered the room and after glancing around, made her way to Sawyer's desk. She sat down across from him and leaned back in her chair, folding her arms across her ample chest.

"I suppose Amerson sent you."

"No," she chuckled. "Nobody *sends* me anywhere. But I did hear from him about your little adventure and thought I'd come and see how you were."

Maizy directed him to a small conference room for privacy, and though he just wanted to get back to work and forget about the whole affair, he followed her. After sitting down he immediately began.

"He doesn't appreciate what I've done."

"Did he say that?"

"No, he didn't, but I could see his disappointment. It was pretty obvious."

Miss M smiled softly and said, "So he was disappointed with what you found then."

"Well, no," replied Sawyer, aware of where the conversation was going. "He's angry because I didn't do what I was ordered to do. I get that."

"Do you? Because what I'm hearing is you're troubled about the evidence you uncovered, not the fact that you disobeyed orders. To understand where your captain is coming from, you're going to have to think this through. We've talked about being honest with yourself, and that applies to this instance. Yes?"

"Yes, yes, I know. I'm angry with myself for doing what I did. I knew what I was doing when I took the DNA and fingerprint kits from Forensics. I just can't stand being at a desk all day when there's work to be done."

"I understand that, Sawyer," smiled Miss M, "and that is to be expected. No one likes desk duty. But you currently have consequences from inappropriate actions that you're working on. Those have to be addressed before you can be given the all-clear to get into the field again. We've talked about this, yes?"

"Yes."

"Well, I'm glad we've had a chance to have this little chat. Your next appointment is…Monday? Right?"

"Right."

Miss M stood and headed to the door. "I'll see you on Monday, then. Have a good weekend."

Sawyer nodded and rose from his chair, watching her walk through the bullpen and back down the hall. *What a mess I've gotten myself into. What a mess.* He returned to his desk and sat down once again. He pulled his first form from the stack when something caught his eye. At the corner of the desk, was a piece of paper with red edges.

Sawyer stood and walked slowly around his desk, bending over for a closer look at what was there. This had to be somebody's poor idea of a prank. The red looked like blood, the paper, mostly buried beneath other papers, appeared to be crumpled. He decided to ignore the prank, however tasteless it was, rather than make a big deal of it. People could be so stupid.

However, as he headed back around to his seat, the hair on the back of his neck suddenly sprang up. This was no prank. Could his gut be sober and back in action…finally? Before sitting down he pulled a couple of exam gloves from his desk and forced his hands into them as he walked back around the desk. He reached tentatively for the crumpled sheet and pulled it slowly from beneath the others, holding it by one tiny corner. There was a message scrawled across the paper in what appeared to be blood, probably the same blood as was splattered over the remaining page.

"What have you got there?"

Captain Amerson strode through the room and stopped abruptly where Sawyer stood.

"I don't know. I thought it was a stupid prank, but I don't know anyone in this department that would be this heartless. This is something else."

The office was gradually filling back up with officers returning from lunch. The normal buzz of voices and phones ringing hung in the air as the captain turned and addressed the room. "Did any of you see anyone at Kingsley's desk today?"

Murmurs of 'no sir' filled the room and the captain returned his gaze to Sawyer. He lowered his voice and said, "My office. Now."

Chapter Seven

Sawyer cleared his throat and followed Amerson, quickly pulling an evidence bag from his desk. He placed the letter in the evidence bag as he walked and once they were seated, Sawyer handed him the bag.

"I'm thinking you'll be wanting this."

"You think correctly. Now sit."

The message on the page was definitely written in the same red substance that covered the rest of the page, all of which would be tested in the lab to determine exactly what the substance was. It certainly looked like blood, but was it animal or human? And if it was human, whose was it? The message was taunting and even more so if the words actually were written in blood. Taunting and eerie, the note simply said, "WANNA PLAY?"

Captain Amerson picked up the bag and read the note. He tossed it onto the table, the distaste on his face apparent.

"Someone is playing a sick joke, or an even sicker game. Which murder are they referring to? The lightheartedness of this note makes my skin crawl. What kind of a human being does this?"

Sawyer's mind raced through the events of the last few days. He'd really done it when he went and investigated the window at the Rank and File without permission. Then he just happened to find the murder weapon, right there, right under the window in the alley. That certainly would have been seen by CSI whether or *not* anyone checked the window for evidence. This is a sharp group, and the CSI department was completely anal about their investigations, as they should be. Something wasn't right here.

Sawyer's eyes grew large as a thought popped into his head.

"He knows who I am. He knows I'm Jack's partner and he's toying with me." He sat forward in his chair as the thought permeated his brain. "I think that knife wasn't found the night of the murder because it wasn't there. I think it was planted there after the fact, and I'd be willing to bet the killer wanted *me* to find it. Why? I mean *if* that's even the case, why would it be important? I'd be willing to bet the killer was banking on my finding it."

The captain eyed him suspiciously. "Why do you say that?"

"I just find it highly suspicious that I'd discover evidence at a crime scene that hadn't already been found. The window is a good example. I really think if we were to talk to all the investigators on scene that night, we'd learn the window *did* get checked. But nothing was found on the window, so no evidence bag was ever used. Which means, the things I found weren't there the night of the murder."

"It would have been logged, though, as having been checked."

"Yes, it should have been. But that was a chaotic, emotional night. What if whoever was working the crime scene logged it on their clipboard, but never got it logged formally into the required paperwork. Something like that could easily have been overlooked with all the emotions of that night."

Captain Amerson picked up his phone and dialed a three-digit number.

"Hey Larry, I want the video feed from the bullpen for the last four days, and I want it now." He'd hung up the phone almost before he finished his sentence.

The captain wasn't a man to be messed with. There was only so far he could be pushed and Sawyer knew this killer had pretty much met that limit. His intense gray eyes could hold your attention like a loaded nine mil aimed right at your head. And at this minute, his eyes were about as intense as Sawyer had ever seen them.

"There are three things we know, as I see it," began Sawyer as he sat back in his chair and ran his hands through his hair in frustration.

"Only three? That's about right for these two murders."

"But think about it. First, this couldn't have been a mugging gone wrong. Jack would never have allowed that to happen. Ever. No matter how drunk he was when he went in that bathroom, there was a 'wildcat' part of him that he somehow kept sober and alert when things got tense. He could sense a problem in his sleep. And second, we know he wasn't killed in the alleyway. He was killed in the bathroom and no one heard a sound. Third, there wasn't a shred of evidence to be found at either crime scene. Nothing. That literally never happens. So, what does that tell us?"

Sawyer sat back in his chair. He laid his head against the seat back and stared at the ceiling. They were missing something. He knew it like he knew he had hands, but he couldn't figure out what it was. This was the one thing about the case that made him crazy. There was an answer; and he had a feeling in his gut that it was right in front of them.

"This killer is toying with me. I'm telling you, he wanted me to find that evidence, he wanted *me* to find it. But why? Why do I matter?"

"We need fresh eyes on this one. Someone who's not familiar with either case, with this department or with the town, and I think I know just the person." Captain Amerson sighed heavily and linked the fingers of both hands together, resting them on his pile of gray hair. "I want you to hear me out on this one."

"That sounds incredibly ominous."

"I mean it. Just hear me out. I have a partner for you, a five-year veteran of the Brooklyn police department. Hard worker, good follow-through, and tough as nails. I don't even know if you're strong enough to deal with this one."

"What's his name?"

"Well, now, that's the kicker. She's not a man."

Sawyer's eyes widened and his mouth fell open. "You're saying he's a *woman*?"

The captain sighed again, but couldn't help the smile that crossed his lips. "The last time I checked there was only one other option if an individual wasn't a man. And I said hear me out."

60

Sawyer lifted his hands and dropped them into his lap helplessly. Once the captain got something into his head, there was no changing his mind. But this woman wasn't the bottom line. There was a deal somewhere in here...he could feel it coming.

"This isn't a topic for discussion," said the captain firmly. "I've decided if you want back out there to investigate these murders, you'll go with this new detective, or you won't go at all."

There it was. The deal.

"I'll tell you what," said Amerson. "She's not due in town for another three weeks or so. That'll give you some time to get used to the idea before you're in the middle of it. I want you to give this some thought, but think all you want, Kingsley. She'll be your new partner when she gets here, like it or not. You'll stay at desk duty until she gets here. Understood?"

"Please tell me she's not going to be my babysitter."

"I'm telling you she's going to be your new partner. But, just so you know, I will not unleash you on the good citizens of Blakely without a partner. Take that however you'd like."

Sawyer stood to go. He walked to the door, turned to glance back at his captain, and then to stared at the floor with a smirk. "So...is she decent looking?"

"Will you get outta here with that!?" Captain Amerson snatched a paperback from his desk and pitched it at Kingsley. The book hit the wall as Sawyer stepped quickly out and shut the door with a chuckle.

Picking up his jacket from the back of his desk chair, Sawyer slipped into it and headed for the door. He stood on the large concrete porch between the two marbled pillars that graced the entry into the station.

He glanced around their small town. Not too big, not too small; just big enough to keep two police departments busy, but small enough to keep those officers safe, until now.

The crime rate was low in Blakely, Iowa, and so was the census. New business was welcomed as a way to decrease unemployment and increase the tax base by hopefully bringing new families into the community. Still, farming was the largest industry in town. A lot of corn was grown in Blakely and a lot of beef. On the hot muggy days of summer, the manure smell was strong enough to ruin any appetite, no matter how large or small. Fortunately, it was spring right now, and the heat hadn't cooked the manure enough to make the smell permeate the town. Maybe his new partner would hate it here. That would be just fine with him.

Sawyer was hungry and decided to get some lunch. There was a diner not far from the station that he enjoyed, so he walked the two blocks down Main Street and took a seat by the window. He settled in and picked up the menu from its place at the end of the table. He already knew what he wanted, but he perused the menu anyway to kill time while the waitress made her way to his table. When she arrived, he ordered his usual cheeseburger and fries and continued watching the scene outside his window.

Gazing lazily out at the quiet town, Sawyer's eye was drawn to an old maroon sedan parked across the street. A middle-aged man sat in the car, watching people go by through sunglasses worn high on his nose. He was also wearing a baseball cap low, over his forehead. He seemed somewhat familiar, but most of the town did, so that wasn't particularly unusual.

Slowly sunlight caught on the end of a gun barrel the man concealed in the crook of the arm he rested in his open window. Never changing its aim from the diner, he raised the gun.

"GUN! Everyone on the floor. NOW!"

People screamed and hit the floor just as a bullet shattered the glass in the diner's front window. When the shooting stopped, Sawyer jumped to his feet and ran out the door as the shooter sped away, firing off a couple more rounds as he went.

A police cruiser with uniformed officers had just left the station, saw the shooting and screeched to a halt in front of the restaurant as another cruiser squealed after the shooter. The officers jumped from their vehicle and rushed to Sawyer.

Was that guy shooting at me?

"Is everyone okay?" Officer Teltzing asked as he scanned the broken window and the people inside the restaurant. His partner, Officer Miller, ran into the diner as Teltzing continued. "What just happened?"

Sawyer was brought back to the present by the sound of Teltzer's voice. He stared at his coworker.

"I'm not sure. I think it was probably a random shooting. Interestingly, the guy looked vaguely familiar, but I couldn't see enough of him to be sure. I happened to be watching him and saw the gun as he raised it to fire. I ordered everyone onto the floor about the time the bullets started coming through the window.

"You probably saved lives by doing that, Kingsley. Good thing you were here. No one else would have noticed that gun."

"Yeah, I guess," said Sawyer, still wondering if his being there wasn't just happenstance, but part of a

63

plan. Was it a good thing he was there? Or did his being there put everyone in the restaurant at risk?

"You okay, Kingsley?"

"Yeah, yeah, I'm fine. Just, you know, wondering what that was all about."

"For sure. I'll head back to the office and file a report. Captain will probably want a statement from you. I'll have Miller stay here and interview customers, see if anyone else saw something besides you."

"Sounds good. I'll...I'll head back to the station."

"You're sure you're okay? I can give you a lift."

"No, I'm good. The walk will do me good."

As he headed back to the station, Sawyer thought about the strange note on his desk and the shooting he'd just experienced. The chilling words 'Wanna Play?' made his skin crawl.

Sawyer wanted to play. Yes, he certainly did.

Chapter Eight

The basement apartment was old, as evidenced by the peeling paint on the cement walls. The walls themselves were covered with old and current newspaper articles featuring the duo, Baker and Kingsley. Headlines reading "Kings of Convictions – Baker and Kingsley at it Again", or "Bad Guys Beware – Daring Duo Hits Pay Dirt" made up much of the articles.

A gloved hand holding a red permanent marker reached up to each article, slowly and deliberately drawing a red line through the form of Jack Baker in each picture. With each mark a soft chuckle escaped his mouth.

You both think you're so special, strutting around town like you own the place. You bleed and die just like we all do. I've proven that haven't I? Let's just see how well you do when there's only one of you doing the hunting.

During the weeks Kingsley was drinking and missing work, the killer was wonderfully gratified. Certain he'd made his point and hopeful Kingsley would realize how useless he was without his partner, he'd hoped the detective would leave the department for good. However, now the pathetic excuse for an investigator was back to work, on desk duty. The killer was disappointed, for sure, but he realized it was quite heartwarming to see Kingsley's frustration and humiliation. Kingsley's actions made it obvious how much he hated desk duty.

Still, the situation was a bit frustrating because, if his point was going to be made, it was necessary to get the detective out into the field so Kingsley could actually see how low his level of efficiency truly was without his 'esteemed' partner. This was going to be fun to watch. But what could he do to get Kingsley out of the office and back into the investigation?

Suddenly, a deep, throaty laughter filled the room. The man had to sit down to keep himself from falling over. This was going to be good.

He moved his chair closer to the desk, pulled out a piece of paper, and began writing a little note. This had to be good; it had to be the note of the century, one that would make Kingsley unable to stay where he was, doing what he was doing. How did he want to word this?

Chuckling at the whole idea, the writer could hardly contain his joy.

***

The investigation into the shooting at the diner went nowhere in a very short time. Bullet fragments were scrutinized, but there was nothing special about them. No one had seen the license plate; the car was an early model Chevy, of which there were dozens in Blakely.

Sawyer kept wondering if those bullets were meant for him, but why would he think that? This whole investigation was beginning to feel very personal. Why? He had no reason to believe it was, and yet that's where every round of questions brought him. He kept musing over the idea that if he'd not been in that diner, would there still have been bullets flying? He would love to have an answer to that question, but there was none. And so his frustration and determination both reached new heights.

As he sat at his desk on this sunny, late spring day, he stared out the window. His head was full of questions but he wasn't allowed to seek out any answers for them. He was stuck filling out forms while a killer walked the streets of his town. Something had to give here, and soon. He didn't know how much longer he could take doing nothing.

***

Captain Amerson strode purposefully into his office. He went straight to his desk and laid the file he was holding on the desktop. He stared at it, unable to move. Having been forewarned by the guys in the lab, he was now both curious and apprehensive. He'd been told this was a result no one expected, and his stomach knotted at the site of the file. It wasn't very often the lab guys were affected by lab results. They'd seen it all; but apparently, they'd never seen this before.

He shook himself free of the thoughts that raced through his head and hung his uniform jacket and hat on the coat rack. He turned back to his desk, pulled the chair out and sat down. He moved the chair closer to the desk, picked up the file and tenuously opened it. Pulling the lab sheets from the folder, he laid the folder back on the desk, leaned back in his chair with a heavy sigh, and began to read.

As he read, his mouth went completely dry, while the impact of the words on the page burned in his brain. He rubbed his hand over his face and reread the report again and again and again, his stomach coming closer to losing its contents with each read-through. Who *was* this killer? Heartless and cold as stone, he was sick to his core. He had to be stopped, and to stop someone like this it was going to take the likes of Sawyer Kingsley. Amerson knew it, but he also knew when he told Detective Kingsley the results of the blood work, he might just lose him again. There was no way around it. He had to be told, and as his captain, the job fell to Amerson. There were days he hated his job, and this day would be at the top of that list.

He picked up the phone and rang Kingsley's desk.

"Yeah."

"My office."

Sawyer hung up the phone and Amerson watched him approach through his office window. Trying his best to put on a good face, he knew by Sawyer's look he'd failed miserably.

"You look awful. What's up?"

"Sit."

Sawyer sat down across from his captain and waited.

Captain Amerson ran his hand through his hair, picked up the papers and began. He could feel the color draining from his face.

"The blood test on the note from your desk is back. I have it right here in my hand. It's not pretty. I've asked the counselor to join us."

"Miss M? What for? Come on Captain, it can't be that bad, can it?"

Miss M came through the door just as Amerson responded.

"It's that bad."

"Good morning all," she said cheerfully, then changed her tone when she saw Amerson's face. "What's happened?"

"Nothing," began the captain. "Well, something. Just…please…sit down. I wanted you to be here for…for Sawyer."

"Captain," began Sawyer, "I think I can handle this. What is this all about? It's a DNA test to see if the blood was human and to determine whose blood it is, if we can. Right?"

"The blood is human, Sawyer, and it belongs to Jack Baker." That came out a lot faster and a lot harder than he'd meant for it to.

Miss M's hand flew to her mouth and she stared at Sawyer.

"No…that's…that's…wrong. You *tell* them to do it *again*. They did it wrong."

"Sawyer, listen to me," replied Amerson. "There are three results in this folder. The lab had a difficult time believing the results themselves, so they ran the test three times. It's Jack's blood. Each test confirmed that."

Sawyer's jaw clamped shut, every muscle in his body tensed and he turned his head away from both the captain and Miss M. He rubbed his jaw with one hand and held the other in a fist on the armrest, to keep shaking.

"Breathe, Sawyer," said Miss M. "Just breathe. I know this is hard, but finding Jack's body was harder than this, and you made it through that. You'll make it through this as well. Just keep breathing."

Sawyer forced air into his lungs, forcing it back out again. He turned his head to the side and then the other, cracking his neck.

"I want in on this one, Captain. You said if it came back related to either case you'd let me in. I need to do this for Jack."

"If Maizy clears you for duty, I'm good with that. But, Sawyer, you're going to have to get a handle on this. You can't investigate anything with a chip on your shoulder. We need you on this investigation, but we need you at full speed, with no fists. Am I clear?"

"I need to go. I…I have to walk. I need some air."

"Go home," said the captain. "Go home and stay there. Walk around your block if you have to, but stay close to home. That's an order."

Sawyer nodded to Amerson as he stood and walked swiftly out the door, closing it softly behind him. The effort it took to do that wasn't lost on his captain.

"He's going to need you in the next few hours. I'd appreciate it if you could make yourself available to him."

"I can do that," replied Maizy as she stood. "I'll clear my calendar for the day. He can come in any time tomorrow as well. I'll fit him in."

"I don't know if he's going to make use of that, but I appreciate your willingness."

"We'll talk later."

Maizy left the office and Amerson sat quietly at his desk. He knew there hadn't been an easy way to break this news to his detective, but he certainly wished he could have found one.

What is it that turns people into monsters? Were they good people to begin with, or were they born monsters?

***

Sawyer didn't go to his car right away. Questions filled his head as he moved along the sidewalks and down quiet streets. The world seemed to be folding in on him, and he felt powerless to stop it. With nothing to go on, how would he ever find this killer? How would he identify a man who knew his way around a crime scene? Was he a stalker? Had he somehow figured out what led investigators to a perp? Did he watch forensics shows on TV that talked about how a killer is found? Where did he learn how to clean up a crime scene so completely there wouldn't even be hair left...anywhere? Who *was* this guy?

On he walked, through town and around the neighborhoods until night fell, not realizing how long he'd been at it. When he saw streetlights coming on, he was approaching the station again. The light was still on in Captain Amerson's office, and he thought for a second about going back in, but what was left to say? He didn't feel angry any longer, he felt exhausted...emotionally exhausted. As much as he wanted to stop thinking about these murders, stop examining and re-examining the evidence from the two scenes he had, he couldn't. There was some kind of emotional motor inside him that pushed him along, keeping him moving in the same circle over and over and over.

Sawyer's need to see his evidence board grew. He desperately had to see the pieces to the first puzzle in the hope they would lead him to pieces of the second…Jack's puzzle. He had so little to go on and such a fierce compulsion to put the pieces together, but it was no longer just for Jack. He'd been leaving the Franz family out of the equation, but something told him both crime scenes needed to be in there. He would figure this out, and he'd do it for Jack and for the Franz's. They were depending on him to find their killer, and he would find him. That was something he *could* do.

Chapter Nine

Sawyer came through the door, slamming it angrily behind him. He'd not come home immediately like the captain ordered, but lost himself in the walk around town. Couldn't be helped. He needed the air. If this cost him his job, he'd have to live with it.

He stood in the entry for a while, gazing into the living room when his eyes came to rest on the engagement ring still lying in the carpet by the chair leg. He leaned back against the door, giving in to the thought he'd fought since he left the captain's office.

"I need a drink."

He strode through the living room and into the kitchen, opening several cabinets before remembering he'd thrown out all the liquor in the house weeks ago. Good thing, because he knew he'd have emptied every bottle. Sawyer slammed the last cupboard door shut, and strode through the living room, hurrying past the ring on the carpet then stormed down the hall to his bedroom.

His thoughts returned to his friend, lying in the alley that night. Was Jack already dead when he was thrown from the window? How had the demented killer taken enough blood from his body to write a note with it? He stood before the evidence board, glaring at the pictures and pages of evidence, hands unknowingly clenched into angry fists. He could feel his brain creeping back into the pit he'd worked so hard getting out of. He didn't want to go there.

Forcing his hands to relax at his side, he studied every photo, every piece of written evidence now tacked to the board. Each photo he saw of the Franz family turned into the same picture in his mind…the scene from the alley and the blank death stare of his partner, Jack. Sawyer blinked and then blinked again and still Jack stared out from every picture.

Thinking he needed that drink after all, Sawyer went to his car and drove to the Rank and File. He *really* needed a drink. However, when he entered the tavern, it wasn't the bar that drew him in, it was the men's room. Unable to keep himself from it, he marched determinedly to the door of the bathroom and pulled it open.

The voice he'd heard those weeks before popped into his mind again. *It's here. Look closely. It's all here.* Frozen in the entry, his back to the door, Sawyer took in every detail of the room…the stalls, the drain in the middle of the floor, the pipes through the ceiling, the window and sill, the mirrored sinks, hand soap and towel dispensers. Silently he waited for the room to speak to him, but the room said nothing.

Sawyer turned and moved in the direction of the window. He opened it up and inspected the sill, waited, and inspected it again. There was nothing there. He gazed out at the place in the alley where the killer had left Jack's body. In his mind's eye, Jack was still there. But this time, Sawyer inspected the placement of the body. His mind was clear and focused and he was able to recall every detail of the body and the night, Jack's vacant stare, his hair, the tone of his skin. It all came back to him in perfect clarity.

There was something about Jack's body, something about the way it was placed that was all wrong. Sawyer shook his head. *Don't be stupid. He'd just been dumped out a bathroom window. You think his body is going to be perfectly placed? Get a grip.* But the feeling wouldn't leave him. He gazed back out the window, picturing his friend once again.

Perfectly placed. What was he missing? Jack's arms were wide; the left hand made a fist, the right hand...the right hand...*pointed into the alley*. His right hand was definitely pointing into the alley. Happenstance? Sawyer didn't think so. His friend hadn't died in the bathroom, he'd died in the alley, but not before he'd left a message for Sawyer.

Sawyer hurried from the men's room, out the door and into the alley. This time, he walked slowly, heart pumping, but it was far too dark to see anything. He jogged to his car, grabbed a flashlight from the glove box, and headed back to the alley. Inch by inch he scoured the end of the alley, the wall and the ground. He moved stinky piles of junk, turned over every piece of whatever he found. In the end, he stood staring at the brick wall that signaled the end of the alley. He moved the beam of his flashlight slowly across each row of bricks. The first time through there was nothing. Second time through...there it was. One of the bricks had no mortar around it.

The brick was eye level, making it easy to reach. He pulled it from its place in the wall with his heart pounding out of his chest. He could feel beads of sweat forming on his forehead. In the spot left vacant by the brick and tucked deep into the wall lay a small recorder. He pulled some gloves from his pocket and wriggled his now shaking hands into them. Sawyer quickly removed the device and inspected it for explosives. It was just a voice recorder. Dare he listen to it without turning it in as evidence first? He'd screwed up enough on these two investigations. As much as he wanted to take this on himself, if he ever hoped to investigate these murders again, he'd better not touch it.

Heart still pounding, Sawyer placed the recorder in an evidence bag and ran back to his car. He hoped Captain Amerson was still at the office. It was now after midnight and he realized he'd have to explain why he'd once again disobeyed a direct order and not stayed at home. Why hadn't he gone right home? He'd needed air, lots of air, and the time just slipped away from him. He'd gone right home as soon as he'd realized the time, but obviously he'd not stayed there. He hadn't come to the Rank and File to investigate; he'd come to extinguish the searing pain of the DNA results from the note with as much hard liquor as he could consume.

None of that would matter. He'd disobeyed a direct order. Again. He glanced at the evidence bag on the seat beside him. It wouldn't have been found if he hadn't disobeyed that order, and it needed to be found. He hoped the captain would understand that and see how strong his need was to be part of finding Jack's killer. He couldn't understand what it was that made him feel the way he did, but he was certain Jack's killer was also the killer of the Franz family.

Captain Amerson's light was still on when Sawyer drove into the station parking lot. He would do what he had to do to get this investigation going. There was no turning back now; he'd simply give Captain the evidence bag. At least he could honestly say he'd not listened to the recording, if there even was a recording. With that thought, his heart sank just a little. What if it was nothing?

Sawyer strode through the bullpen and to the captain's office door. He paused briefly before knocking.

"Come in, Sawyer."

Sawyer opened the door and walked to Amerson's desk. He laid the evidence bag in front of his boss and sat down. "How did you know it was me?"

Captain Amerson gave him the 'duh' look and Sawyer forced a grin.

"I didn't go right home, I went for a walk."

"I know."

Sawyer continued without even hearing his captain's reply. "I needed a drink and I'd thrown out all the liquor I had at the house, so I drove to the Rank and File for a drink."

"I figured."

Again, not really hearing the response, he continued, "I don't know what happened, but I ended up revisiting the crime scene. I know I shouldn't have, and I didn't go there for that purpose, I swear."

"I know."

"It's just that--" Suddenly Sawyer realized he'd been ignoring Amerson's responses. "You do?"

Captain Amerson smiled softly. "Yes, I do. I knew there was no way you were going to go home; you were far too upset. And I figured you'd not be able to stay away from the crime scene, *and* I was fairly certain you'd find something, which--" he picked up the bag, examining it with a smile, "it looks to me like you have. I get it, Kingsley. I knew the minute I said the words there was no way you were going to be able to do what I asked."

Sawyer visibly relaxed in his chair.

"I was fighting with myself all the way over here because, once again, I'd not followed a direct order. I didn't mean to do that, it was just that my mind took me for a ride and I went along. I apologize. It wasn't deliberate. It was more…I don't know…almost zombie mode."

"I get it. What have you brought me?"

Sawyer explained how he came to be in the alley again and how he'd found the recorder.

"Well," began Captain Amerson, "what say we have a listen?" He donned the familiar exam gloves and pulled the recorder from the evidence bag.

"I checked it and didn't see any signs of tampering," said Sawyer, not realizing he was whispering.

"Okay then, here we go."

Captain Amerson hit the play button and a hissing noise came from the device. It sounded like air, or wind interference. A gravelly voice, low and rough came through the speakers.

"I figured you'd probably find this, Kingsley. I was hoping you would. Oh, don't worry-- I've wiped it clean *and* disguised the voice…you'll find no evidence in here. Just me telling you this time you're not going to make the front page of the paper for your superior investigative skills. You're going to lose on this one. (Garbled laughter) Yeah, you're going to lose on this one."

Amerson turned off the recorder and stared at Kingsley.

"I'd be willing to bet," said the captain, "that he arranged Jack's hand so it would point to the back of the alley."

"So, it wasn't a message from Jack after all." Sawyer sat back in his chair, his eyes focused and angry. "You know, the *worst* thing he could've done is challenge me. I'll find him now, for sure, and if he's a real good boy, I'll let him live to see the inside of a courtroom. Then I'll make sure I have a front row seat at his execution."

He stood and strode from the room without another word. Nothing else seemed to matter now. He was back. His focus was clear; his gut was awake and ready for work. Tonight he would sleep very well, as he would every night from here on out, because tomorrow and the day after that and the day after that, he would need to be at his most efficient. This man would pay for what he'd done, and yes, the game was on.

As predicted, he was out the minute his head hit the pillow. His dreams were flooded with images of Jack and the Franz family following him everywhere he went. They weren't especially frustrating dreams, but more like reminders. It was as if they were asking him not to forget them, asking that he help them, that he find their killer and give them peace. The feeling of the dreams, it seemed, was about their need for peace.

He lay in bed the next morning for several minutes before sitting up. *I hear you. I hear all of you, and I'll find your killer. I promise you that.*

Chapter Ten

At a slender and shapely five feet seven inches tall, Esley Rider was a firecracker that picked her explosions carefully, and when she exploded, it wasn't soft and lovely. She was a do-it-yourself kind of woman who had no need for a man in her life; she liked living alone. Not big on words, she was sure of her abilities, and that's all anyone needed to know about her. Her dark hair and intense brown eyes set off her small oval face perfectly. She had a simple beauty that she cared little about. Yes, she wore her makeup, but it was minimal, as her long dark lashes didn't require much help. Her dark hair was pulled back into a ponytail. Functional…and it seemed to fit her personality.

She strolled into the captain's office on this morning with all the attitude of a lioness. She owned the room. Still respectful to her captain; she was confident and sure of herself. Sawyer disliked her immediately. He'd already been with a woman who thought she knew what was best for, not just her, but the known universe as well, and he wasn't impressed.

She was simply a shorter version of Jillian, and she irritated him right off the bat.

Captain Amerson introduced Sawyer to his new partner.

"Sawyer Kingsley, I'd like you to meet Esley Rider, your new partner." He beamed with all the excitement of a new parent.

Sawyer forced a grin, but his handshake pretty much said it all. He could tell by the look on her face she was aware of his lack of enthusiasm. She smiled a somewhat sarcastic 'this is going to be fun' smile and sat down in the chair beside him.

"I want you two to play nice out there. Rider, you're going to have to keep Mr. Kingsley here from killing the suspects before they have a right to due process."

"Captain--" Sawyer began his protest, but the captain held up his hand, stopping him before he'd begun.

"We've talked about this Kingsley. I believe you'll both work well together. As a matter of fact, I'm sure of it. The reason being, for both of you, it's pretty much your last chance."

Sawyer shot a surprised glance at his new partner and she twisted uncomfortably in her seat.

"Kingsley, you'll take point on these two investigations. You'll be working the Baker and Franz killings exclusively, and as a *team*. Any questions?" Amerson looked expectantly at both detectives.

"Well, for starters," began Esley, her large dark eyes inspecting every inch of Sawyer as she spoke, "Mr. Kingsley is not thrilled with the prospect of working with me. How is this investigation supposed to be successful if we're opponents instead of partners?"

"Don't kid yourself, Rider," said the captain flatly. "You should be used to working with people who don't want to work with you. The chips on both your and Kingsley's shoulders are so big I can see them from here. I expect you to deal with your issues and get the job done."

Sawyer said nothing, but knew right away Captain Amerson hadn't been totally honest with him concerning this new detective. "Crème de la crème, eh Captain?" he frowned.

"You're a fine one to talk, Kingsley," replied the captain. "I suggest you both stow your attitudes and get busy. There's a lot of work to be done on these cases. Dismissed. Both of you."

The two detectives left the captain's office and went to Kingsley's desk. He saw a new desk had been set up so the front of both desks met, which meant they both had to actually *look* at each other. *Things just keep getting better and better,* Sawyer thought.

"Bring me up to speed on these investigations," started Esley, as she strode purposefully to her desk and sat down. "Where are we with them? Who are the victims? Are there any leads on the perp or perps? You know, all the usual." She pulled a writing tablet from the top of her desk and grabbed a pencil, looking expectantly at Sawyer, and waited.

Sawyer looked at her with no expression. His placed his elbow on the desk and rested his head on one fist trying to decide if he wanted to answer her. He remembered the captain's words and began. "The *victims* are a family of five, Mom, Dad and three kids, all shot execution style with a handgun at close range. The bodies were arranged in the middle of the living room floor, face down, heads placed toward the entry. The second murder is my former partner, Jack Baker."

Esley responded before he could continue. "Ah," she said, nodding, "makes sense. No wonder you're so rude."

"Right." Sawyer was gritting his teeth. "What's your excuse?"

Esley stood, shoving her chair back with her legs. "Watch your tone."

"I can certainly do that," replied Sawyer, happy to have gotten some emotion out of her. "Who's watching yours?"

The conversation went downhill from there, and when Sawyer stood to go, Esley stayed put.

"You planning on helping with these investigations?"

"I'm trying to decide." Esley stood and shot him a disgusted glare as she walked through the door ahead of him.

The twenty-minute ride to the Franz farm was spent in complete silence. Esley stared out the side window watching the farms go by. The stalks of corn were about two feet high, as summer was about to start. Rows and rows of corn covered most of the fields.

Sawyer thought he should probably take the high road and try to ask her some questions about herself, but he couldn't bring himself to do it. She was a pain in his butt with a big city attitude that, unless she shrunk it down about ten sizes, wouldn't fit in the town of Blakely. But he knew he couldn't tell her that. Still, it didn't stop his desire to do so.

Sawyer thought back to the last time he'd driven out to the Franz farm. He hadn't actually done the driving. Jack was in the driver's seat, and it was Jack's car. He remembered their conversation and wished he'd paid more attention. He missed his partner and confidante. The counseling sessions with

Miss M had pretty much saved him. The therapist turned out to be someone he could really talk to, and without Jack to bounce his thoughts off of, he'd needed that.

He glanced to the passenger seat and saw only the back of Detective Rider's head. It would never be the same without Jack and he knew it. Having a new partner made that fact painfully clear and he disliked her all the more.

He pulled into the drive and continued to the house. The area was still a crime scene and hadn't been cleared, except for the outbuildings where the daily care of the farm animals still needed to be done. So far, the neighboring farmers were doing the chores, but soon the animals would go up for sale once the probate process was complete. From Sawyer's understanding, that could take months. He had no idea how probate played out because that was never part of his investigation, and he was glad about that. It seemed like a sticky process to him. *Jillian would've been all over it--*. He stopped himself from thinking more about that as they came to a halt in front of the farmhouse.

They left the car and walked up the steps to the front door. Sawyer took a set of keys from his pants' pocket and opened the door. Everything was the same as before; the crime scene tape was still up, blood spots on the carpet in the living room; everything was in the same place as it was the day the family was found. Two pair of coveralls lay folded neatly by the door and they slipped silently into them, pulling on the shoe covers before entering the living room. The house was silent with only the swishing the crime scene coveralls made when they walked.

Sawyer was the first to enter the living room, bending over and going under the tape. His eyes missed nothing this time. It was as if his senses were heightened by the taunting he'd heard on the recorder that night with the captain. The walls were white, too white, yet there was no smell of new paint. There was, however, still a fairly faint smell of bleach and he walked to the wall and sniffed it. The smell was stronger. This was something he'd not noticed before.

"I think the perp washed the walls with bleach. There was no blood spatter anywhere and the assumption was they were killed somewhere else and brought in here. I think the killer may have washed the walls down with an oxygen-based bleach. Doesn't stink like bleach, nor does it leave trace evidence. Which makes me wonder if the walls were checked for blood. I'll have to ask."

"Check this out," called Esley from the opposite corner of the room. She was pointing to a spot in the corner where two walls met. Until he got right up to it, Sawyer saw nothing, but then he could make out a very faint spot of what could've been blood.

"Keep checking, see if you can find more of that. I'm going to call the department and see if I can get some CSI's out here. I want to make sure nothing's been missed."

Once he called and got CSI on its way, he called Captain Amerson.

"Amerson."

"Captain, I'm out at the Franz house with Rider and we think we may have found some blood spatter, possibly missed in the initial investigation. I've got CSI on the way."

"Okay." There was a warning tone to the captain's voice. "Just remember, he's messed with crime scenes before. The placement of Jack's hand pointing to the wall and the evidence in the windowsill, are a couple of examples. If he's come back to the site and decided to mess with us, this could be part of his 'fun.' Just be wary."

"Will do."

Sawyer returned to the house and didn't see Esley. "Rider!" he called out, walking into the kitchen and then to the pantry. With no response from the detective, he began to worry. Soon he was running from room to room first downstairs and then upstairs, checking out each window to see if she was outside. He ran back down to the kitchen and heard a low moan from the mudroom. He raced to the mudroom and found Esley lying on the floor holding her head, just coming around.

"What happened?" he asked, helping her sit up. He glanced quickly to the back of her head. "Go slowly, you're bleeding back there."

"I...I think someone hit me from behind, or maybe I bumped into something."

"If you bumped into something, you had to hit it pretty hard. You didn't hear anyone come up behind you?"

"No, nothing. Maybe he was already in here when I came in."

There were footprints on the floor around her. Sawyer pulled her to her feet, careful not to disturb the footprints and walked her into the kitchen. He sat her down at the table and returned to the mudroom. The footprints were there, clear and dark with mud, and definitely not Esley's.

"You're sure you didn't hear anyone behind you?" he said, as he returned to the table where Esley was seated. She was gingerly feeling her head where there was now a large bump growing under the cut.

"This isn't my first rodeo, Kingsley. No, not a sound. I think he was already here and we interrupted whatever he was doing." She winced as she touched the lump.

"He was planting evidence, which he's become very good at." Sawyer looked at the blood on her head and grabbed a bunch of paper towels from the roll on the counter. "Here, put some pressure on that." Then he continued with his thought. "I'm pretty sure he knew we were coming, but I can't figure out how he would know that."

He stood staring at Esley as his mind raced over what he'd just said. Only two people that he knew of were aware they were planning a trip to the crime scene...he and Esley.

"When CSI gets here, I'm going to have them go over this house completely, again. I want every inch re-examined. If he was here, and we interrupted him, he may not have had enough time to clean up the scene. We might catch a break. If they find nothing more, if the blood is planted, then we'll check my desk for a bug and see if someone is listening in on our conversations. Then we'll have a whole new set of questions."

The CSI team arrived and Sawyer took Esley to the Emergency Department to have her checked out, in spite of her rather loud and forceful protests. It had already been a long day, and it was only noon.

Chapter Eleven

By the time Esley was cleared for duty and they were back at the station, it was mid- afternoon. It had been a full day, but there was much paperwork to do, many reports to be filled out and turned in. The nagging question in Sawyer's mind was still there and had plagued him since Esley was injured. Did the killer know they were coming and waited for them? Did he not know they were coming and was caught off guard while planting evidence?

The spot in the corner turned out to be human blood and was sent off for DNA testing. There was a hair found in the pantry that hadn't been there before, but it could belong to the Franz family, to Esley or even to Sawyer, or it could have been planted there by the killer. Until they had results of the tests on those two pieces of evidence, they were back where they started…with nothing to go on in either investigation.

As much as he hated admitting it, Esley presented another set of eyes, and that could be a good thing in stalemated investigations such as this one. A rancid taste ran up from his belly just thinking about actually turning to her for help, but he would do anything to help find Jack's killer. Anything...

After finishing the paperwork, Sawyer wondered if Esley was up to checking out the alley where Jack died. He was about to ask when she spoke up.

"So...what about that second crime scene? An alley, wasn't it?"

Sawyer looked up from the final form he'd just signed. "Yes, I didn't know if you'd be up to examining another site. It's been a pretty eventful day already."

"I don't like being treated like a baby, Detective," she said flatly. "We have a job to do. Let's get it done."

Her tone was demeaning, which made him sorry he'd not demanded she go look at the crime scene. Gritting his teeth, he kept his thoughts to himself. Without acknowledging her 'Wonder Woman' persona, he rose, grabbed his coat and headed to the car. She quickly followed after him with a look of stubborn determination.

He immediately felt bad, especially since she'd suffered a pretty significant blow to the head.

"Listen," he said softly, "this is going to take some getting used to for me, and probably for you as well. Let's try this again. I think you could use some food, don't you? You probably need some more rest before hitting the case again. Let's go get some lunch."

"I'm more than capable of knowing when I need rest. I--"

"We're going to get something to eat. Now."

Sawyer heard no more from the passenger seat and he took her to the diner by the station. The window had been repaired and had he not been there on that day, he wouldn't even have known there'd been a problem.

They took a seat by the same window and sat across from each other in the booth.

"So, tell me about yourself," he said. "How long have you been a police officer?"

She stared at him for a moment before speaking. "It doesn't matter. I'm a police officer. Now, actually, a detective."

"Okay," Sawyer sighed. "What do you do for fun?"

Esley snickered pathetically. "Like detectives have any time for fun."

Sawyer made a couple more attempts at conversation and was finally saved by the waitress. They ordered their meal and once the waitress left, Sawyer stood and walked to the rack that held the daily paper. He picked one up and returned to the booth. He couldn't remember the last time he'd read the newspaper. If Esley wouldn't talk to him, he'd enjoy some reading.

He plopped back down in the booth and started on the front page. He paid little attention to Esley, who was now scanning the restaurant. If she didn't want to be partners, then he wasn't sure what they'd be. *I guess we'll just be co-workers.*

Sawyer lowered the paper a tiny bit so he could see what she was doing. She stared out at the street and watched the passersby, apparently content to be left alone. He continued reading until their lunch came, then they ate in silence.

Once they finished lunch, the two detectives rode the few minutes to the Rank and File and parked on the street in front of the alley. He first took her inside the tavern and she waited while he checked to make sure the men's room was clear. As they entered he explained where everything had been at the time of the murder and what they'd discovered about the killer, which was nothing much.

"Are there photos of the crime scene?"

"Of course," he replied looking at her like she'd suddenly grown purple hair. "There are always photos of the crime scene."

"I'm aware of that," she said, somewhat sarcastically. "What I want to know is if there is any way to determine if our killer is left or right handed from the blood patterns on the floor. I need to see the drag marks, how the body was positioned in the alley, if there were fingerprints on the window grip that would tell us which hand he used to open the window. I need to see the wounds on the body. That is usually a good indicator of which hand the killer favors."

"He was right-handed, and of course we checked that out. Are you kidding me? You think big cities are the only place where law enforcement actually uses their brains? We happen to have a top-notch CSI division here. They know what they're doing, and so do we as investigators."

Esley turned to face him, her lips pursed and her jaw set. "I wasn't questioning your ability or your department's. I was simply stating I want to see for myself so I can draw my own conclusions. It's that whole 'fairy tale' idea that the more fresh sets of eyes you have on a crime scene, the more chance you have of finding things. Sorry to ruffle your feathers." She was in full sarcasm mode by the time she finished.

"You know, you and I have to come to some kind of truce if this partnership is going to work."

"Just do your job and I'll do mine. Other than that, I want nothing to do with you."

"Wow. You're a piece of work aren't you? What a delight it will be to solve these crimes with you on board."

"I need to see the alley. And I need some fresh air."

She strode to the door and pulled it open. She left without another word.

"Jack, where are you when I need you? We had a good thing, you know?" Sawyer moved to the door and pulled it open as he thought to himself, *why'd you have to go and get yourself killed?*

By the time he reached the alley, Esley was already there with gloves donned checking through all that had already been checked. Sawyer tried to acknowledge her right and her need to see things first hand. He said nothing to her and simply used the time to further investigate what had already been gone over at least a hundred times. He hated this alley. He hated the memory it induced in him. But he forced himself to look and look again at the same things he'd already seen dozens of times. Clearly, as the months had passed, there was new garbage and new items in the alley. Because the area was used for loading supplies and products for various businesses, the department couldn't keep it blocked off forever. Little by little they'd lost much of the original crime scene; what remained was now pretty much useless.

"The killer has planted evidence from day one, but only what he wants us to see. He taunts us, especially with this scene. He left us a recording that was found at the back of the alley only recently. You can listen to it if you want, the recorder's in lockup."

"I'd like to go see what they have in the way of evidence now."

It was a demand, not a request and Sawyer turned and headed to the car. She acted as if she was expecting him to protest. He didn't and her irritation made him smile.

Once they were in the evidence lockup, Sawyer led her to the desk. Sergeant Lenny Carson, an old-timer with the department, was the Officer in Charge in evidence lockup and had been for the past ten years.

"Hey Lenny," Sawyer called out. "How's it goin'?"

Lenny looked at Sawyer with a brief distaste, replaced immediately by a welcoming smile. "Goin' great down here, always a swingin' joint to be stuck in. And who is this lovely lady?"

Esley stuck out her hand. "I'm Esley Rider, and you are?"

"Clay Carson…uh, *Sergeant* Clay Carson. Nice to meet you."

Before Sawyer could jump in, Esley spoke up. "I hear you've got evidence down here for the Franz and Baker murders."

"Little lady, we've got evidence down here from every murder committed in this town since 1923. And, yes, we have the Franz and Baker evidence as well."

"Just to be perfectly clear, I'm *not* a 'little lady,' and I'm relatively certain you have all the evidence I've asked for. There's little need to tell me you have it. Now, may I see it?"

Lenny shot a 'whoa' glance at Sawyer who shrugged and looked away.

"I'll be right back," he mumbled, and quickly retrieved the requested evidence boxes. They were light.

"Is there anything in these?" Esley asked as she picked up the boxes and nearly tossed them over her head. She obviously expected them to be much heavier.

"There's a few things, but nothing that tells us anything we need to know," conceded Sawyer. Lenny nodded in agreement.

"That's a sly one, that guy," he said softly. "About as sly as they come."

Esley carried the boxes to a table in the corner while Sawyer signed for them. She cut the tape and removed the lid from the Baker evidence box. She stared into the box in disbelief. There was a recorder, the one Sawyer brought to the captain, two evidence bags with hair in them, a note laid out in a larger evidence bag, a bloodied knife, and blood samples. She held the letter up to the light.

"*None* of this is helpful?"

"None of it. The hair and blood samples both belonged to Jack, the blood on the note belonged to Jack as well, and the rest of the alley was clean. I found the recorder a few days ago when I went back to the Rank and File for one more look. There wasn't a fingerprint to be found on anything or anywhere. He was probably wearing gloves, but there was no blood spatter, no hairs, not so much as a speck of dandruff. The perp cleaned the whole bathroom except for Jack's blood that he managed to smear throughout the whole room, and he also cleaned the alley. Don't ask me how you remove evidence of any kind from a public alley, but he did it. He made no effort to remove the victim's blood, however. He wanted us to see *all* of that, for sure."

Esley continued to peruse the contents of both boxes, muttering to herself as she went and making notes on a small spiral notebook she took from her jacket pocket. She'd ask a question every so often and then return to her muttering. The look of concentration was impressive. It was as if she had no idea there were other people in the room, like she could talk to the box and the box would answer her. Somehow, Sawyer understood that. It didn't seem weird to him.

It was late when they finished and Sawyer dropped Esley at her hotel, where she was staying until she could find a place, and then drove to his home. He pulled up the driveway but stopped himself before exiting the car. He had a garage, but he never used it. It wasn't that it was full of boxes or storage; it was pretty much empty. He just never bothered to use it; he didn't know why. That little bit of information was of particular interest to Miss M, so, just to impress his therapist, he parked the car in the garage.

Sawyer slipped the key into the doorknob of the house and turned it. He opened the door, dropping the keys into his pants' pocket as he came through. The garage entry opened into the kitchen and once inside he stopped cold. Something was off. He drew his gun and backed out of the house, exiting the garage. Moving stealthily around the windows on the front of the house, Sawyer carefully peered into each room. From what he could see there was nothing out of place, nothing amiss. But he'd learned from experience, when the hairs on his arms and the back of his neck snap to attention like they had in the entry, it always meant there was something wrong whether he could see it or not. He continued on around the house and into the backyard, still finding nothing. He wondered to himself if he was getting a little spooked by these two investigations.

Shaking his head, Sawyer holstered his gun and headed back around to the front of the house. He looked up to see Esley exit her car and walk across the lawn toward him.

Great. What could she possibly--

Without warning, a huge explosion ripped through the night air, sending Sawyer flying into Esley, knocking her to the grass and landing directly on top of her. He remained where he was, covering their heads with his arms. Once the debris settled, he pushed himself part way up and half smiled down at Esley.

"Welcome to my humble home."

"Get off me."

Scanning the burning residence as he struggled to his feet, Sawyer said half heartedly, "I'll bet you say that to all the boys."

Chapter Twelve

Esley shoved Sawyer off of her as sirens screamed up the street. Sawyer stood and watched as blistering, hungry flames devoured his home. In reality, there was nothing he cared about except his evidence board, but now that he had free reign of all the evidence, he could watch everything else burn, especially the memories.

"It's a do-over," he muttered as he dusted off the front of his pants and jacket.

"It's a what?"

"Never mind."

The captain pulled up, lights flashing and siren blazing. He leaped from his car and jogged to where Sawyer and Esley were standing.

"The report said you were dead. I'm certainly happy to see that was in error."

"Who called that in?" laughed Sawyer. "We've been standing right here outside the house since the thing blew...well, not exactly standing, but still, right here."

The captain shot him a confused glance and whistled softly as he surveyed the still burning home. "Report came in from an anonymous caller. I hope you've got insurance."

"Yes, I do, actually. And now I'm going to have all new stuff. Funny, though, I didn't see anyone around here but Esley and I. Interesting."

Esley was standing a few feet away, fuming. The captain took one look at her and said softly to Sawyer, "I see you've already managed to tick off your new partner."

"Yeah, well, it didn't take much. I only had to have my house explode and that seemed to do the trick."

"She's mad because your house exploded?" Captain's eyebrows shot skyward.

"Something like that."

Still confused, the captain shook his head and headed off in the direction of the fire chief to ask him some questions. Sawyer turned to Esley and smiled. "Are you okay?"

"Fine. Thanks for asking." Her voice was thick with sarcasm.

Sawyer smiled, struggling to keep his mouth from getting him into more trouble with her than he already was. This was a good thing. Suddenly he felt like Sawyer again, like the sarcasm and the irritating charm was returning. The smile broadened and he returned to watching his memories burn.

Something odd happened inside him when his house exploded. Something he could feel but couldn't name. It was as if all the pain of the past several months blew up with the house. He felt a weight lifted from him, from his heart and his shoulders, from his back and his legs. He knew Jack was gone, but somehow he'd found a place in his heart where Jack could 'ride along' with him from this day forward. He could feel his old partner always beside him; sometimes he'd swear he could hear his voice. Either way, it was Jack, and Sawyer hoped he would always be there. The thought brought with it a sense of closure Sawyer had looked for these past months. Events in his life he'd once thought would forever haunt him, now quietly settled into the back of his head, out of the way, yet forever a part of who he was. Jillian was gone, and though he'd known it for a long time, he could finally own the feeling that it was a *good* thing, both for her and for him.

"What's the matter with you?" Esley's voice and the sharpness that fit around the edges of it shook him from his thoughts. "Who stands there grinning like a fool while their home and all their belongings burn to the ground? Who does that?"

Sawyer's grin broadened even more. "Apparently, I do," he said, turning back to the fire. "Sometimes it's nice to clean out the closets and start over."

"You're insane."

"Yes. Yes I am, and I've worked hard for it."

Esley turned and strode to her car, shaking her head as she went. Captain Amerson returned to where Sawyer stood and looked at him expectantly.

"What?" asked Sawyer, in mock defense.

"You tell me," he replied. "I take it you two are feeling closer and closer as the days go by."

"You could say that, I guess, considering this is our first day."

"Make it work, Kingsley. She's your last chance." The two men were quiet for a moment before the captain spoke again. His dark eyes bore a hole right through Sawyer's head. "Now, about this mess," he said nodding toward the house. "What do you think happened?"

"I would guess it's no more than an exploding furnace. When it cools and we get the fire investigators out here, we'll know better. I think it's just a fluke."

"You don't think there could be any connection between this and your killer?"

"Nah. He's into murder, not arson."

The captain sighed and turned to go. He stopped and looked back at his detective. "I'm afraid I have to disagree. Had you been in the home, this would be a crime scene."

Sawyer raised his eyebrows and stared back at the house with dark concerned eyes. Not once had it occurred to him that this could be connected in any way to his investigation. Maybe the fire *was* more than just his home burning. He had to admit, if he hadn't listened to the hair on the back of his neck, he'd be a dead man.

Still, there was a part of him that wondered if the captain was being a bit overdramatic. He didn't want to think there was someone out there who wanted him dead. That thought begged the questions: *Was I getting too close? Am I making the killer nervous?* It was all Sawyer could do to keep himself from laughing. He had *nothing* of consequence in his investigation. Nothing he felt was bringing the investigation to a close. But if the killer thought he was close…

Sawyer scanned the front yard looking for Esley.

"Esley!"

Esley heard him call her name from the car and got out, approaching him from behind. "What?"

Sawyer turned to face her. "We have to take a closer look at the evidence. Now. Right now."

Esley looked at him like he'd gone soft in the head. "What's the matter with you? You might have a concussion. We should have you looked at."

"I don't have a concussion and I don't need a doctor. Think about it for one minute." He paused for a moment and glanced back at the remains of his home. "If the killer did this, he had a reason. What if his plan was to kill me? If it was, I can't help but think we've missed something. This guy thinks I'm onto him, and he could be feeling like he needs to shut me down. Why? What could we know that would make him feel that way?"

Esley's eyes widened and then filled with discouragement. "But, what could we have missed? You've been over the evidence dozens of times."

"I'm telling you, if the fire investigation rules this as arson, there's only one direction this can go. *We've missed something.*"

"Let's go then," she said, turning toward her car.

"I'll drive, or I can--"

Sawyer was already pulling his keys from his pocket when he stopped abruptly. He stared at Esley as the realization of where his car was hit him. "Uh...my car...is...*was* in the garage."

They both stared in the direction of what once was the garage, now was fully engulfed in flames. The remains of what was once Sawyer's car could be seen under the debris from the fallen roof.

He shrugged and headed toward Esley's car. "Looks like I'm looking for a new car tomorrow."

***

Both Esley and Sawyer were stopped on their way to her car by the fire chief. There were questions to be asked, and scenarios to fill in. They spent two more grueling hours answering those questions and explaining over and over again where they were positioned when the explosion happened, where they'd landed when they were blown into each other, were they injured, had they been looked at, did they see anyone or anything prior to the explosion? The last question made the skin on his scalp tingle, remembering the captain's words.

The list of questions seemed as if they would never end and Sawyer was tired, his muscles were aching and he wanted to get his hands on the evidence. He was certain they'd missed something important. Even as he reviewed the evidence in his head, he could find nothing of consequence. His frustration level was rising and he needed the evidence in his hands, inspecting every inch of it.

Esley had tried unsuccessfully to get Sawyer to check into a hotel room prior to reviewing the evidence, but he refused to hear it. He could tell by the look on her face she was going to pull out her gun at any moment. They were both exhausted, but her exhaustion looked far more dangerous. Her dark eyes were angry, and her usually well-kept medium length dark hair was out of control and looked like it hadn't been combed in a week. All things considered, she wore 'dangerous' quite well, and Sawyer's mind wandered often from the evidence to the woman driving the car. He forced his mind back to the evidence, which seemed safer.

By the time they finished being questioned at the house and arrived at the station it was nearing 1:30

a.m. Checking into a motel first was out of the question. His mind was focused on the evidence and he refused to spend one minute more doing anything but studying that evidence. In spite of the time, and their fatigue, Sawyer was nearly jogging to the evidence lockup. Keys were issued to those who had active cases and would need access around the clock. The FOB keys kept track of who entered and the time they came and went. Their little police station was becoming quite uptown.

Sawyer ran his key over the 'eye,' identifying him and releasing the lock. Sergeant Carson was gone for the day and they hurried into the room. They pulled the boxes from the shelf for both the Franz murders and Jack's murder. Esley set to work on the Franz file while Sawyer took Jack's box.

Once they'd gone through the boxes, making notes of anything they'd not noticed before, they switched boxes and began the procedure again. Sawyer's eyes were burning and watering as he placed the lid on the Franz box and rose to return the box to its place on the shelf. He knew Esley had to be exhausted as well and remembered that she'd actually received a nasty bump on the back of her head. She had to be exhausted. He glanced up at the clock. It was now 4 a.m.

Before he returned the box to the shelf, Sawyer turned to his partner to see how she was doing and found her fast asleep, drool slowly falling from her mouth and landing gently on the table. He stifled a laugh, trying to give her some privacy. As tough as she was, as hardcore and mean as she tried to be, she could drool with the best of them. He knew he needed to wake her, but somehow he had a hard time disturbing her. Maybe it was because he was getting so much ammunition for his sarcasm file from watching her that it was hard to give up the opportunity. Or maybe it was the bump on the head. Still, he turned and set the box on the table, softly removing the lid and pretended to be examining a piece of evidence as he spoke loudly.

"Have you found anything useful?"

His voice broke the silence enough that she snapped to attention, quickly wiping the drool from her mouth and the table. He was certain she was checking to see if he'd seen her, making it even more difficult for him to keep a straight face.

"No, no, nothing. What time is it?"

"It's four. Best to get some shuteye before the day begins. Can you give me a lift?"

"Yes, as far as my apartment. I'm too tired to take you downtown to a hotel. You're going to have to make do with the couch in my living room."

"Well, how nice of you to invite me to sleep over. You're just full of surprises, Ms. Rider. I would be happy to oblige."

"Cute. The couch. You're sleeping on the couch and only because I'm far too exhausted to go any further than my apartment. Just so you know, I'm a black belt and I know how to kill you five different ways."

"You are *such* a sweet talker. Let's go."

Chapter Thirteen

In the week since the fire, Sawyer had moved temporarily into a hotel while he waited for the apartment in Esley's complex to open up. In her own home, she wasn't as stiff and as angry as she was once she stepped out the door. She was actually quite likeable, until she changed into her superhero persona. Then she was a bit hard to take.

Sawyer stood outside the charred remains of his home, as the young insurance investigator approached him with a broad smile.

"You'll probably be happy we found this," he said handing him an engagement ring, charred but intact.

Sawyer took the ring and smiled. "Are you married?" he asked the investigator. The man was young, in his early twenties, with sandy colored hair and dark eyes. He was a couple inches shorter than Sawyer.

"Almost," he said grinning. "Saving up to buy one of those." He pointed to the ring then returned to writing his notes.

"Well then, this is your lucky day." The young man looked up. "Take this to a jeweler and have them clean it up. If it cleans up well, it's yours. If not, toss it or sell the stone and the gold. It didn't do me any good and I'm not interested in dealing with it. Maybe you'll have better luck with it than I did."

The young man didn't know what to say, but took the ring when Sawyer handed it to him. "I...I'm not sure I should accept this. I mean..."

"Then toss it. It's yours to do with as you please. If your superiors need me to confirm the gift, here's my card. I'd be happy to do that."

"Th...Thank you," he said, obviously stunned. He took the card as Sawyer cast one more glance at the house before heading to his newly purchased sedan. Esley was waiting in the car, having watched the exchange between the two men. As Sawyer slid into the driver's seat her curiosity got the better of her.

"What was that all about?"

"Oh, nothing. He found the engagement ring my fiancée threw on the living room floor before she left. Somehow it wasn't destroyed in the fire, which to me indicated it must be meant for someone else. The kid said he was saving for one, so I gave it to him. Seemed like the right thing to do."

Esley's eyes softened and she stared at him for a moment, but before she could speak another fire investigator approached the car. He was maybe a year or two beyond middle age with salt and pepper hair and a nice round stomach. His eyes intense blue eyes stared through the glass. Sawyer rolled down his window and the man leaned in.

"You got a minute? We've found some things that might be of interest to you."

"Sure," replied Sawyer, turning to Esley, "Come on, this could involve the investigation. You may want to hear what they have to say."

The man wasted no time and immediately introduced himself. "My name is Bradley Simkins and I'm the lead investigator on this case. What we found in your garage might be important. At the very least, it's fascinating."

Sawyer and Esley both followed Bradley into the charred remains of what was once a garage with a car in it. Bradley led them to the back of the garage where the furnace stood, barely.

"This is probably the most interesting case I've ever come across. Here is where the furnace was, as you probably know," he said motioning to the corner area in front of the car. "Do you see the metal piece there?"

Sawyer nodded.

"You'll see lying beside it what looks like a bunch of metal legs. I counted six of varying lengths.

Sawyer nodded again. "What is that?"

"I'm not exactly sure just yet, but off the top of my head, I would say it's a home grown rocket launcher. I know that sounds crazy, but that's not the craziest part. I'd bet my paycheck it was set up to fire through that door into the kitchen and to the front entry of the house. From the fire and blast patterns I'd say the middle of the home, about where the entry is, took the biggest brunt of the explosion. It's as if the rocket was very, very short range and set to go off when the door was opened. We found a trigger wire in the entry, but it doesn't look like it was hooked up correctly. The trigger was still intact, but of course, charred in the fire. I feel fairly confident in telling you, this was someone's attempt to kill whoever went through that door first. Fortunately for you, it didn't work as intended."

"It's the first time in a long time I didn't use the front door. I came in through the garage. Wouldn't I have seen a rocket launcher when I parked in here?"

"It could have been hidden under or behind any number of things. It's hard to tell at this point, and we may never know, but it was probably well concealed."

"Can you keep this information quiet for a couple weeks?" Sawyer looked questioningly at Bradley, his dark eyes intent on the investigator.

"That won't be a problem. I'll get our final report to Captain Amerson in a couple of days. This is going to take some time to weed through, I'm afraid."

"Thanks for the heads up, I'll let the captain know the preliminary info you've shared and that the full report is coming."

They shook hands and Sawyer and Esley headed back to the car. Sawyer was deep in thought, remembering his conversation with the captain the night of the fire. He'd believed Captain Amerson that night and that's why he'd gone back to the station with Esley to review the evidence. But he'd believed him in a disconnected sort of way, with more emphasis on the case than on the concept that someone was trying to kill him. The events of the day just made that emphasis chunk into place like the door on a large vault.

As he slipped the key into the ignition and turned it, he felt a little numb as all the angles of the two cases they were investigating came at his brain. It was as if the one piece, the *one piece* they needed to bring all these mismatched angles together was missing. And if it was missing, what was this killer worried about?

His thoughts were interrupted as Esley began to speak. "Sooo...someone is trying to kill you? I'm assuming it's the same killer we're looking for."

"I can't think of anyone else who would want me dead, in fact, I can't even figure out why he'd want to kill me or Jack. If it is our bad guy, it sounds like he thinks we know more than we do. But why would he think that? What in the world could we possibly have that would make him think we could find him?"

The car fell silent as they made their way through town and back to the station. Sawyer parked the car and the two detectives entered the front door and headed up to the captain's office. The captain was speaking with someone, so Sawyer and Esley waited at their desks, updating their files with the new information from Mr. Simkins.

"Let's go over the list of items in evidence. Do you have your list?"

Esley flashed him an irritated look and pulled open the drawer. She pulled out the file and dropped it on her desk. "Of course I have it." She opened the file. "What are we looking for?"

"I have no idea, but maybe if we look at each item individually, it could tell us something."

"Well..." Esley began. "We have the hair and blood samples first on the list..."

"Okay, let's think about that," Sawyer was looking at his copy of the same list. "What did we learn from those samples?"

Even though the evidence list from each of the two crime scenes was not long, reviewing each item individually, as he was doing, was going to take an eternity and Sawyer knew it.

"Listen," he said, thinking again, as he sat back in his chair, "I'm going to take these home tonight and go over them myself. You can do the same if you want, but I'll write down anything I think of that could mean something. Fair enough?"

Esley looked at him thankfully. It was obvious she wasn't in the mood for a long evening at the station.

As they were putting their folders away, the captain finished with his meeting and called out to Sawyer. He'd seen them come to his office earlier.

"Did you two need to see me?"

Sawyer and Esley stood and headed to the captain's office. Once they were all seated Captain Amerson began. "What's up?"

Sawyer recited what they'd been shown at the scene of the fire. "We've gone over the evidence dozens of times and found nothing. Does he think we have something we don't have? It makes no sense when you look at the evidence we've got. Which begs another question. How does he know what we've got?"

"I'm not liking the direction this investigation is going. It's not exactly making me feel warm and fuzzy," the captain stood and walked to his window, gazing out at the traffic. "We got the DNA results back from the hair found at the Franz home. It doesn't match any of the DNA so far, which means, it could be our killer. They're checking the NCIC database right now. We'll see if we get a hit. If we don't, then it's going to take a miracle to break this case."

Sawyer thought for a minute and said, "Captain, there is something in the evidence we have that's making this guy nervous. I'm going to take my evidence list to the hotel with me tonight and go through it. If it takes all night, I'm going to find what's got him so worried."

"I'm not so sure he should be alone any longer," said Esley. She felt herself blushing and forged on with her thought. "I mean, if this guy is trying to kill him, he should have someone posted outside his room, if not in the room with him."

Sawyer grinned softly and threw his arm casually over the back of his chair. "Just what are you saying, detective? You want first watch or something?"

"Oh would you grow up!? We're talking about protection here!"

"I definitely believe in protection. I mean, for sure."

Esley glared at him and turned to the captain for support. "I give up. He can get himself killed for all I care. I'm done with this fool." She stood to leave.

"Sit down Rider. Kingsley, stow it. This isn't working for the two of you and if you can't work together better than this, I'm going to put someone else on these two cases. Now grow up, both of you, and get your eyes where they need to be. Yes, study the evidence, I like that idea, and watch your backs. Esley, I don't think you're any safer than Sawyer is. I don't have the manpower to post watches at both your places. We're too small for that kind of detail, but you can watch each other. See that you do. If you have to combine your homes for a while, do it. But keep your eyes on the case and keep it professional, or I'll have both your badges."

Esley sat down in her chair, her mouth hanging open in astonishment. "You can't order me to live with this...this...complete slob. You can't make me do that. That is unprofessional at the very least, not to mention the man is a complete... Seriously. No way."

"Hey, I'll have you know I'm incredibly tidy. I stayed at your place one night," then looking at the captain he explained, "We worked here really late the night of my fire and I slept on her couch because she was too tired to take me to a motel and I didn't have a car." He said the whole sentence quickly, without a breath, like he was talking to his father.

Captain Amerson was still staring out the window and able to mask the knowing smile on his face. He cleared his throat, and his face, and turned to look at the two of them.

"You're partners. The purpose of partners is to watch each other's back. You do what you have to do to make that happen. I don't care what it is, but you keep each other safe. This killer has, for some reason, stepped up his game. Who is he? What does he do for a living? Is he a local? Why you? Why Jack? Why the Franz family? I want some answers and I want them yesterday. Now get out there and get me what I need. Stop wondering and start finding before someone else gets killed. Are we clear?"

Both detectives were staring at the ground and said in unison, "Yes sir."

Chapter Fourteen

Sawyer stood in front of what was once his home. It was early in the day and a soft drizzle coated the burned wood, making the whole neighborhood smell like it had burned. He stood with an architect who had drawn plans for his new home, to be built on the same spot. The man was young, younger than Sawyer, he guessed. He stood just under six feet tall with sandy and blond streaked hair in, what Sawyer could only guess was styled by a two year old. Such was the style of the day, but he didn't like it much. Just looking at the mass of hair made him wonder if the kid was old enough to *be* an architect.

The architect introduced himself as Manny Jones, a partner with his father in the architectural firm of Jones and Jones. They'd discussed the floor plan Sawyer was most sold on and now were making sure the home would work for the size and shape of the lot. They were just finishing up the final details when Sawyer's phone rang.

"Excuse me for a minute," he said as he walked a distance away while pulling his phone from his pocket. "Kingsley."

The voice on the other end of the line belonged to Captain Amerson who'd called to tell Sawyer he was needed at the station immediately. Sawyer hung up the phone and hurried back to Manny.

"I'm sorry Manny, but I've got to run. You'll get those plans drawn up so I can have a look? I'm kind of anxious to get this process started."

"Yes, I'll do that, and I'll give you a call and set up a meeting so you can review them when they're ready."

"Thanks," he called out as he jogged to his car. "Thanks for all your help."

As Sawyer drove to the station, his thoughts wandered to his partner and whether or not she would like the design. He shook his head in disbelief at the thought. *Why should she care about the design of my home? Why should I care if she cares?* Her face kept popping into his head, and the memory of how great she always smelled wandered through his brain. He really hated when he did this.

Sawyer shook himself back to reality and realized he needed to come to grips with the concept that he would live alone. Women were nothing but trouble…nice trouble, soft trouble, easy on the eyes trouble, but *trouble* all the same. He wondered, as he pulled into the station, how long it was going to take him to get that through his thick skull.

***

Esley stood in front of her bathroom mirror putting the final touches on her soft, dark hair. She wondered, as she stared at the reflection, what would have happened if she'd actually been able to enter the Olympics. She'd been in line for the USA Track and Field Team as a runner, but two weeks prior to the tryout she tore her hamstring, and that was that. She'd gone into Karate from there, once the leg healed, and obtained her black belt, thinking that she'd go into law enforcement and put her black belt to good use there. Now here she was in Smallsville, USA having never used any of that training and fairly certain she never would. Why hadn't she listened to the warnings of her captain back in Brooklyn and cleaned up her act while she had the chance?

Sawyer was nice enough, a bit of an egomaniac, but not bad to look at. Good build, quirky sense of humor, not a bad partner overall. *It could have been so much worse.*

She was just putting her things away when her phone rang. Captain Amerson sounded stressed, so when he told her she needed to get to the station, she quickly grabbed her coat and keys and headed out. Hopefully this would finally be some good news.

***

The three of them sat down around the captain's desk, and Amerson began.

"The DNA from the hair found after Esley's attack at the Franz home has come back. The hair doesn't belong to anyone in the family or on the force. It looks like it could be from our killer, but there's a hitch."

"A *hitch*?" both detectives answered in unison.

Amerson held up his hand as Sawyer and Esley started talking at once. "Let me finish."

The two stopped, both mid-sentence, and Captain Amerson began again.

"The hair belongs to one Marston Finch...and he's been dead for fifteen years."

There was a stunned silence. Captain Amerson continued. "This could mean several different scenarios, but the most promising one is that Mr. Finch is alive and currently living as someone else. You can't change DNA. You can alter fingerprints, change your outward appearance, change your name, but the one thing you can't change is DNA. So, if Mr. Finch is alive, he's done something to change his identity. I'm guessing he lives in or around Blakely, making it easy for him to tamper with our crime scenes like he has. He's got a grudge against you, Kingsley, just like the one he had against Jack Baker, proving he knows our community and more importantly our police department. This may put you in the middle of something incredibly dangerous, Ms. Rider. I'm worried about that, but want you to make your own decision when it comes to your involvement in these two cases."

"This is the first even semi-break we've had in the case. This could be the reason the guy's been trying to kill me. It makes so much sense. Why would someone want to kill Jack or me? We checked everyone we could think of that might have a grudge and why they would and couldn't find a thing. I think you should take Esley off the cases. It's too dangerous."

Esley raised her eyebrows and tried very hard not to grin. "You're kidding, right? I'm a cop...a detective, and you're telling me I should run and hide because it's too *dangerous*? It's what we do. We didn't sign up to be safe, now did we? We signed up to keep *others* safe, to protect our communities and keep them safe. How could you even suggest I be removed from these investigations?"

"Precisely why I said it had to be her decision, Kingsley," said the captain, shrugging his shoulders.

"Right," sighed Sawyer, turning to Esley. "I see your point. I didn't mean to infer you weren't up to the task, I was just, well, saying, you didn't…you probably couldn't…"

The more he talked, the deeper he fell into the pit he was so successfully digging, and the light at the top was getting smaller and smaller. He decided he'd best keep his mouth shut. "Never mind. I just thought…I was only trying to…I mean you didn't really know…never mind."

"Where are you living now, Sawyer?" The captain looked at him expectantly.

"There was an apartment available in Esley's building, so I took it. Had to talk a blue streak about not wanting a lease but when she found out we were both cops, she was glad to have the protection in her building and let me rent month to month. It worked out pretty good."

"And where would it be in proximity to Esley's apartment?"

Sawyer glanced at Esley who was smiling nonchalantly at the captain. "They're across the hall from each other. It was the only one available and you *said* we should have each other's backs, so I thought the best thing was…"

"Stop, Sawyer. I get it," replied Amerson, maintaining a straight face. "That works. Are you getting furniture and clothes, everything you need?"

"Yes," said Sawyer, still squirming a bit. "My insurance has paid for all my clothes and bought enough furniture to do me...no, not do me, but you know, to do until the house is re-built."

"Okay, then," said Amerson. "I'll expect you to get something done on this and start making some headway. Investigate this Finch character. Find out who he was, how he died, where he's buried, if he has any family... I want answers. The more we know about this man, the more we know about our killer. Hopefully. Dismissed."

He handed the DNA file to Sawyer and the detectives turned, leaving the captain's office and heading to their desks. Sawyer stopped. Esley heard his footsteps stop and turned to see him scanning the office.

"I'll tell you what," he began. "I say from now on, anything, and I mean *anything* we say about these cases will need to be in a conference room. Let's take the files we have to the small room and see what we can hash out."

Esley shrugged and they continued to their desks, picked up the files and headed to the small conference room.

"What's with all the secrecy?" Esley eyed him suspiciously.

"I'm not sure, but something about this feels entirely too...wonky."

"Wonky?"

"Yes, wonky. Funky. Weird. Hinky. Out of sync. Call it whatever you like, but there's something about this whole thing that feels wrong. My gut is screaming at me to listen."

Esley shook her head slowly and dropped the file onto the table. "And just when I was beginning to think I could work with you, you go all crazy. Great."

"I'm serious! Don't you think something is wrong with this investigation? Don't you see how every move we make is countered with some kind of checkmate? I'm pulling my hair out over this. Just after Jack died, I thought I heard him tell me something."

"WHAT??"

"Just, hear me out. It's true. I heard Jack say to me, *"It's here. Look closely. It's all here."*

Esley slid into the chair at the end of the table and studied Sawyer's face. "You know, if you believe in that sort of thing it's actually kind of sexy."

"Really?" Sawyer's eyes lit up.

"Really."

"There's a 'but' in there somewhere."

Esley smiled and placed her elbows on the table, clasping her hands in front of her. "*But* you're sounding a little too crazy for my liking."

"That's it? You don't like my crazy?"

"Not particularly. A crazy detective isn't exactly someone I would feel comfortable with in a dangerous situation."

Sawyer couldn't help the chuckle that escaped him as a sly smile slid across his face. "Well, how about non-dangerous situations?"

"Eye on the goal, Cowboy, eye on the goal." He liked the glint in her eye as her smile slowly faded.

And then... the moment was over. Sawyer shrugged and pulled out the papers from the file Captain Amerson had just given him.

"So, let's plan some forward movement with this information," said Sawyer, struggling to keep his mind on the task at hand. "We need to find out everything we can about this guy," he glanced at the paperwork, "Marston Finch, for a start. What do you say? Shall we slice it up and each take a piece of the pie or shall we work all the angles together?"

"I say work it together. There's less catching up to do if we come at it that way."

"Agreed."

With that, the two of them set off researching Mr. Finch from birth to fake death. The more they looked, the less the information made sense. After hours on the phone, Esley was writing down some notes when Sawyer ended his last call.

"So, this guy was a cop." Sawyer was musing, rubbing his jaw and thinking out loud.

"He was a *cop*?" Esley's jaw dropped as her mind roiled with the possibilities.

"Yeah, and he requested a closed casket service. He'd planned his funeral out in quite a bit of detail, who would officiate, where it would be held, it's all got a weird feel to it."

"Well, not really, a lot of people plan their funerals early. It makes them feel more prepared for whatever life throws at them. And some people plan ahead just so their children know what they want. Did this guy have a family? Kids? A wife, or ex-wife?"

"Nope. Single. Not so much as a traffic ticket, either. Didn't own property, never took out a loan of any type, which is odd by itself. Everyone takes out a loan at some point, at the very least to purchase a car. But he's got nothing. It's like he went through life totally invisible."

"Well, that's not a good thing. Invisible people make great sociopaths, you know."

Sawyer nodded his head. "True."

Chapter Fifteen

The air outside had taken on the fall chill typical of this time of year. On some days it felt as if it could snow, but being the end of September, it was still a bit warm for that. Still, it was cool and the air smelled of dry hay and falling leaves.

It was lunchtime and Sawyer suggested lunch at the diner. He and Esley sat down at his favorite spot in front of the window and picked up their menus from the end of the table.

"Okay, I've got a question for you," said Esley, eyeing him suspiciously over the top of her menu.

"Shoot. I can take it."

"Why *this* window and why *this* booth? You sat here like it had your name on it. I believe we sat in this booth the last time we ate here, too."

"Actually, it's pretty special to me. I mean, I was shot at while sitting next to this window. And I eat well in front of windows. I don't think I could have a dining room in my home without a large window in it. Makes me feel like I'm eating in the great outdoors."

"Uh, huh. You were shot at while sitting here?"

"Well, the diner was shot at. No one really knows *who* the target was, but why not shoot me? I mean, I'm dangerous, I'm mysterious, and having been a target, well that just adds to the mystery, don't you think?"

"Uh, no, not really. But since you think it does, it adds to the crazy."

They ordered their meals and once delivered, both enjoyed the meal and the company, which Sawyer felt was a very nice change. Maybe he could like this new partner after all.

They'd finished eating and Esley was staring out the window.

"Ten bucks for your thoughts," smiled Sawyer.

"What?"

"Ten bucks...you know, inflation. That was a saying from the turn of the century, or about then anyway. You remember, 'a penny for your thoughts?' Well, I'm giving the modern day, inflation affected version."

Esley shook her head with a smile. "Okay, so I was wondering what would happen if we ordered an exhumation?"

Sawyer paused for a moment. "I would be willing to bet we have enough evidence to show a need. What we need to see is-"

Esley helped him finish his sentence as they spoke in unison. "...if there's a body in that casket."

After a discussion with Captain Amerson, the captain contacted a judge and applied for an exhumation order. Due to the high profile cases the department was working on, the order was granted quickly and within the hour, and Sawyer and Esley were on their way to a small Iowa town named

Thornton. Marston Finch died in the town of Thornton, about 200 miles north of Blakely.

"Has anyone ever told you...you look just a little Native American?" Esley cocked her head as she stared at Sawyer's profile.

"No, I'm surprised you even noticed it. No one does. But yes, I'm like one tenth Native. Native Alaskan, actually, and that is the sum total of what I know. Although I have a cousin...well, let's say a fifth cousin, like a million times removed...something like that, who's full Native Alaskan and lives in Alaska. He works for the forest service and he does some amazing tracking. I hear he's pretty good, but that's only through the family grapevine and you know how family inflates the good parts of the family history."

"A tracker? Like a hunting animals type of tracker?"

"Well, yes, he does well there, but from what I understand, he is amazing at tracking down fugitives and has helped law enforcement several times. I guess it's what he does for the forest service in Denali Park. We knew each other as kids and would play when the family got together, but as time went by we saw each other less and less and I barely know him now."

"That's too bad," she said staring out her window. "It's sad that families do that. Mine has done the same thing-wait, you said he's tracked fugitives? Really? You think he could help us find our mystery killer? I mean, do you think we could use him on these two cases?"

Sawyer thought for a moment and shifted uncomfortably in his seat. "I really don't even know if what I've heard is true. It could all just be blown out of proportion because of a single instance. I don't think he could pick up on cases this cold. I mean, it's been almost six months."

The two rode in silence for a while before Esley picked up the conversation. "I think you should talk to him."

Sawyer had been paging through the evidence from both crime scenes in his head and had long since lost the train of thought regarding his cousin. "Talk to who?" he asked, his mind lost in the investigation.

"Your cousin? The tracker guy?"

Sawyer sighed. "I don't even know how to get a hold of him. Let me think about it and see how I feel."

Silence fell once again, but this time it was broken by Sawyer who asked the questions. "You know, I know absolutely nothing about you. Where is home? Do you have brothers? Sisters? Are you close?"

Esley smiled softly and turned her head away. "Home is...well...*was* in Idaho, Northern Idaho."

"Why do you say 'was'?"

There was a long sigh from the passenger side of the car and Sawyer wondered if he'd asked the wrong questions. Maybe there was a reason she didn't talk about her family. "Listen, I'm...I'm sorry if I poked my nose in where it doesn't belong. We can talk about something else. We don't have to talk about your family."

"No, no, really, you're fine." Her eyes seemed larger and darker than they had been, as if she was fighting tears, but there were no tears. "My family was killed in a house fire when I was twelve. I'd gone to spend the night with a friend or I'd most likely be dead, too."

"Esley, I'm so sorry. Where did you go after that?"

"I lived with family; I was kind of passed around a bit, until I turned sixteen. Then I was better able to take care of myself. I got a job at a local pizza place, and a year or so later I moved up to manager and thought that's what I'd do for my life. But not long after the fire, word came back that the fire was arson. Someone had set a fire in my home and killed my family. As time went by at the pizza place, I realized what I really wanted to do was catch bad guys. However, while I was in Brooklyn, the chip on my shoulder grew pretty big and I had a hard time obeying orders and sticking to protocols. So, I ended up here."

"How many were in your family?"

"It was my parents, my brother, Chesney, and two sisters, twins, Vivienne and Dianna." She chuckled softly. "I always called them Vi and Di and they *hated* that. I was the oldest at twelve, then Ches, he was ten, and the twins were eight. We were all close, except when I called the twins Vi and Di, then they'd try to kill me." She smiled at the memory. "But we were a close family. So, you can maybe understand when I heard the Franz family had twins, it was a little rough for me."

"Yes, I do see that. You turned out amazingly strong for someone who's been through what you've been through."

"I've had to learn the difference between 'strong' and 'overbearing,' but once I got that down, well, maybe I haven't quite gotten that down yet, but I'm working on it, and things have become a little better. Still, there isn't a day that I don't think about my family and miss them."

"I'm sure. I apologize for bringing up something so difficult."

"It's not a problem, really. I just haven't ever told anyone about it because I didn't want to be treated any differently because of it. I wanted to be my own person. That's what my dad always said when I was small." She smiled sadly. "I can still hear his voice as he'd say it."

"Well," began Sawyer, "he'd be very proud of you. How could he not be?"

"Thanks."

Esley rolled her head as if shucking off the negative feelings and turned to Sawyer. "What about you? Do you have family? Sisters? Brothers?

"Uh, yeah. I have two older sisters. We're pretty close now, but not so much when I was younger. My sisters, Anne and Lisa, got these *huge* Raggedy Ann and Andy dolls for Christmas one year. I was just a toddler and they delighted in dressing me up and parading me around the house. I didn't mind so much then, but as I got older, it was the pictures they'd taken that irked me," Sawyer shook his head at the memory. "They insisted on 'sharing' them with my *bros* who came to *hang* at my house. Of course, I was then teased mercilessly by these 'bros' until I wanted to choke both my sisters."

Esley was laughing, obviously not sounding very sympathetic to his plight, but she couldn't help it. The pathetic look on his face made it even funnier.

"But that wasn't all," Sawyer quickly interjected. "When I started dating, until my mom put a stop to it, both girls would bring the pictures to school and show them to my dates. Thankfully, that only happened a couple of times, but somehow the picture made it into the high school yearbook."

"Oh, they were *genius*!" Esley laughed, leaning her head back on the headrest and holding her stomach. "Merciless, but genius."

"Easy for you to say. When I was five, they took pictures of me when I got into their tampons, unwrapped two of them and hooked the string over each of my ears for earrings. They took *multiple* pictures of *that* as well."

"Being the only boy with a houseful of sisters can't be easy." Esley was attempting sympathy, but she could barely hold back the fit of giggles that threatened to take over.

"Things change when we grow up and move away from the family. I wanted to strangle them when I was at home, but when I was thirteen and they wouldn't let this stuff go, my dad pulled me aside. He told me that one day I'd appreciate what I learned about women from my sisters. I had no idea what he meant until I turned twenty and started dating women more seriously. As my relationships with women became more involved, some things made perfect sense, other things, not so much. I will admit, however, I did learn how to communicate with women from living with my sisters. I'll have you to know I'm very in touch with my feminine side because of them, and *that* has come in very handy."

"Really…?"

"Yes, really. I'm the perfect male specimen."

That brought another round of laughter from Esley and her arms collapsed in her lap, too weak to lift.

"I have to meet these women. They sound seriously amazing."

"Yeah, well, *now* they're amazing."

As the laughter died, both of them became lost in their own thoughts and the car fell silent. Afraid to ask any more questions, Sawyer drove the rest of the way wondering what her life must have been like. He felt instantly bad for the way he'd teased her and for making her so angry. And yet, she didn't want to be treated with kid gloves. She said as much. No, he wouldn't change how he treated her. She wanted to be treated professionally and he could do that, with a bit of unprofessionalism thrown in for laughs.

They pulled into the Thornton Police Department about noon. With exhumation order in hand, they entered the station and were directed to the captain's office.

***

Esley watched as Sawyer approached the captain and shook hands. Her partner's manner was smooth and friendly. She admired how he put others at ease as he spoke to them, and watched while a rapport was formed as Sawyer and the captain talked and joked. She liked this man, but as suddenly as the thought appeared in her mind, she shoved it out of her head. She was not the kind of person he would be interested in. He was way out of her class and she had no business thinking the things she was thinking. Even if there was a chance he could care for her, the truth was, they were partners and a relationship between the two of them was not allowed. It was best to keep her feelings completely professional. It did her no good to become romantically involved with someone who had no interest in someone like her. The thought tore at her heart. The pain was real, and it bit like a venomous snake.

***

Arrangements were made for a backhoe to meet the detectives at the cemetery. Sawyer and Esley followed the small forensics team, and both cars arrived as the backhoe was being unloaded from the large flatbed truck. The caretaker directed the group to the gravesite. In moments the casket sat on the ground next to the gaping hole it was taken from.

Each member of the party donned white crime scene coveralls along with facemasks and exam gloves. The forensics lead, Greg Hardman, walked to the side of the casket, broke the seal and lifted the lid. Gasps raced through the small group. The casket was empty.

Chapter Sixteen

Esley was staring at Sawyer and Sawyer was staring at his feet. He looked up and turned to her, speaking slowly.

"Now we know it was the DNA evidence the killer didn't want found. He knew the DNA would lead us right to this empty casket and then to him. The man killed a cop...almost killed two cops. He killed *families.* We're gonna find this guy, Esley, and then we'll finish this."

"Yes, we will find him," said Esley, moving in beside him. "But the thought occurs to me, how do you suppose he knew we had DNA evidence?" There were so many conclusions drawn by the empty casket and none of them were good. She hesitated to state the obvious, but couldn't help herself. "We either have a mole in the department, or a cop killer who's a cop."

Sawyer shook his head. "That's impossible. It can't be. No cop would do to another cop what this killer did to Jack. Killing him was bad enough, but throwing him out the window like he was so much garbage...it wouldn't be done by another cop." However, as the words flowed from his mouth, he knew, somewhere inside him, that it had to be one or the other. The thought twisted his gut and made him want to empty his stomach.

Sawyer strode to the casket and inspected the lining. His eye caught a glint off of something in the lining and he bent over for a closer look. Peeking out from a part of the pleated lining was a small piece of paper, neatly folded and secured with cellophane tape.

Carefully pulling the note from its hiding place, Sawyer pulled the tape away from the note and slowly opened the folded paper.

> *"I am a reptile that has shed its skin,*
> *I am a chameleon, blending into its surroundings.*
> *You have invaded my secret place.*
> *You will die like the rest of them,*
> *Never having seen my face."*

Greg stood at the head of the casket only inches from Sawyer. Without looking at him, Sawyer whispered, "Check your watch. In two minutes, I'm going to ask you to call your department and make some arrangements. When you do, I want you to get some officers down here as quickly as you can, but do it quietly." He folded the paper and replaced the tape. Still whispering he said, "I want these grounds searched for anyone who seems suspicious. Tell them to use unmarked cars, no sirens." Greg nodded his understanding. He handed Sawyer an evidence bag.

Sawyer gingerly slipped the note into the bag as if he were holding something unclean. Once the instructions were given, he spoke again, this time without whispering.

"Would you have room in your lab to store this casket until we can get a transport up here to bring it to Blakely?" Sawyer nodded his head in the direction of the casket.

"Yes, we could do that. I'll call and make those arrangements." The forensics team lead stepped back from the casket and began to unzip his coverall to access his cell phone.

"Thanks. I'll get my department on that right now, as well," replied Sawyer. The two men separated and made their calls. Minutes later, Sawyer watched as the casket was lifted and placed on the back of a truck for its trip to the police station's forensics lab.

Sawyer looked up as three cars pulled slowly into the cemetery and took different routes through the grounds. He directed Esley to his car and they waited for the search to be completed. Greg also waited in his car for the officers to report back to him if they'd found anyone.

The cemetery was small and the search took only a few minutes. Soon, one of the cars pulled up beside Greg's car and rolled down his window.

"We found nothing. There's no one else on the grounds but your group."

"Thanks. I'll let the detective know."

Sawyer heard the exchange and exited his car. "Thanks, Greg. You saw the note?"

"Yes, it's pretty creepy."

"Yeah, it is. We're going to head back to Blakely," he said, handing the man his card. "If anything comes up, call me. There will be someone up here in a couple days to transport the casket."

"Sounds good. Drive safe."

Once the casket was on its way, and the party had left the cemetery, Sawyer and Esley headed back to Blakely, both with several possibilities of who the author of the note could be, running through their heads.

"Are you going to tell me what the note said?" Esley watched her partners' face with intense interest.

Sawyer stared out the front window, his eyes a mix of anger and frustration. "It was written like prose, really dark prose, and said something to the effect that he's a snake and a chameleon who both sheds his skin and changes to fit his surroundings. Then he said whoever opened the coffin would die 'like the rest of them.' "

"Nice. Just what this world needs, another psycho."

They drove toward Blakely, and it was a little past lunchtime when they decided to stop at a small diner along the side of the road. Sawyer didn't realize how hungry he was until he stepped inside the restaurant with Esley and smelled the wonderful aromas that filled the room. Part of him wondered how he could be hungry at all.

"I'm starved," said Esley as she walked into the diner. "You buyin'?"

"I guess it would be the gentlemanly thing to do, yes?" he laughed.

"Well, you did say you were the…and I quote… 'perfect male specimen.' "

"I did say that, didn't I? Then I guess I'm buying."

They found a booth and sat down across from each other. Sawyer felt his back and shoulder muscles finally begin to relax as he gazed out the window and visited quietly with Esley. After ordering their drinks, they perused the menus left for them by their waitress. They were quiet for quite some time as they made their choices and waited until the waitress returned to take their order.

Sawyer began to speak with frustration in his voice. "I just don't understand how someone can bury an empty casket and not know it's empty. There weren't even any weights in there to make someone *think* it had an 'occupant.' "

"I wonder if we should have someone from that station speak with the funeral home that handled the arrangements. Was there an embalming? Are we missing a body, or was there never a body? If someone *saw* a body in that casket, if originally there *was* a body, then how did it get buried with no one in there? And if there never was a body, how did the thing get buried at all?" Esley picked up her soda and took a small drink.

The way her hand held the glass and how her lips touched the straw made his mind wander. Her eyes never left his, as if she were waiting for an answer… Suddenly he was aware she *was* waiting for an answer…and waiting…and waiting... Sawyer snapped out of his trance and cleared his throat.

"Yes, yes…they…it…" He was barely aware his lips were moving.

"What's the matter with you? Are you okay? You better not be having a stroke because you have to pay for this lunch first. Do you hear me? No stroking out until you've paid for lunch."

Regaining control of himself, he said casually, "Nice. I would never leave a damsel in distress at a diner with no dinero."

"That's the most ridiculous thing I've ever heard," she chuckled. "No wonder your sisters tortured you."

"Hey, that was pretty clever for spur of the moment, I think."

"That's what you get for thinking," she said, raising an eyebrow and tossing a smirk in his direction.

Their waitress came with their meals and set the warm plates in front of them. They'd ordered hamburgers and the meat tasted fresh off the field. The vegetables were crisp and good…Sawyer had never had a better burger. They continued discussing the cases as they ate.

"What I don't understand," said Sawyer, wiping his mouth with his napkin and picking up a fry, "is how anything like this could ever happen. Obviously the guy is still alive or we wouldn't be finding his DNA at the Franz crime scene." Then as if switching gears completely, Sawyer's thoughts landed on a memory from his and Jack's first trip to the Franz crime scene. "You know, Jack brought up an unsolved murder in Smithville when we were out at the Franz farm and how similar it was to the Franz murders. He wondered if there was a connection. Neither of us thought much of it at the time, thinking it was a long shot at best. Now I wonder if he was onto something."

Esley's dark eyes looked thoughtful. "How far are we from this Smithville? Maybe we should stop in and have a chat with that police department while we're out here."

"I've been thinking about that," said Sawyer. "We'd have to call Captain Amerson and get it approved because I don't know that we could make it over there and then home at a reasonable hour. He'd have to approve the hotel room. I mean, rooms."

Sawyer leaned back and rested his hands on top of his dark hair, grinning like the he'd just eaten the canary. His green eyes never left his partner's face.

"Yes," she said. "Rooms. And don't try anything funny."

"Hey, it would be far from funny! I mean, if I tried anything. Which I wouldn't because I'm the perfect male specimen, and though I'm funny, my 'technique' is not. It's quite serious and quite impressive, if I do say so myself."

"You should quit while you can." Esley smiled at him and his stomach almost came up through his throat. He shifted in his seat and stared out the window.

"What's the matter with you? You're acting like you're going to be sick."

"No, I was just thinking that I should probably call the captain. I'm gonna go do that and see what he thinks. I'll be right back."

***

Esley watched Sawyer swagger away and couldn't help looking at how nicely his jeans fit around his…

Stop this. That's ridiculous. You've had this conversation with yourself a dozen times now. He's not interested. You're just jumping in where you don't belong. Back off and show some professionalism.

When she was thinking with her head again, she wondered why he felt it was important to have a 'private' conversation with the captain. It was like he couldn't wait to get away from her. Oh, this was good. *It's going to be a wonderful evening alone in my room flipping through television stations while he's out at the local bar having a great time.*

He was standing in the alcove, straight down the aisle from their booth. She loved how long his legs were, and those green eyes. Seriously, she was going to have to do something about those eyes. *Cut it out. Just stop!*

It's just that when he was resting on one leg, his hand in his pocket, well…the way his jeans formed around him, and how sure of himself he was, how…he was…so…

She snapped back to reality when he opened the entry door and exited the glass enclosure of the entry. Esley realized it probably was a good idea to make sure the details of this case remained private and that was why he'd chosen the alcove. It was pretty smart, really.

He scooted back into the booth. It was hard for Esley to decide which was his strongest trait. Right now, she was admiring his confidence, among other things.

"Captain feels like it's a good idea to check it out as long as we're already out this way. If you're ready, we can be on our way and maybe be there before dark."

"Sounds good to me. Did you tell him what the note said?"

"Basically. We'll go over it when we get back to the station tomorrow."

Sawyer motioned to the waitress for the check and she brought it right over. He left the tip on the table, and paid the check on their way out. Even the way he left a tip made her blood pulse just a little faster. Maybe she should go back to hating this guy. That might help. Yeah, no…it was too late for that, she was certain.

***

They drove on to Smithville, which was northeast of Blakely. The stop at the diner was the perfect place to make the change in direction. Sawyer thought Esley seemed a little nervous and he was sure she was worried about his intentions.

"Listen, I want to make something clear. Okay?"

"Sure."

"I know this partnership needs to stay professional. I have no intention of ever making it anything else, okay? I really mean it. I feel like you're concerned about that."

"Oh, no. I couldn't agree more. I'm glad you said something because I feel the same way. Really. Thanks."

The levity of earlier in the day was definitely gone. Suddenly, Sawyer couldn't think of a thing to say and he was beginning to think his partner had now officially crawled back into her ninja persona. Hopefully she was just tired; hopefully he was too. Right. Like he was even going to be able to sleep tonight.

Smithville was a small town, just a little smaller than Blakely. They arrived in time to catch the department captain still in the office and were able to speak with him regarding the Martin murders.

This case involved an older couple found dead in their home, killed execution style, just like the Franz family. Also like the Franz murders, the whole house was reportedly wiped clean. The house was nearly sterile.

The captain, Captain Douglas, was about the same age as Captain Amerson, same amount of gray in his hair, but much lighter hair than their captain's. He was more trim as well, with no stomach to speak of, and a wedding ring on his left hand. He was warm and friendly and very happy to share the information they needed.

When they left the station in Smithville a couple hours later, they had several boxes of copied files and evidence. Sawyer placed all the information in the trunk and drove to the hotel where they would stay for the evening.

The clerk handed them the keys to their adjoining rooms and directed them to the easiest access. The man didn't even smirk. Sawyer wasn't sure why he thought the man would smirk in the first place. After all, they were two detectives, professionals, trying to get a job done. There was nothing odd or out of place in that.

You're SUCH a schmuck. Sawyer took the keys and they headed to the third floor of the hotel and found their rooms. He handed Esley her keys and her face reddened, making him wonder if he'd done something to embarrass her. He couldn't believe what a child he felt like, as if everything he said and did was from the mouth of some junior high juvenile. In addition to that, it seemed like after every conversation he'd had with her, he was forced to pull his foot out of his mouth and pretend nothing happened. Any way you cut it, he looked and felt like an idiot.

Chapter Seventeen

Sawyer sat at the desk in his hotel room and searched the files, one page at a time. He'd given half the files to Esley so she could work on them for the evening. Why weren't they working together and discussing what they were finding? He decided working together and discussing as they went would take too long. As an afterthought he wondered if it would also be…too…dangerous.

Seriously? It was too dangerous to work with your partner? Too dangerous to be around the one who's supposed to have your back, and whose back *you're* supposed to have? Sawyer fought with himself over the semantics of the whole situation, trying to ignore the emotions of it. It was all emotions. He knew it, but he didn't know if she knew it.

This was Mr. Smooth talking here. The guy who always had plenty to say when it came to women, and if nothing came right away, there was always a joke to be made out of the situation. He just couldn't seem to find anything funny about this situation and that made the whole thing feel like…mud. He wished he could just go back to disliking her. *She's quite bossy,* he reminded himself, *and very sarcastic. At least...she was in the beginning. Why can't she just go back to that ninja persona and be done with it?*

Sawyer sighed, instead of pulling his hair out in frustration, and returned to the file he was reviewing. This was going to take an eternity.

***

Esley sat on her bed, propped with several pillows, yet still feeling uncomfortable. What was happening to her? She'd had this conversation with herself a thousand times. At least it felt like a thousand times.

"You know what?" she said to the quiet room. "This is ridiculous. If it's going to work out, it's going to work out. If it's not, it's not. I'm good with either."

She returned to the file and groaned, hating that she couldn't trust her own words. Standing up beside her bed, she stretched and picked up the file. She paced slowly back and forth across the room as she continued to read the pages of the file.

Suddenly, she gasped and stopped in the middle of the room. She looked back at the bed and bent over the end of it, grasping at pages she'd already seen, looking for one specific page. She found it and stood up, comparing the two pages. Was she reading it right? Had she skimmed and not gotten the whole story? How could she have missed this?

She hurried to the adjoining door and opened hers, but Sawyer's door was locked. She started pounding on the door, still looking at the page in her hand.

Sawyer opened his door and a wide smile split his face. "Are we dressing down for some physical activity or are you just showing off?"

Esley looked down and realized she was in her bra and panties, so engrossed in the paper work she'd forgotten. With a screech she shoved the paperwork into Sawyer's hands and slammed her door shut. She ran for her jeans and shirt and hurried back to the door, buttoning up the blouse as she went. With a deep breath, and ears still burning hot, she opened the door once more.

"Aw, now what'd you have to go and do that for?" he said chuckling.

"Never mind. Did you read the papers I gave you?"

"You mean the ones you shoved at me just before you slammed the door in my face? Oh, and nice job on the buttons. You might want to try that again. Can I help?" He started toward her and she pushed his hands away.

"I can handle this myself, thank you very much. Now read those sheets I just gave you. Tell me what you see."

"Okay," he said scanning the pages. His placid green eyes read the lines quickly. "Looks like they were longtime Smithville residents, the parents of..." Sawyer's eyes widened. "They were the parents of Marylisa Franz! This could be the link we've been looking for. I've got to call Captain Amerson. This is big. This is really big."

"No, wait before you call the captain, Sawyer," Esley finished aligning the last button with the correct buttonhole. "We need to examine more of this file. Somewhere on that sheet it says the parents were estranged from their daughter. Marylisa never spoke of her mother, never included her in forms that asked for parentage. Nothing. Maybe there is more to that relationship than the little we've read. It doesn't make sense that with the deaths of the Franz's and the Martins, someone wouldn't have contacted next of kin, you know?"

"Unless," mused Sawyer, "unless no one knew who the next of kin was."

"Right!" said Esley. "You see what I'm saying? It wouldn't look good to call the captain every time we find some important information. We need a timeline…how long before the Franz family was murdered was this couple, the…the..." she leaned into him and quickly found the names she was looking for, "the Martins, killed? We have too many questions with no answers yet. Bring your files in here and let's see what we can find out. Maybe if we form a succession of events, we'll get further than if we jackrabbit all over the files."

The excitement of finding a lead, no matter how insignificant, was quickly taking over the mood in the room. Sawyer returned to his room long enough to grab his files and head back into Esley's room. She sat on the bed and Sawyer sat at the table with the information he had. The feeling between them was so different now. Esley was smiling. *This was more like it.*

***

The morning light was but a muted glow through the blinds on the window of Esley's hotel room as her brain slowly struggled into wakefulness. She snuggled into the body next to her, which caused her eyes to fly open as she jumped from the bed with a shout.

"What are you doing in here?" she yelled at the still sleeping figure of Sawyer, fully clothed on her bed. He'd been the body she snuggled up to and looking down, she realized she, too was fully dressed. Still, his arm had been over her waist and that had been...really, really...nice.

Sawyer opened his mouth and smiled. "Is it morning already? I'm starving. I need food."

"What are you doing sleeping in my room? You have your own room. How are we ever going to be taken seriously if we act like horny high school students?"

"Hmmm," he said mulling over what she'd just said, "Who would know? And furthermore, who would care? You fell asleep first, and we were both going over the files and I kept working, but I guess I must have fallen asleep not long after you. It's not that big a deal, you know. We're both still dressed. That has to account for something...or nothing, depending on what you're accounting for." He grinned again and winked at her as he rolled over and stood, stretching. "Let's pack this stuff up and head out. There's probably a restaurant not far from here where we can grab some breakfast while we review our findings."

Esley fiddled with her hair, thinking she probably looked a mess, and that brought a chuckle to Sawyer. Slowly he moved around the bed and walked to her, placing his arm around her waist and pulling her to him. She made no effort to stop him. There was no way her knees would hold her up if he wasn't right there.

"Admit it. This was a nice way to wake up." His eyes bored into hers, and the messy pile of hair on his head only added to his rugged good looks, which in turn, added to the weakness in her knees. "I could easily get used to this."

He brought his face to hers and their lips met, causing Esley's stomach to lurch and her knees to completely give out.

"Whoa," he said, catching her before she fell to the floor. "Are you okay? What's wrong? I've never really had a reaction like *that* to a kiss." His arms steadied her, making sure she was solidly on her feet before he released her.

"Uh, no, I'm just a little hypoglycemic, that's all. I...I need some food. We should go eat."

She knew she'd just told him the biggest lie ever, and from the telling look on his face, she was painfully aware he knew exactly what had happened when he kissed her, and he liked it.

She rushed to pick up the files still on the bed.

"I'll...just...go get my things together and we can be on our way. You're sure you're okay?" The twinkle in Sawyer's eye when he spoke only added to her feeling like a schoolgirl.

"I'm fine, really, I just need to eat."

They hauled the boxes back out to the car and Esley waited there while Sawyer went back inside to pay for the rooms.

She remembered the kiss in her room and goose bumps formed on her arms and legs and the back of her neck. She was stunned to realize she'd said and done nothing to even acknowledge he'd kissed her. She'd started picking up the stupid files like nothing happened. *What was that about?*

Sawyer approached the car and opened the door. As he slid into the driver's seat, he said, "There's a restaurant up the road about a half mile, I guess. We can eat there. Does that work for you?"

"Yeah...yeah, that will be just fine. Thanks."

"I don't know what time we actually conked out, but we made a lot of progress on those files. We know the Martins were killed about nine months prior to the Franz family killings. We know there *is* some kind of connection between this guy that supposedly died but is still alive and these two families. We'll run DNA when we get back to the station and see what comes up."

"Yeah, that sounds good."

Sawyer and Esley were silent as they turned into the restaurant parking lot. They got out and walked to the front door.

Once inside, they were ushered to a booth where they sat down, still in silence. Finally the awkwardness was more than Sawyer could handle.

"Listen," he began, "I'm sorry if I offended you back in your room. I just thought-"

"I wasn't offended," she said softly, staring at her hands.

"You weren't?"

"No, I wasn't," she smiled, looking up at him. Her hair was back in the signature ponytail, which made her eyes seem all the larger and deeper brown than before. "I was a little surprised, that's all, and it actually answers a lot of questions."

"Ah, you were wondering if a guy like me could kiss like a movie star, right?"

"Yeah, right. That's what it was. Exactly. Couldn't have said it better myself."

"So, was it like a movie star then?" he teased.

"No, not really. The *last* movie star I kissed made it last longer. Theirs was more like, *Stars and*

146

Stripes Forever, you know? Like, *The Longest Yard.* Sort of like *Free Willy*." She set her chin in her hands and smiled.

Sawyer threw his head back and laughed heartily. "*Free Willy*, eh? I think I could arrange that."

Maybe someday she would tell him exactly what questions his kiss answered. For now, it was Esley's turn to laugh. This was a man she could get used to laughing with.

***

Watching them laugh and enjoy themselves made him angry, *so* angry. Sawyer Kingsley wasn't going to get another chance at love. He wasn't going to have another chance at picking up where he and Jack left off. From watching them, he knew they were both feeling like they were going to crack this case. That wasn't happening. The killer rubbed his hand over his face and tried to plan his next move. *Kingsley had his chance to show off for the whole town. There are others of us that could do that as well as or better than Kingsley and Baker. Everyone thought Sawyer was the golden boy; that he and Jack would 'clean up' the town singlehandedly. Well, let's see how Esley Rider figures into all of this. Let's see what happens when she's out of the picture.*

Chapter Eighteen

One of the things Sawyer liked about Esley was her strong will. She'd taken care of herself most of her life, and that made her independent and strong. However, the part of her that showed itself once she got to know you, the part that wasn't afraid to show empathy and compassion, that part was important to him. It was the combination of those things that made him respect the person she'd worked so hard to become.

They arrived in Blakely in the late afternoon and checked in with the captain. They filled him in on what they'd discovered and on the connection between the not-so-dead suspect and both the Smithville couple and the Franz family. It felt good to actually have some *new* information to share, but now they had to figure out what direction this information would take them, if indeed there was any direction to go.

But the most interesting piece of evidence was the note from the casket.

"Here's something you're going to want to see," said Sawyer, putting some fresh gloves on and removing the note from the bag. "It's a bit macabre, but considering who it's from, it's not so abnormal. This man is our killer, Captain, I know he is."

Captain watched as Sawyer opened the paper and laid it on the desk. The words were typed in a font size big enough to fill the whole page. Amerson shook his head as he read the words. "He's a snake, all right. And a coward."

The frustration in the room was felt by all three of them. Still, somehow Sawyer felt like this last trip was the beginning of the end of all their frustrations. Still, there was something discomforting, even ominous, floating in the back of his mind. Sawyer let it go. There was nothing to be done about a 'feeling.'

Once they finished with the captain, Sawyer and Esley left to grab some dinner and then head home to work some more on the information they'd obtained in Thornton and Smithville. Sawyer felt there had to be *something* in those pages that would point them in at least *some* direction.

They were seated in the diner and Esley was the first to speak. "You mentioned a cousin you had. You said he was a tracker. Maybe you could find out just what kinds of things he tracks and just maybe he could be some help to us on these cases. I really am beginning to think if we solve one of these cases, we'll solve all three; Smithville, Franz, and Jack. Would it be worth it to find out?"

Sawyer studied her for a minute before speaking. "I suppose it would. I really have no idea if what he does would be helpful to us. We haven't been in contact for…it has to be twelve to fifteen years, at least. Last I heard he worked with a ranger up in Denali National Park. I'll see if I can get a hold of him through the ranger station."

Their meal was delivered, and they reviewed the information they'd found while they ate. So much of it remained unexplained, including whether or not the link between the Franz and Martin families was even relevant. Maybe the killer knew of the relationship between the two families. There was no way to know. It was just as probable this was just a random link he chose for no reason. But then again, maybe it wasn't.

They drove by Sawyer's new home to see how the build job was coming, and it looked good. They'd put the roof on and it looked like they were making progress on the inside of the home. It was late and quickly getting dark, so they didn't try to walk through. Mostly, Sawyer just wanted to keep tabs on where they were. There was a walk through the following week and he would have any questions he had answered then.

They drove back into town, to their apartment complex and walked up the stairs, both feeling the emotional and physical fatigue of a long day. With their apartments right across the hall from each other, Esley looked a little tentative, but Sawyer couldn't have been more pleased with the arrangement.

Sawyer put one arm around Esley's waist and lifted her chin with the other hand. The kiss was sweet, but brief, and Sawyer looked at her with surprise. "Okay, so that felt more like Snow White kissing Sleepy the Dwarf."

Esley giggled and laid her hand on his chest. "I...I just think we need to do as the captain warned. We need to keep this professional. We have a really important job to do and I don't want anything to take our minds from finding this killer. It's...it's important to me, and I know it is to you."

Sawyer smiled at her, let go of her waist and stepped back. "There's nothing wrong with that logic. Nothing at all." He waited for her to go into her apartment. When the door closed he turned and opened the door to his place and went inside. He thought he heard a thump, but couldn't figure out if it came from the apartment above or beside him. *I'm too tired to care,* he said to himself. *It's probably just kids in another apartment.* Shaking his head, he thought of his new house and couldn't wait to get his privacy back.

***

As soon as Esley stepped into her apartment and shut the door a figure stepped silently up behind her. Before she ever saw the man, she felt a needle go into her neck and the room faded to black. She dropped to the floor, unconscious, but still alive.

Her assailant checked the door and made sure the hallway was clear. He placed her over his shoulder and quickly made his way to the back stairwell and out to where his car was parked. It was dark enough now that he didn't worry about being seen as he threw his burden into the backseat without checking to see if she was okay. He climbed into the driver's seat, started the car, and drove away.

Esley woke drugged and freezing. In nothing but panties and bra, the room was obviously unheated and she felt the chill to her bones. She shivered in the cold, trying to force her brain to remember how she'd gotten here and why she wasn't wearing any clothes. She tried to open her eyes, but the second the light hit them, what felt like a knife shattered her skull and a moan escaped her mouth. She tried it again and again.

Each time she was able to leave them open a little longer. Still the pain in her head was crippling. Each movement of her arms or legs brought the same pain crashing through her skull. Shivers shook her and she felt stabs of pain in her ribcage that threatened to steal her breath.

She forced herself to lie perfectly still, hoping whatever was causing the pain in her head would lessen and she would be able to think. Think. That's what she needed to do. She hoped if she could keep her eyes closed, the pain wouldn't be as strong and she could think.

I said goodnight to Sawyer, I walked into my apartment and closed the door. From there her mind went blank. The obvious truth was she'd been taken. But who took her and for what purpose? It had to be their killer, and if that were the case, she was in deep trouble.

She tried once more to open her eyes; this time the pain was less. It wasn't gone, but it was softened enough that she could at least slowly study her surroundings. Her hands weren't bound, neither were her feet. She tried to sit up, but let out a cry and quickly lay back down, holding her head, hoping it would help.

She returned to scanning her prison. It appeared to be a basement. There was something on the walls, if she could just make her eyes focus. Something…papers? Posters? Pipes of different sizes ran across the ceiling, as much as she could tell without moving her head. Maybe if she could force herself to stand and push through the pain it would pass. She tried once again to push up on one arm but the pain was so great she let out another cry. Surely if she didn't stop doing that her attacker would return.

She had to keep silent until she could protect herself. Hopefully he would stay away until then. Exhausted and cold, she slipped back into unconsciousness.

Esley had no idea how much time had lapsed since she'd been taken, or how long she'd been out, but when she opened her eyes the sharp pain she'd felt before was now only a dull roar. She winced, trying to keep quiet while still trying to see more of her surroundings. The room was still a blur and she struggled to identify what she was seeing. Gradually, the room began to take shape and she saw the papers on the wall were newspaper clippings. The clippings had red circles and lines all over them, making it difficult to see who they were about until she was able to read the headlines. Most of them displayed the names Kingsley and Baker as part of the title, but her eyes wouldn't let her make out anything else. Circles and lines seemed highlighting parts of the articles, but what they were accenting, she couldn't tell.

Gingerly she moved her legs. No change in the pain level. She slowly moved her hands and arms with the same result. Pushing herself to a sitting up position, she was then able to stand, but the room spun around her. Certain she would fall, she stumbled to a wall and leaning against it, waited for everything to stay put. It didn't take long, but the movement made her feel as if her stomach would lose whatever contents it still carried. Was it night? Was it morning? There was no clock in the room and no calendar to help her determine what day it was.

Esley did an inventory of herself; her legs felt like long blocks of ice, with huge bricks for feet, but there was no blood anywhere that she could see. She slowly searched the room for her clothing and found nothing. She rubbed her arms and legs as vigorously as her head would allow in order to get the blood moving again.

There was a click in the hallway and the sound of shuffling feet. Esley's training switched into gear and she hid silently behind the door. The pain and exhaustion were gone, replaced by a sudden surge of adrenaline, anger, and rage, as she anticipated confronting her assailant. The man opened the door and didn't find her right away, obviously not thinking she'd be conscious when he entered the room. He stopped short, and that split second gave Esley the time she needed to kick him hard in the small of his back. He stumbled and turned, grabbing her by the throat with a growl and throwing her against the wall. His eyes looked wild and crazed, filled with surprised fury. She planted her feet and using the ball of her hand hit him hard in the face. She could feel the cartilage in his nose crumble against the impact.

The man let out an enraged scream as he punched her in the face. She felt her eye begin to swell, but returned the blow with a jab to his ribs and felt a crack. She slugged him hard with her other hand, forcing him away from her. She hoped she had enough balance to use her legs. Turning to the side, she raised one leg and kicked him in the face with the ball of her foot. He screamed with rage and stumbled toward her, hitting her in the rib cage with a large fist. She felt the pain of bones breaking, and with one last effort, brought her foot up again, slamming it into the side of his head. The man collapsed in a pile on the floor, unconscious, but still breathing. His face was familiar, but she couldn't place him and didn't want to stick around long enough for him to come to. She opened the door and ran as fast as her unsteady legs would allow. Her ragged breathing added to the pain in her ribcage, but she could not stop. There was no noise behind her, but she had no idea how long that would last. She bumped into the wall, stumbled, and nearly fell before she finally reached some concrete stairs leading to an open cellar door. Holding onto the wall, pain pulsating through her, Esley climbed them as quickly as she could. She wanted to throw up, but didn't want to stop and forced her stomach to be still. She felt her lip swelling and her eye was nearly swollen shut. She had to find a place to hide and hope someone would find her.

Nearly naked, Esley stepped out of the cellar into a snowstorm. *It's not even Halloween! How could it be snowing this early?* The icy pieces hit her body, stinging her exposed skin with each step.

I have to hide; I have to find a dry place to cover me. I'll die from exposure if I don't.

Ignoring the pain and pressing forward, Esley raced down a long drive, hoping to find someone, *anyone* on the road. The snow was piled up nearly two feet and the sky was heavy with clouds, telling her it was daylight, at least.

Frozen and trembling, she ran for what must have been a mile before she came to a field with giant rolls of hay. Exhausted, her feet bleeding from the cold and the rocks, she felt her head swim as she stared at the bales. She was about to fall into a lump on the side of the road when suddenly she felt arms holding her up.

"Let me help you." The voice was deep and comforting and his touched warmed her body from head to toe. She could feel the heat rushing to her feet, her legs and her arms. Esley looked up and into the face of a total stranger, but felt no fear. He helped her through the fence, then lifted her into his arms and carried her to the first large bale. Quickly, he began pulling huge pieces from the roll of hay and laying them on the ground.

"Lie down on the hay. I'll cover you and go for help."

She did as she was told and felt the warmth of the hay cover her. The snow was stopping and as more and more hay was piled over her, she felt herself slipping into sleep with the knowledge she would live.

"Wait," she called weakly. "Who are you?"

"My name is Jack. I'll get help as quickly as I can."

Chapter Nineteen

Sawyer stared into the snow from his captain's office window. Snow had been falling for a day and a half and was finally only just beginning to let up. Since the night before last, he'd not seen nor heard from Esley. With no sign of a struggle and only a pinprick of blood found on her entry carpet, there was little to go on. His body felt cold, like all the caring, all the good in him had been sucked out. Numbness filled him.

Will this mad man take everything I care about? Was it even the killer who took her? Could it have been just a break in and she's...she's...

Nothing seemed to make sense. Knowing Esley's training, her kidnapper would had to have completely incapacitated her, to take without a trace of a fight. The sound of that made the blood freeze his veins. He knew better than to panic in situations like this, but it was taking every ounce of will he possessed to not tear the town apart looking for her.

Ordered to come to the station and stay put, Sawyer now stared vacantly out the window. Captain

Amerson didn't trust his judgment when his emotions ran high, and so he waited for answers, a victim of his own bad choices.

This was not going to work for him. He had to *do* something, and he had to do it now. What was he supposed to do? Which way should he go? Where would he start to look? Indecision paralyzed him, but he knew if he didn't start looking, Esley was going to die, if she wasn't dead already.

He shifted his shoulders and turned, heading for the door. As he left the captain's office, Sawyer was stopped by Dan Johns, the officer in charge of making sure Sawyer didn't leave.

"I can't let you go, Sawyer, you know that."

"Johns, move aside. I can't stay here any longer. You wouldn't be able to if you were in my shoes and you know it."

"I can't do that, Sawyer, I have my orders. You know what that means."

"I don't want to hurt you, Dan, but I'm leaving here one way or another."

Dan sighed and stepped aside, having been informed that this could happen. "He's going to fire you, you know."

"Yes, I'm sure of that. But I'm not losing another partner. If she's already dead, then I won't be coming back to the department anyway. If she's alive, at least she'll be coming back."

Sawyer grabbed his coat from off his chair and hurried to his car. He had no idea where he was going, but he knew he couldn't stay still and do nothing. He had to find her. He had to.

Head North.

The instruction was clear and to the point, but was it just his wishful thinking or was it…something else? With nothing to lose, he backed the car out of the parking place and headed north. He'd driven for about three miles when he decided to turn around, feeling the search was pointless.

Turn left.

What? There was a feeling in his gut he'd grown accustomed to listening to, and this feeling...these words he was hearing were coming straight from the gut. He listened and turned left at the next road.

He was out into the country around Blakely now and farmlands lay as far as the eye could see. Hay bales covered with snow seemed like soldiers guarding their fields. He drove another mile before he heard his gut again.

Stop. Look right.

Look right? Sawyer looked to the field on his right and saw a hay bale torn apart with very little snow on it. There was a pile of freshly pulled hay obviously from the bale beside it. He opened his door and stood, staring at the pile of straw before heading to his trunk and grabbing a blanket. He trudged through the thigh-high snow and began calling Esley as he approached the pile of hay. If this was her, how many hours had she been in there? He had no way of knowing.

"Esley? Esley, are you there?"

Sawyer heard a soft moan from the pile and began running as best he could to the hay. He dropped to his knees and lifted the hay, frantically throwing it aside and grabbing more. Under the layers, he found a cold and shivering, but very much alive, Esley. Her face was swollen and bloody, her left eye was swollen shut.

"Sawyer…." She whispered, without opening her eyes.

"Yes, it's me, I'm here. I'm going to wrap you in this blanket and carry you to my car."

He carefully placed the blanket around her, grateful for the hay that had most likely saved her life. She cried out in pain as he lifted her from her bed.

"I'm so sorry, I know it hurts, but I've got to get you warm. Forgive me." He held her as closely to him as he could without hurting her more, hoping his body would provide at least some heat. Struggling through the snow with Esley in his arms made a smooth walk difficult. She moaned softly, with each step.

He opened the passenger door and laid her across the two front seats as gently as he could. She cried out again and lost consciousness. Quickly removing his coat, he slipped it over the brake that lay between the two seats to offer at least a little padding. He slid under her and onto the driver's seat, picking her up and holding her tightly to him with one arm. He cranked the heat as warm as he could get it and headed back to Blakely.

"Sawyer…" she whispered again, returning to consciousness.

"No, Esley, don't talk. I've got you."

"Jack…did you…talk to…Jack?"

"Don't talk Esley. Just be still. You're safe now."

She moaned softly in his arms. Sawyer held the steering wheel with one finger and stretched his other arm across the seat, making sure her feet were covered. He struggled to find his cell phone in his jacket pocket that was now stuffed under Esley.

Somehow he found the right pocket and pulled the phone out and auto dialed the station.

"Blakely Police-"

"Evelyn, it's Sawyer. Tell the captain I've found Detective Rider and then call the emergency room at the hospital and tell them I'm on my way with her. She's going to need some medical attention. She's alive, but she's been pretty badly beaten. I need you to get some officers and a forensics team out to the coordinates I'm going to send you. They'll find a bale of hay there where I found Detective Rider. Maybe the snow stopped before her footsteps could be covered. Just tell them to see what they can find."

He hung up the phone and immediately sent the coordinates he'd recorded when he pulled up to the site. Sawyer cradled her even more tightly than before. He drove carefully through the unplowed roads, making sure he could get her to safety as quickly as possible.

With time to think now, he felt the knot in the center of his stomach begin to loosen. She was in his arms and she was safe. But who'd done this to her? What had she seen? Did she see her attacker? How did she escape? He smiled softly. *If she looks this bad, I'd hate to see what the other guy looks like.*

He felt her stir and she whispered softly, "Did Jack call you?"

"I don't know what you mean," said Sawyer. He only knew on person named Jack, but he couldn't have been there.

"Jack...the man...who...who...helped me."

"Don't think about that now. We'll talk about it later and you can fill me in. For now, just rest. We'll be at the hospital in just a few minutes."

Jack? Did she mean Jack Baker? Sawyer shook his head in denial. That would be impossible,

Jack was dead. There must have been some other guy named Jack. His old partner wasn't the only Jack in the world. Still there was something nagging him about how he found her. He knew he'd heard his 'gut' give him directions right to the spot where Esley was hidden. He'd had hunches before, but nothing that he could ever remember as being that specific.

Was that really you, Jack? Do I owe you for saving Esley?

There was no answer, not that Sawyer expected one, but he was certain the 'Jack' Esley referred to was Jack Baker. He'd heard of stories such as this before, but never had one hit so close to home. He felt incredibly grateful and knew Esley's safety was not happenstance, nor was it anything short of a miracle.

As he stared down at the face, swollen nearly beyond recognition, Sawyer admitted to himself something he'd not allowed himself to think until this moment. He felt more for the woman in his arms than he'd ever felt for Jillian. The thought surprised him somehow. He knew he had feelings for Esley, but that those feelings were as strong as they were, shook him.

Only one thing mattered now. Sawyer had to find this piece of evil that would kill so many people just to get to him. He still had a difficult time believing all this was for his benefit; that someone had a grudge, or something to prove and it somehow had to do with him. It just didn't make sense. Why would he matter? He was nobody. Wasn't he?

As Sawyer pulled into the emergency bay at the hospital, there was only one thing that mattered. He had to find Esley's kidnapper. His face, hard with determination, registered his intent. *You better be praying I don't find you, because I'm going to make you pay over and over and over...*

He opened his door and eased out of the drivers seat, lowering Esley gently. As he came around the car, a gurney with two male nurses came through the door.

"Detective Kingsley?"

"Yes, she's in the front seat."

They carefully removed her from the car and placed her on the gurney, hurrying back inside. Sawyer started to follow them through the door into the treatment rooms. One of the nurses stopped and the gurney continued on.

"It's going to be better for her if you wait here. The minute I know something or have an update, I'll come and tell you."

Sawyer nodded and stepped back. He really hated this part...the waiting and wondering. But he waited and wondered all the same. In a few minutes the waiting room was swarming with police officers, there to offer support, take his statement and do whatever they could to aid in the investigation. Captain Amerson approached him.

"I know I'm fired," said Sawyer.

"No, you're not fired, nor are you placed on administrative leave," he said, placing a heavy hand on Sawyer's shoulder. "I need to learn to stop giving you orders that you cannot obey. You saved her life. You did the right thing."

It was almost an hour and a half before someone came out and called his name. Sawyer rose and the doctor came to meet him.

"She has several broken ribs. Though her face looks bad, the bones in her face are unbroken. The swelling will go down in time. She's one tough lady."

"That she is," replied Sawyer. The relief he felt was so strong he could barely speak

The doctor nodded and continued. "She's stabilized and in her room." He said handed Sawyer a slip of paper. "This is her room number. She's going to be fine. She's been asking for you."

Sawyer thanked him and practically sprinted to an elevator. He exited on the third floor and found her room. Making his way to the hospital bed, he sat down beside her. She opened her good eye and smiled, then winced.

"Looks like I'm going to have to be serious so you won't smile."

"Probably a good idea," she swallowed with an obviously dry mouth.

Sawyer found the water pitcher and poured her some water, then held the cup and straw to her mouth so she could drink. She drank nearly the whole cup before she released the straw.

"You *were* thirsty," he smiled. "Need more?"

"No, I'm good. I didn't realize how dry I was, I guess."

"How are you feeling? Do you feel like talking about it?"

"I'm okay, but pretty sore all over. I...I think I know the guy who attacked me, but I can't place him. His face looked so familiar...until I broke his nose."

Sawyer muffled a laugh, clearing his throat. "I'd have paid good money to see that."

Esley giggled and winced. "I think I got him pretty good, but I didn't want to stick around to figure out who he was. I took off pretty quick. One thing I do remember, I was in some kind of cellar and on one wall there were all these newspaper clippings and every headline was about you and Jack. There were red circles all over each one with big circles around the people in the pictures, I'm assuming you and Jack, but I was drugged and I couldn't see very well."

"This guy had clippings of Jack and I? What in the world would he want with that?"

"After having been there…my best guess…would be jealousy. Someone jealous of your success. It's the only thing that makes sense."

"Who could be so jealous he would kill two families, fake his own death, kill Jack and kidnap you just to prove his point? I can't imagine jealousy would be the reason behind these attacks. One thing's for sure, you've made it very easy to identify the killer if you broke his nose."

Just then Captain Amerson poked his head into the room and motioned for Sawyer to step out.

"Here's the part where I lose my job for sure," mumbled Sawyer as he stood to go.

"What?"

"Nothing. Rest. I'll be right back.

Chapter Twenty

Captain Amerson didn't look angry, and he didn't talk like he was angry. Sawyer was surprised when his captain placed his hand on Sawyer's shoulder, running his other hand through his thick salt and pepper hair.

"I wanted to make you aware of something, Sawyer, and I want you to hear me out before you say anything. Clay Carson, Sergeant Carson from Evidence Lockup, you know who I'm talking about, right?"

"Yeah, I know who he is."

"Well, he was in a car wreck a couple of days ago. He's got a broken nose and some broken ribs. We've checked out his car and he's telling the truth. So just to nip your thinking in the bud, he couldn't have been the one who took Esley because the accident happened the day before her abduction, but he couldn't get a hold of anyone because he lost power at his home and his cell phone was dead. He'd made his way back to the house and as soon as he could, called for an ambulance to come and get him, and reported the accident to the station."

Sawyer could feel his gut swelling with anger. "That means nothing, Captain. He could have easily abducted her and then staged the wreck to match the necessary timeline."

"Calm down, Sawyer. I know this has become personal for you. I spoke with Esley before you were brought in to see her. I know about the newspaper clippings. But Sergeant Carson isn't your guy. We'll keep digging. So far, nothing has turned up where you found her. There was enough snowfall to erase any evidence that could've told us where she'd come from. She's a strong woman. She could have run miles before stopping in that field. Or it could have been only a few yards. We have no way of knowing. Hopefully she'll be able to tell us more when she's a little more coherent."

"Does he live anywhere near where I found her?"

"Yes, yes he does. We've searched his home. There is no cellar; and no room with pipes or newspaper clippings were found. He'll be released tomorrow morning. He won't even be here that long."

"I'm not leaving her here alone, Captain. I'm staying with her until they release her, and then she's staying at my apartment."

"I understand."

"And I'm going to want to take a look at that car and the crash site. And I want to search his home."

"The warrant has already been issued and executed for those searches. We can't search them again unless we have probable cause, so, unless you can come up with new evidence, we can't go there."

Sawyer returned to the room and sat down beside the bed. He gently lifted Esley's hand and held it in his. She was asleep now, her breathing sounded more even and color was returning to her face. Carson was in the same hospital, and since Sawyer didn't believe in coincidences, the man was involved in this up to his broken nose. Sawyer knew he was, and he would prove it. But he would have to have some help.

Sitting beside Esley's bed, he was reminded of his cousin, Grant and the conversation he and Esley on their trip to Thornton. Rumors in the family hailed him as some kind of bigger than life spiritual crime solver. Was there such a thing? How much was rumor and how much was fact? That was what Sawyer needed to know. The stories he'd heard at family reunions, seemed larger than life. He remembered Grant as a kid. They'd had fun playing all the things kids play, but he'd also been a rather serious kid. Grant talked a lot about his uncle and the things his uncle had taught him, which made no sense at all to Sawyer. He knew Grant had a father and they had a great relationship, but it was always the uncle that taught him and disciplined him. Sawyer remembered the Grandfather being part of the teaching, as well, or at least he thought he remembered that.

Grant always encouraged Sawyer to not be afraid of his Native ancestry, that he should 'embrace' it. The two of them couldn't have been more than six at the time and he highly doubted even Grant knew what that meant. It was hard to embrace something that made no sense.

He smiled softly at the memory and kissed Esley's hand.

"I'll be right back." She was out, didn't hear a thing, didn't feel the kiss, but none of that mattered to him.

Sawyer strode into the hallway and found an empty couch. He sat down, pulled his cell phone from his pocket and called his mother. He was certain she'd have a phone number for Grant, or at least Grant's parents.

After thirty minutes and twenty-seven 'bless your hearts,' he ended the call and stared at the number he'd written on the only scrap of paper he could find from his coat pocket.

What do I say to a man I haven't talked to since we were, what…ten? Would he even remember me? I don't even know him anymore, and what do I ask him anyway? "Hey Grant, it's me, Sawyer. I hear you can track…I hear you can smell stuff, I hear you're larger than life and catch bad guys when nobody else can." Sawyer had no idea what he'd say, but he picked up his phone and dialed the number his mother had given him.

The phone rang three or four times and was answered by a strong voice, yet soft and gentle at the same time.

"Mulvane."

"Hey, Grant, this is Sawyer, Sawyer Kingsley. Do you remember me?"

"Of course I do," came the smiling reply. "You are my cousin. One never forgets cousins." There was a soft lilt to his voice, yet the serious nature was still there.

"I…I need some help, Grant, and I understand you do some tracking. Have you ever worked with law enforcement?"

"Occasionally," he replied. "I do a lot of work for the rangers up here in Denali Park. You are in law enforcement now?"

"Yeah, yeah I am. I'm a detective with the Blakely, Iowa Police Department. I'm working on a case that feels like I take one step forward and two back with every lead. What would you think of flying down here to Blakely and lending me a hand? I'll buy your ticket and talk to the Captain about payment for you."

There was a chuckle from Grant before he spoke.

"There is no need to speak of payment. You know our culture, Sawyer; you know you have only to ask. I would be honored to come and I hope I can be of some help. Give me your email address and I will send you flight information when I get it."

"Thanks, Grant. But…what's so funny?" There was playfulness in both Grant's chuckle and Sawyer's response to it.

Grant chuckled again. "I guess it is because I never thought you would grow up and choose such a serious career path. To me, it seemed you were destined to become a stand-up comedian or something."

"Well, for the record, I'm still pretty funny, but I have come to appreciate my more serious and classy side as well."

"You? Classy? I'll believe *that* when I see it. You will pick me up at the airport?"

"Yup, I will, in my new car."

"Just out of curiosity," said Grant with a smile in his voice. "What happened to the old car?"

"It got burned up when my house exploded."

The line was quiet for a moment, but there was a hint of levity. "Just cannot wait to see that class act of yours. This is going to be good."

The cousins exchanged email addresses and Sawyer ended the call. There was something strangely calming about the conversation...or maybe it was the man. It felt like they'd never been separated and like the concept of family still rang very strongly in Grant. Sawyer liked that. He was looking forward to seeing his cousin again.

Sawyer returned to Esley's room to find her awake and sitting up, with the help of her bed. Her battered face looked awful, and seeing her struggle to smile and to eat or drink made him angrier than he could let on.

As badly as Sawyer wanted to get out there and find some answers, he couldn't leave Esley alone. He trusted no one with her care, not even his own department. He looked down at his cell phone when it dinged to notify him of email received. He pulled up the email and smiled; Grant would be there in two days. He had a really good feeling about this.

"Where have you been? And why are you coming through my door smiling like the Cheshire Cat?"

Esley's face seemed like it was still swelling. He wondered how big a face could get, but hoped he'd not have to find out. The swelling would go down, but her broken ribs were what would keep her laid up for some time to come. Sawyer knew that, and he was glad to have her out of the fray for at least a little while. If she ever knew he felt that way she'd skin him alive and show him what real 'fray' was about.

"You look like you feel better," he said, happy to see her looking a little livelier. "I've actually been talking to my cousin Grant."

"Grant?" Esley's face was a swollen blank.

"Grant. Remember the Native Alaskan I told you about?"

"The tracker? I thought you said that was mostly family myth."

"I guess we're going to find out if that's true. I hope he really is larger than life, because that's what it's going to take to solve these cases."

Sawyer gave Esley a thoughtful look. "You're coming to my apartment when you're released from the hospital. I don't want any arguments about it, either. With three broken ribs, you're not going to be able to get around and take care of yourself. I'm taking care of you because…because that's what partners do."

Esley started to argue with him, and then realized he was right. Frustration filled her one good eye and she frowned. "I…I'm really not used to being 'taken care of,' Sawyer. I'm sure I can take care of myself. What would I do if you weren't my partner? I'd be taking care of myself."

"No, you'd have home health in there until you could get around on your own. You know that's true. But, we're partners, and partners look out for each other. I'll also have a guard at the apartment when I can't be there."

"Oh, come on, Sawyer. Don't you think that's a little over the top?"

"No, actually, I don't. You're pretty helpless to defend yourself with those ribs the way they are, and until we catch this guy, he has no idea how much you saw of him and whether or not you can ID him. He doesn't know you can't remember the house or which way you ran. He doesn't know any of that. So, as far as the killer is concerned, you are an imminent threat to him. We'll have guards undercover watching the complex, even when I'm there."

Esley laid her head back on the pillow and sighed with a wince. "This whole thing stinks. It would all be over if he hadn't drugged me. I would've been able to ID him, show you right to the house he lives in and we'd be done with it. But, now I don't think I could identify him if I tried. Once I started moving, everything became a mishmash of wavy, blurred images. I'm lucky I was still on the floor when I saw the newspaper clippings or I wouldn't be able to remember those either."

"Well, he *did* drug you and it's *not* over so there you are, and it's not your fault. It's just the way this act played out, but fortunately, the play isn't over yet, and I have a really great feeling that our ace in the hole will be on his way here in a couple of days."

"I hope so. I'm a pretty lousy patient and an even lousier prisoner. You won't be able to keep me secluded forever, you know."

"I'm well aware of that fact. I don't plan to have you 'secluded' any longer than I have to, trust me. I need my partner. But I need you to be ready, and that's going to take some rest first."

Esley reached out and took his hand. "Thank you, Sawyer. I really don't know what to say."

"I do have one question for you. Who is Jack? You kept asking me if I'd talked to Jack."

Esley thought for a minute. "It's hard to remember, but I know someone helped me. He carried me across that field and pulled the hay out of the bale for me to lie on. Once I was lying down, he pulled more off the bale and put it over me. He said he'd get help and when I asked him his name, he just said, "Jack." That's all I know. No one ever called you?"

"No, no one called me."

"Then…how…how did you know where to find me?"

"I just…I thought it was my gut. I kept hearing where to turn and how far to go." Sawyer smiled. "Maybe I did talk to Jack. Maybe that voice in my gut…in my head…*was* Jack. He must like you a lot."

Chapter Twenty-One

From the time Esley and Sawyer had been assigned to each other as partners, he'd experienced very little time without her beside him. Being partners they spent the better part of everyday together and often those days went far into the evening. Now, with her recovering in his apartment, Sawyer had even less time without her. The living arrangements gave him even less time to think through how he felt about Esley the woman, not Esley the partner. He didn't want to jump headfirst into a relationship that would end in disaster; he'd been there and done that. There was really only one thing to do in order to find out what his feelings were. He would ask her out.

This wouldn't be an opportunity to discuss the case; this would be an official date. He wasn't sure when, he just knew he needed to do it. Timing was difficult right now, though. Grant was landing in a couple of hours and it would take about forty-five minutes to get to the airport to pick him up. Esley had been released from the hospital with strict instructions to lay low for a few weeks and allow the broken ribs to heal correctly. Sawyer was determined to make sure that happened. She was at his apartment now, and he'd been caring for her and sleeping on his couch. He was thankful it was a comfortable couch, because with Esley sleeping in his bed, that was about all the options for sleeping arrangements he had.

Having her in the apartment had been easier than he'd originally thought. It seemed so natural to him to have her there, like she was *supposed* to be there. He couldn't remember a time when he'd felt like that about a woman.

On this day, there was a home health nurse watching Esley as Sawyer drove to the airport. It was early morning, about 6 a.m., when he left. He hadn't wanted to leave her alone, and the nurse seemed like a great idea. There were undercover police officers parked at both the front and the back entrances to the building, along with two uniformed officers outside the door of his apartment. Still, he worried.

Who was this guy that had done this to Esley? Was Carson really an innocent coincidence? It appeared to be so, but there was something about the guy that bothered him. Something about that whole situation that wasn't right.

Sawyer arrived at the airport and found his way to the waiting area. The plane was coming to the gate, so his wait wouldn't be too long. He was aware it'd been a very long time since he'd seen his cousin, and wasn't sure they would recognize each other. However, the minute Grant came through the door, Sawyer approached him and stuck out his hand.

Grant ignored the hand and gave him a warm hug. "I thought that was you, Cousin," he said with a soft, humble smile. "You have not changed much, just grown taller."

"I see you still wear that ponytail."

"Yes, I do. It is my strength. If I cut it I will be weak as a kitten." His eyes sparkled as he slapped Sawyer on the back playfully.

They chatted about old times and the tricks they played on each other as young boys, laughing at the memories. It was good to have him there, and Sawyer felt a strong kinship to this quiet, gentle man. There was no luggage to wait for, since Grant travelled light, so they continued their conversation as they made their way to Sawyer's car.

"I guess I'd better fill you in on what these cases are about." Sawyer glanced sideways at Grant. His cousin's skin was much darker brown than his, his black hair shined in the sun and was held back in a ponytail that went down to the waist of his jeans. He wore a t-shirt, plain, no logo or graphic. Everything about the man was simple, humble and...quiet.

"First, tell me how your family is doing. It's been a long time since I've heard about them. I know my family would want to know how they are."

Sawyer gave him the quick version, sisters are married, Mom and Dad are aging, but still able to care for themselves, the usual information. He then moved right into the cases he and Esley were working on and ran through the events, starting with the Franz family. He told Grant of Jack's death, about Marston Finch and his disappearing act, and ended with Esley's abduction.

Grant listened carefully until Sawyer finished his monologue. He sighed and looked out the window.

"I do not mean to pry, cousin, but you have left something out."

Sawyer did a mental review of all he'd told Grant. "I...don't think so, Grant," he said slowly. "I've told you everything I know."

"You care for her."

Sawyer was thrown back in time to a day the two young boys were playing together and Grant said Sawyer knew something he wasn't telling him. About eight at the time, Sawyer knew exactly what he hadn't told him, but couldn't bring himself to say it out loud.

"You know, just because your parents have an argument, it does not mean they are getting divorced."

Even so young, Sawyer was stunned that his cousin could be so insightful. The memory yanked him back to the present and the current question that hung in the air.

"I...don't...it's not so much that I...I mean, she's my partner and of course... but it's not what you think."

"Yes, it is exactly what I think. You care for her." Grant continued to stare out the passenger window and Sawyer could feel the slight smirk that graced his lips. "Lying to yourself will solve nothing, and only cause more problems. Does she know how you feel?"

"Yes. Yes she does. I think."

"Make sure. The investigation will go so much smoother when you tell her. Secrets kept between partners make working together difficult. Talk to her."

Grant turned and faced Sawyer. There was no smirk, no accusation on his face. No judgment, no shame, no ridicule. Just a *knowing* look. Sawyer suddenly felt he was going to really enjoy working with this man. There would be no pretense, nothing unspoken.

"Gotcha. So, Grant, tell me what you do."

"I track. My grandfather said I was born with a gift. I believed him, and here I am. It's difficult to explain, and so I do not try. My grandfather worked with me and taught me everything he knew, and I added that to the gift I was born with, and so I track."

"Okay. Well, let's hope you can help us find this killer."

"I can help you, and I will."

Suddenly, Sawyer remembered he'd not even told Captain Amerson about his invited guest. "We better run by the station and introduce you to my captain. I pretty much forgot to tell him you were coming."

A small grin spread slowly across Grant's face, but he said nothing.

They pulled into the station parking lot and the two men headed up to the captain's office. He was in and Sawyer rapped on the office door.

"Come."

Sawyer and Grant entered, and Sawyer motioned for his cousin to take one of the chairs in front of the captain's desk.

"Captain, this is my cousin, Grant Mulvane. He's here to help with the Franz and Baker investigations."

Amerson's eyes widened and he coughed and sputtered for a minute before standing and heading to the door of his office. "You," he said, pointing to Sawyer, "follow me."

Sawyer glanced at Grant who had that same small, unassuming smile. Sawyer shrugged and stood, following his captain into the bullpen area. They didn't stop there, however, but went to the conference room next door to his office; Amerson closed the door behind them.

"Do you have any idea what someone like Grant Mulvane is going to cost this department? Did you even *think* about cost? I'm the one who's got to balance this department's budget and report to the Chief. What do you think you're doing?"

"Captain," said Sawyer, a little unsure where to begin. "Grant is my cousin. He's here as a favor to me. Wait…he's *expensive?* You *know* my cousin? How could you know Grant?"

The captain's eyes were growing larger with each word from Sawyer's mouth. "Everybody who's anybody in law enforcement knows who Grant Mulvane is. Are you kidding me? He's your *cousin?*"

"Uh, yes, he is, but we haven't been in contact during our adult lives. I wasn't even sure he'd remember me, let alone come here. But, he did remember me and he was more than willing to help."

Captain Amerson shook his head with an incredulous smirk and headed to the door. He headed back to his office with Sawyer mumbling behind him.

"I'm somebody in law enforcement, and he's my cousin, and I didn't know about Grant Mulvane. Obviously, not everyone knows about him."

They entered the office once again and Captain Amerson reached out and introduced himself. "Mr. Mulvane, I'm honored to have you come and help our department. Thank you so much for that."

"It's Grant, Captain, just Grant, and I'm more than happy to help. Just point me in a direction and we can get started."

"I will leave that to the capable hands of Detective Kingsley here," he said, nodding to Sawyer. "Keep me apprised, and I mean that, Kingsley. Don't be going off half-cocked."

Sawyer shot his captain a respectful but wounded look and headed to the door. As they walked down the stairs to the exit, Sawyer couldn't help staring at his cousin. "Who *are* you, anyway?" he asked, not bothering to mask the shock and awe in his voice.

"I am a tracker," replied Grant, softly. "I am just a tracker."

Sawyer decided to take Grant to the Rank and File men's room first and see what he thought. In the back of his mind, he couldn't get rid of the feeling that there was something in that room he was missing. It would be interesting to see what Grant thought of it.

He found an open parking spot on the street in front of the Rank and File, and the two men proceeded into the building.

"Hey Stan," called Sawyer, as he entered. "We're just going to have a look at the men's room." Stan tossed him a nod and they continued into the hallway.

As the door into the men's room opened, Sawyer saw a look of mild revulsion sweep momentarily across Grant's face. "What?" he said quickly, "What is it?"

Grant just shook his head and continued into the men's room. Sawyer started to explain about where the blood was and the window and how the body was dumped into the alley through it. Grant put his hand up to stop him.

"It is okay," he said quietly. "If you could wait outside and give me a minute, I will be able to tell you more."

"Oh...okay," stammered Sawyer as he exited the room. Grant was an old soul, even as a child, and maybe that's what gave off the 'weird' feel. Still,

Sawyer couldn't help but wonder at his technique. *I hope he isn't a kook. Apparently he isn't, if what Captain Amerson said was true, and there's no reason believe it's not.*

***

The room filled Grant's nostrils with a putrid smell of a violent death, of dying and of massive amounts of blood. It was so strong the tracker pulled a cloth from his pocket and covered his mouth and nose. He followed the blood trail as clearly as if he'd been there the day it happened. The smell, mixed with the horrendous remnants of emotions in the room, was a sickening mix of sensory data that threatened to overload his brain. Grant turned off the lights and took a moment, closed his eyes and chanted softly in his native tongue. It worked; slowly the chant faded from his lips and he could focus on the room. He kept the lights off, allowing only the light from the alley window to illuminate the room.

He walked to a stall and discovered the death had happened there. Surprise and anger, mixed with sadness and torment filled the stall, along with a strong sent of gratification, obviously from the killer. Other than the killer's scent, there was no way to separate who felt what, but the feelings were all definitely there.

Something…someone… Was it the spirit of Sawyer's best friend and partner he was sensing? There was a need here, a cry for help that had yet to be discovered. Something in the room, possibly left in the room, he was sure of it. He checked behind each toilet, swiped his hand along the top of each stall, and under. He searched corners and cracks and finally ended up on his belly, finding the scent he was looking for, and slowly crawling to the wall under the window.

He moved with a grace that few possess, stalking the scent, knowing exactly where the scent was placed. A prayer of thankfulness, to those from whom the gift of tracking was given, ever so humbly escaped his lips. He had found what he was looking for. It took only seconds.

Chapter Twenty-Two

The boot print stood out like a neon light, if you were at an angle to see it, and if you were blessed with the sight and smell of a wolf. He stood quickly, formulating a picture of the boot in his mind, noting the size and also the type of tread. He would need to identify that boot at some point, but proving the print was there would be difficult. It wouldn't be admissible in court; he'd been through that before. Best to say nothing and use the information to confirm the killer for himself when he was found. The killer's scent was strong. He would be found.

Grant turned the lights back on and opened the door inviting Sawyer back in. "I am sorry to make you wait in the hall, but I have to focus, and it is easier for me to concentrate if I am alone.

"Did you find anything?"

"Nothing that can be used in court. Can you show me the other crime scene, please?"

"Yeah, sure." Sawyer studied Grant's face and knew there was something he wasn't saying. He would allow the man his space, but he needed some answers and wasn't sure how long he could wait.

They drove the fifteen minutes to the Franz farm in silence, with Grant lost in thought. Sawyer didn't want to disturb his thinking so he kept to himself as well. They turned up the drive and parked in front of the home. The crime scene tape was still in place; and as they walked up the porch steps, Sawyer removed the tape and opened the door.

Sawyer watched Grant step back and place his finger under his nose. Grant turned his head and stared out at the fields, finally dropping his hand to his side. Taking a deep breath, he entered the house and scanned the room. The tracker walked from room to room, slowly taking in every aspect of the home with his eyes and his nose.

"You smell something, Grant. What is it?"

"It is the same scent I found at the Rank and File, but it is not as strong here. This was the first crime scene?"

"Yes."

"And Jack was here...with you, yes?"

"Yes."

"He is still here, and in the men's room, as well."

"I *knew* it! I heard him tell me all I needed to crack this case was in that men's room, but I could never find anything. I figured it was just my imagination. I looked several times to be sure, but there was nothing there."

"The spirits of the dead walk this earth with us. We can learn much from them."

Again, Sawyer found himself studying his Native cousin. *Is this guy for real? Or am I being taken for a ride...I guess I'll see.*

"You doubt me." Grant gazed at the detective. No accusatory tone, no judgment, just a statement of fact.

"I haven't decided yet," replied Sawyer. "But I feel I have no choice but to trust you. I can only hope my faith is not displaced."

"You speak like my grandfather. He would have liked the man you grew to be." Grant laid his hand firmly on Sawyer's shoulder, then turned away and let it slide slowly off. "Both murders were done by one man. A man who is not who he says he is. He gives off an uncertain scent, but it is always the same uncertain scent."

"You lost me."

"Yes, well, I am not lost. I will continue my search." Grant smiled softly and returned to his slow progression through the house. Occasionally, he would stop and touch something then lift his hand to his nose and shake his head as if in disbelief. He examined door jams and sinks, bathtubs and couches. He studied every inch of the home and finally stopped back in the living room.

"He comes here often." Grant peered around the room, as if hating what he was seeing.

"Jack?"

"No, the killer. He comes here to gloat, and to steal things."

Sawyer knew he'd come back at least one time, but according to Grant he came a lot. Had he taken more things from the house? Was he planning to plant more evidence somewhere?

Sawyer's cell phone rang; he quickly excused himself and went out onto the front porch to answer it.

"Kingsley."

It was Esley. "Just checking on you. How is it going with Grant?"

"It's good," he said tenuously.

"What do you mean? You sound unsure."

"He's just really different and takes some getting used to. But he's a cool guy, a good guy, and I think this is going to work out nicely. How are you feeling?"

"Sore." Esley sounded irritated.

"I'm sure. Just do what the doctor says and you'll be better in no time."

"Right. I've never been very good at doing that kind of thing, you know. I want out of this house," she lowered her voice and angrily continued. "But Nurse Killer Bee is having none of it. She barely lets me talk, let alone move!"

"A little strict, is she? Well, good. If that's what it takes to keep you there, good. I gotta run. I'll call you later. Behave."

He heard a frustrated grunt and the call ended.

Sawyer stepped back into the house to find Grant lying on his stomach, his face flat on the carpet, his long ponytail fanned out behind his head.

"What happened? Are you alright?"

Grant chuckled. "I am fine. I was just checking footprints. There has been a lot of traffic in here, but the killer's footprints are unmistakable." Grant stood up and stared at the spot of the carpet where he'd been laying.

"I don't see any footprints." Sawyer bent over and studied the section of carpet.

"I know."

"I want to take you to evidence so we can take a look at what little we have from CSI. Are you up for that? We can go get some lunch afterward and take some to Esley. You can meet her then. You'll probably be staying in her apartment. It's just across from mine. Are you ready to go?"

"I am." The two men walked to the door and Sawyer was the first out. Before Grant exited, he turned one more time, scanned the house quickly and then stepped onto the porch, closing and locking the door behind him.

Pulling out of the driveway, Sawyer stopped before continuing onto the highway. "You found something in the men's room at the Rank and File."

"Yes, I did."

"It was a footprint, just like the one you found in the house, wasn't it?"

"Now see? You are not as white as you think you are." Grant chuckled at his own joke and stared out the front window.

Sawyer couldn't help laughing softly as well. This was a strange man, so deep and so full of knowledge. If Sawyer were asked to describe him, it would be hard to know where to start. The one thing Sawyer did know was this was a *good* man, an honest man, and Sawyer could trust him, and *would* trust him.

They arrived at the station and Sawyer led Grant to the evidence lockup. They walked through the door; Sawyer was halfway to the Sergeant's desk when he realized Grant wasn't behind him. He stopped and turned to find Grant staring at Sergeant Tarynton, the man who had replaced Sergeant Carson while he recovered from his car accident. Tarynton was tall, youthful looking with blond hair and grey eyes, probably in his late thirties or early forties.

"What's wrong?"

Grant said nothing, but his eyes remained fixed on Sergeant Tarynton for a brief second longer. "Nothing. Show me the evidence."

Something was definitely off. Sawyer would have to discuss it later, as now it seemed a monumental task just to get him through the door. He eventually did follow the detective over to the table to check out the meager box of evidence Sergeant Tarynton brought them.

Grant didn't look at the Sergeant again, didn't even move his eyes in his direction. He focused on the evidence, but that inspection didn't take very long.

"You can see we have little to go on." Sawyer's voice resonated off the evidence lockup walls.

"I see that," he said quietly. "This man is not usually here, am I correct?"

"You are," Sawyer replied, keeping his voice softer as well. "He's covering for Sergeant Carson. That's a story for over lunch. Are you ready to go?"

"I am."

Sawyer signed out on the sheet and they left.

"Okay, what's up? You're acting strange…well, more strange that you usually do."

Grant was quiet. "We can talk over lunch."

Sawyer led him out the front of the building and they got in the car. As they drove to the diner down the street, Grant was contemplative. He was like a vacuum, sucking in all the information he'd gained during the day and rolling it around in his head. Sawyer could almost hear the wheels turning.

The short trip to the diner took only seconds, and Sawyer parked the car. They walked into the diner, and to 'Sawyer's seat.' Grant was beginning to come out of his cocoon and as they sat down he stared across the table at his companion.

"Tell me about the other sergeant."

Sawyer recited the whole story of how both Sergeant Carson and Esley ended up in the hospital on the same day and how his injuries had been very close to the same injuries Esley thought she'd inflicted on her abductor. When he finished, the look on Grant's face hadn't changed.

"You left nothing out?"

"No, nothing that I can think of."

Grant started to speak, then stopped. He stared out the window for a moment. "The evidence room is wrong. I cannot feel why, or how yet. I only know it is…wrong. And it is not just a little off, it is *all wrong.*"

"I wish I could feel what you feel. I found nothing out of place. I don't know Sergeant Tarynton; he's only been with the department for a couple months. Those months were pretty hectic for me, so not much opportunity to stop and chat with the new guy."

Their lunches were delivered and Sawyer ordered Esley's lunch to go. They would stop there once they'd eaten so he could make sure it was okay for Grant to stay in her apartment. Of course, she needed to meet him, as well, and most likely size up who it was that was temporarily taking her place as Sawyers partner.

"Tell me again about Thornton, and what you found there."

Sawyer recited the trip again, what they'd found, the empty casket and the link between the couple killed there and the Franz family. Grant digested the information like it was a burger and fries.

He was focused and concentrated on every word Sawyer spoke; like he could actually *see* the words leave his mouth. It was a bit disconcerting.

Grant continued to eat while he listened, but still Sawyer felt like he was more focused on listening than eating. He wondered if Grant actually tasted his food.

"And you read the files on this Phillip and Sylvia Martin? You are certain they are related to the Franz Family?"

"Yes, they were the parents of Marylisa Franz."

Grant took another bit of his burger and chewed thoughtfully, continuing to stare at Sawyer's mouth. Only this time, Sawyer wasn't talking, he was eating.

"Do I have food on me or something? You keep staring at my face."

"Sorry, sometimes I focus on something without realizing it. I close out the rest of the world and concentrate. Did Mrs. Franz have any siblings?"

"No. Only child. Which is sad, because that means the whole family line is gone. That is really a tragedy. I hadn't even thought of that before."

"So, it was the intent of our killer to clear out a whole family line. Two generations. To prove…that he can…" Grant paused, thinking.

"Do genealogy?" Sawyer interjected the line before thinking. "Sorry, that was rude."

"No, not really. He had to do some investigating into the family tree or he wouldn't have known how far reaching his killings would be. You are sure the Martins had no other children?"

Sawyer stared at his fries. "No, actually, I'm not sure they didn't. I…I never thought that was an angle of any importance or it would've been made clear there were other children. I saw one child listed on their obituary and just figured that was it."

Grant picked up his napkin and wiped his mouth. He now stared at the table, his brow knit, his dark eyes focused, dark hair shining from the lights in the diner. He had a rugged handsomeness to him, which made Sawyer wonder why he'd never married. Maybe he *was* married. Sawyer had never asked.

"So Grant, are you married?" Sawyer laid his napkin on the table and stretched back in the seat.

"No, I have never had time to find the right woman."

"That's not the reason and you know it."

Grant smiled slyly. "You think you know? Tell me your thoughts on why I am not married. I believe my mother would have great interest in your words."

Sawyer chuckled, happy to accept the challenge. He placed his hands on his head, covering his dark hair. "Okay. This is what I think. You're waiting for that perfect Native Alaskan princess. She's a little shorter than you but her hair is much longer, down to the back of her knees. Her skin is like chocolate milk, smooth and easy to look at. Her eyes are large and round with long lashes that nearly lay out on her cheeks. *She's* the one you're looking for. And you just haven't found her yet."

Grant chuckled. "Maybe you are right. I should start working on finding that woman, yes? I need to train my son in the ways of the tracker, hoping he is born with the same gift the Great God gave to me, but for now, I must find my princess. Maybe she's resting quietly in your apartment."

"Cute. Very cute. If you're done, we'll just see if she fits the description."

Grant nodded and Sawyer paid the tab, picked up Esley's lunch and the two men headed to the car. They arrived at the apartment complex in a few minutes and Sawyer led the way to his apartment. The officers guarding the door smiled and shook hands with Grant when introduced. Sawyer unlocked the door and the two of them went inside to see a napping Esley sitting in the recliner in the living room. The attending nurse was quietly reading a magazine.

"How is she?" asked Sawyer softly. The sound of his voice woke her and she smiled sleepily.

"She's doing well, just very sore," replied the nurse.

"Ah, glad I woke you," he teased, smiling down at Esley. "I've got someone I want you to meet."

Esley tried to sit up straighter and winced. "Stay still," warned Sawyer. "This is my cousin, Grant. You remember we talked about Grant, right?"

"Yes, I do remember." She smiled at Grant, her dark eyes shining up at him. She attempted to lift her arm to shake his hand, but decided against it.

Grant smiled down at her. "Do not do anything that causes you pain. You will heal faster that way." He bowed his head slightly. "It is very nice to meet you."

"Hey, do you mind if Grant stays in your apartment, since you're hogging mine?"

She smiled again, sleep tugging at her eyes. "No problem. It's probably a mess and the sheets haven't been changed…" Her voice faded and her eyes gradually closed.

Sawyer turned questioningly to the nurse.

"It's the pain pills, Sawyer. You should be used to that by now."

"Right," he said, "pain pills. We'll…just…go then."

The nurse nodded. "She needs to rest. The only way to keep her down is to continue giving her the pain meds. Otherwise, I think she'd be out there hunting bad guys with you."

"You're probably right," smiled Sawyer. "We shouldn't be too late. Here is some lunch for her, if she's hungry."

"She will be when she wakes up again. I'll keep it warm in the oven. Thank you."

Sawyer took Grant across the hall to Esley's apartment. The crime scene tape had been removed and the lock on the door replaced. When Sawyer opened the door, his cousin stood at the entry and his nose wrinkled with distaste.

" The killer was here," he said quietly.

"Yes, this entry is where Esley was abducted."

"They were here only seconds before he took her," said Grant, his eyes checking every inch of the room. "I will get my things from the car." Grant went to the car and retrieved his bag, leaving it in Esley's apartment.

Once Grant's things were stowed in the apartment, both men returned to the car.

"The files on the Martin couple are at the station. You want to go have a look?"

"I am not much into paperwork," said Grant slowly, "but I could use a look in the Franz's barn. Did you say you chased a suspect into the barn when Esley was assaulted?"

"Yeah, we did, but we never found anyone. I don't know that he went into the barn for sure."

"I would like to have a look, if you are agreeable to that."

Sawyer wasn't the least bit offended. "Happy to have another set of eyes on the crime. Let's go."

Chapter Twenty-Three

His eyes watch the apartment and the unmarked police cars parked at the front and back of the complex. Esley is the key to his winning this game of wits. He's seen how Kingsley looks at her. Kingsley must never be allowed to make that relationship happen. The killer continues to watch, plotting, planning. Frustration edges into his thoughts; he doesn't like being frustrated. He can feel the anger creeping in, filling his brain. He could feel it begin to work its way into his blood stream. Someone is going to die. Someone has to die. It's been too long.

Unsure if he can wait until the perfect moment to strike the apartment, he drives by, struggling to look as if he were just another passing car. But in his heart, he's not just another automobile. He is like a Black Adder, poised to strike. And strike he would.

***

Grant walked slowly into the barn, taking in every nuance of the structure; the milking stalls, the smell of bailed hay, oats, and horses. Suddenly his senses were accosted by a foul scent that made him want to empty his stomach. Now, *there* was something he'd not thought he would ever smell again. Not only could he smell it, he tasted it on his tongue, felt it on his skin. It was an evil he'd not experienced since the Evergreen Killer.

He moved carefully to the horse stall he'd sensed and a beautiful mare lifted her royal head over the half door, gazing at him thoughtfully.

"Do you have something to say to me, my sister?" whispered Grant softly. He stepped closer into the horse and she placed her head gently on his shoulder. "Ah…so you *do* have a story to tell."

Grant stroked the mare's forehead and moved his hand slowly down her glistening neck, feeling the feathery flow of her mane. She was a beautiful chestnut brown with a deep black mane and the spirit of a warrior princess.

"I am here, my friend. Tell me what you know."

The horse stamped her foot and moved away, her hooves clomping on the stall floor as she moved in a circle around the small enclosure to the back of the stall. She stopped, watching Grant with dark, expectant eyes.

Grant could feel the tingle begin at the back of his neck, traveling up and down his spine simultaneously, until his body was enveloped by coldness. Something bad happened in this stall.

He looked to the side of the stall and found a feedbag. He quickly scanned the barn until his dark eyes came to rest on a sack of oats against the end wall. Moving surely, he walked to the sack, placed some oats into the feedbag, and returned to the stall. He gingerly opened the door, holding the bag before the mare. The horse neighed softly, deep in her throat, and walked to him. Dropping her nose into the bag she began eating the oats. Her jaws worked as she chewed, but her eyes never left Grant.

"That is right. We are friends. It is safe for you to tell me what you need me to know. I will listen. Speak when you are ready."

The mare took her time, the muffled crunch of the oats between her teeth filled the air. Grant's eyes never left hers, and she continued to stare back into his as she munched the last of the oats.

Finally, backing slowly away, she moved once again to the back of the stall and pawed the hay on the floor. She stopped, her eyes boring into his. Grant returned the stare, waiting, watching.

She tossed her head gently into the air and moved the few steps to the other side of the stall and again, pawed the hay on the floor. Grant stepped slowly toward the mare and knelt down beside her with one knee directly behind her left front leg. Lifting her foot, he rested it on his knee and inspected the bottom of the hoof.

"Sawyer, bring me a file, or something no bigger than a file."

He could hear Sawyer moving through the barn and heard him pick up something.

"Found...a thing," called Sawyer as he walked toward the stall. "Can't tell you what it is, but here." He entered the stall and handed what looked like a large metal toothpick with a curved end to Grant. "What've you found?"

"I am not sure, but it looks like some hair caught under her shoe. I am fairly certain it is human hair." He picked gently at the hoof, prying the glob of whatever it was from beneath the horseshoe. "Do you have an evidence kit in the car?"

"Yeah, I do."

"Better go get it," he said, reaching up and patting the mare's neck. "And bring a DNA kit in, too, if you have one."

"I actually do," smiled Sawyer.

Grant slowly set the mare's foot on the ground. "You did very well, my friend. I heard you. No words, yes? It is just you and I, and the air around us. We will only be a minute longer and you will be free of this evil."

Grant stood and stroked her smooth neck, cooing and speaking in low velvety tones. This horse had seen evil, she'd had to protect herself and she was still frightened by what she'd seen and done. But he could feel she trusted him, trusted the truth in his eyes that told her he would know what she needed to tell. And she was correct.

"Do you know about Alaska? I think I should bring you back to Alaska with me. What do you think about that? We are brother and sister now, you and I. We should be together, yes?"

Sawyer returned with the kit and evidence bag. Grant stroked the mare's neck again. "Here we go. Be patient, Princess. We are almost there."

Grant knelt one more time beside the mare and lifted her hoof onto his knee. He whispered softly to her and stroked her leg every now and again. Sawyer handed him a pair of latex gloves and he wriggled into them. Using the pick, he continued digging gently under the shoe and finally the glob broke loose. Sawyer held the bag beneath the hoof and the hair, dirt, and blood fell safely inside it. Grant pointed out the blood to Sawyer.

"I do not know if you can see it, but there is dried blood all around the inside of the shoe here." He pointed to the area he was talking about. "We will have to test it to know if the blood or the hair is human, but it is something that has been bothering this mare since it happened. She had a great need to protect herself from someone or something."

Pulling out the long cotton swab from the DNA kit, Grant swabbed around the inside of the shoe and placed the sample into the collection container. He handed the kit to Sawyer and craned his neck to see through the open stall door. "Is there a water barrel out there and a rag? I need to wash her feet."

Sawyer looked puzzled, but didn't question. He grabbed a rag from a peg over the water barrel outside the front of the barn. He dipped the rag in the water and hurried back to the stall. He handed the soaked rag to Grant and watched silently as he washed the hoof he had on his knee. Grant stood and spoke soothingly to the mare.

"You have helped me, now I will help you." He then moved slowly around the mare, picked up each hoof, inspected it, and wiped it clean. There was no other blood or evidence on any of the hooves, but he wiped them anyway so she would know she had nothing of the evil left. When he was done, he stood in front of the mare and gently placed his forehead on hers, stroking the sides of her head and sliding his hands down her neck as he spoke. "It is gone now. You are free."

He lifted his head from her forehead and spoke to her one more time. "I will see you again, and you will know my home. We will work together and be family. Wait for me. I will come for you."

Staring straight ahead, Grant strode from the stall and through the front door of the barn without a backward glance. The mare whinnied softly and tossed her head. Sawyer had no idea what had just happened, but he couldn't deny the warm feeling filling the barn in that moment. He left the stall, closing the door behind him and stared at the mare. Shaking himself from the intensity of her gaze, he exited the structure and saw Grant was already in the car.

As Sawyer slid into the driver's seat, he looked at his cousin. "How do you *do* that?"

"To what are you referring?"

"How do you make a barn feel like a sanctuary?"

"Oh, that was not me," he said, grinning at his cousin. "That was the mare."

"Yeah…that makes no sense to me."

"There is Native in you," replied Grant. "It makes sense inside you, somewhere, but you must find that place."

Sawyer shook his head, not exactly disagreeing with his cousin, but not agreeing either. He started the car and they pulled away from the barn and headed down the driveway.

"You and I both know there's so little Native in me, there may as well be none," said Sawyer. "But you make me wish I was full Native. I envy you and the loyalty you show to your heritage."

"You are part of that heritage, my cousin."

They rode in silence for a moment before Sawyer started asking questions.

"What was the mare so frightened of?"

"Evil. She had done something she did not want to do, the action forced upon her by someone in this stall with her. She was anguished, and could not remove the remainder of the experience lodged between her hoof and her shoe."

"Are you thinking this was done by the killer?"

A heavy sigh escaped Grant as he thought about the question, shaking his head. His next words were hard to speak, and came from his heart. "In part…but the sadness in her was the innocent that was killed."

"Are you telling me she knew the family had been killed in the house?" Sawyer was doubtful.

"She knew something happened in the house, she had no way of knowing what. But what she was burdened with was a killing in the barn. We will have to wait and see what these samples tell us."

"So, you're saying animals can sense killing." Sawyer's tone was more a statement than a question.

"They can sense much more than that. Their senses are far more heightened than human senses are. Most humans are so preoccupied with life they fail to actually *experience* it. It takes a lot of effort on our part to slow down and *feel* the world around us. Animals in the wild live by that instinct. They must feel their world, or they will be killed. Humans used to be more like that, but the gift has left them now."

It was getting late and both men were tired. After dropping the evidence at the station, they decided to call it a day and pick up some dinner to-go and head to the apartments. Esley was in the easy chair in the living room when they walked in. The nurse filled Sawyer in on Esley's condition and how she was doing as he escorted her to the door. The three of them ate dinner together before Grant headed across the hall. Esley was doing better, a little more talkative and less sleep, but still moving slowly. It was good to see her smile, to hear her interact with Grant. She was genuine, interested in learning about his life and lifestyle. Watching her, it infuriated Sawyer that someone would do what was done to her, not only because she was someone he was beginning to care very much about, but because you just don't *do* that to people. The frustration he felt at not being able to find this killer was written all over his face.

Esley saw the look. "Sawyer," she said, in a cautionary tone, "you have to calm down about this. You're going to use up all your emotional resources in the wrong places if you keep getting mad when you see me. Look how much better I am. My eye isn't swollen shut any more."

Grant smiled at her. "You sound like my mother, and that is meant as a compliment. She is a wise woman."

Esley did look better, but ribs take a long time to heal, and the healing process was very painful.

"Nice," Sawyer said with a smirk, "now I'm totally outnumbered. I just…I just want to find this guy and get him off the streets before he can do this to anyone else."

"We are working on that, Sawyer," replied Grant. "Just keep breathing. It is good for the brain cells."

They sat together in the living room eating from TV trays, Esley with a tray in her lap. She hurt too much to laugh, so they kept the conversation on the investigation, and filled her in on what was found. Pretty soon Esley began to drift off to sleep and Grant rose to go.

"We'll head out early tomorrow, about eight, will that work for you?" Sawyer glanced to Esley and then back to Grant.

"Eight is *early*?" chuckled Grant. "I am done with my meditation by six."

"Show off." Sawyer closed the door after his cousin. By the time he woke Esley and helped her into bed, he was exhausted from the day and ready to sleep. Thankfully, the couch was comfortable.

***

Grant entered Esley's apartment and closed the door. He studied the room, nodding knowingly at its contents and how they were organized into a warm and inviting space. The scent of the abduction was barely noticeable. *This space belongs to a bird*, thought Grant. *A bird that longs to be free, to soar. Not a canary or parakeet, this bird is a raptor...a large bird. She is an eagle, but she does not know it.*

The silence of the apartment was so appreciated and immediately Grant sat cross-legged in the middle of the living room to meditate. His hands rested comfortably on his folded knees, palms up. His eyes slowly closed and his mind became a void. He sought it, welcomed it, and relished in the solitude of the moment. He needed this so badly.

Time was of no consequence and he floated in his own heartbeat, feeling the blood rush in his veins, connecting with ancestors long dead. His meditations were his favorite part of the day. When it came time for it to end, he always felt the loss, but knew when morning came, he would repeat the exercise and feel the strength of his own thoughts once again.

Unaccustomed to the speed of life in a city, however small, Grant didn't like the feeling of being pushed from one unhappy circumstance to another. Yet, it seemed that was what he was born to do. With each investigation he took part in, he became so immersed in the work that he felt a loss of small pieces of himself. But then when each case closed, and the family accepted the loss of their loved one, those pieces of himself returned to him, making him whole once again. It was an interesting cycle, but it was his cycle and he'd come to understand it.

With eyes heavy and in need of sleep, Grant showered and prepared for bed. When he finally lay down for the evening, he was ready for sleep. He smiled as he closed his eyes, thinking how Greyson Beauchene, his boss in Alaska, would chuckle at the amount of talking he had done on this day. But Sawyer was his cousin, his childhood playmate, and there was much to remember. Still, the solitude of the quiet apartment fed his soul. Soon he closed his eyes, and welcomed sleep.

Chapter Twenty-Four

It seemed to Sawyer, as he awoke the next morning, that there was something odd about having a woman sleeping in his apartment, in his bed, while he slept on the couch. He wasn't even married. The thought made him chuckle as he walked softly into the bedroom to see if Esley was ready to get up. When he entered the room, not only was she ready, she was dressed and sitting up, reading a book. Sawyer was surprised to see her prepped for the day.

"Hey," he said quietly, "how did it feel getting ready without the help of Nurse Killer Bee? She'll be surprised to see you dressed."

Esley smiled, but avoided the giggle that threatened her ribcage. "I'm feeling so much more in control of me," she said. "I'm thinking I'm going to like this day a whole lot better than the last few. I'm going to be out there in another week with you and Grant."

Sawyer sat down on the side of the bed. "Don't push it. That's the doctor's call, not yours. You'll have to have a release from him to even set foot in the station. You know that, right?"

"Yeah, I know." The disappointment was strong in her voice. "Do you have any idea how sick I am of your apartment? No offense. I'd be just as sick of mine if I were over there."

Sawyer leaned over and kissed her on the forehead. "No offense taken. I can't imagine being cooped up like this. However, if you're watching my back, I want you at full power, right?"

"Yeah, right."

"When I've got a perp with a gun to my head, and I yell 'Shoot! Shoot!' I don't want any," he switched to his best falsetto and continued, "*Ouch, it hurts to pull the trigger on this darn gun!*" Sawyer cleared his throat while Esley tried not to smile. "None of that. You have to be ready to cover me."

Esley tried to punch him in the arm and winced. "Very funny. I'll take you down when I'm over all this. Just wait and see."

"You'll take me down, eh? And how long do I have to wait for that wonderful little exercise?"

Esley gave him a warning look and he laughed. "Okay, I'll tell you what," said Sawyer. "We're going to dinner tonight, just you and me. I'm sure Grant can find something in your apartment to eat."

"What, you mean like a date or something?"

"Don't you think it's about time? I don't kiss everyone on the forehead, you know. Just someone I care about." Sawyer was staring into Esley's dark eyes and she quickly looked down at her hands, now folded in her lap.

"You…I…I just…really?" She stammered trying to voice her feelings. She felt heat travel quickly up from her neck and spread across her face.

Sawyer's laugh came right up from his belly. "You *have* to know I care about you, Esley, right? I don't think I could've been any more obvious."

"It's not that, so much…I mean, yeah, it's that, but I just never thought you'd…"

"Never thought I'd what?"

Sawyer felt his own heat rising as he stared into her eyes, but it wasn't embarrassment. The woman before him was beautiful, and smart, and strong. But her next words caught him off guard. It wasn't what he expected to hear from that full, confident mouth.

"I just never thought you'd care for someone like me." Tears welled up in Esley's eyes and spilled quietly down her face as she stared at her hands.

"What?" Sawyer was more than surprised by her comment. He lifted her chin and carefully leaned into her, placing his mouth over hers. Hungry passion filled him and she touched his face with her hands, pressing her lips to his until he could feel the wince of pain from her. He relinquished her mouth unwillingly and quickly sat back. "I hurt you, I'm so sorry," he said, laying his hand tenderly on her bandaged rib cage.

"No…I'm…I'm fine, really."

Sawyer gazed at her. The pain and the suffering he saw there pulled him deeper into her eyes. He had no idea she was so tormented. In his experience working with her she'd always displayed such strength and focus. It was hard to believe she felt so insecure.

"Maybe you could tell me what's not to love, Esley, because I find everything about you fascinating."

"You do?" Her eyes, still moist with tears, widened in surprise. "It's just that, well, you…you have a family. You grew up in that family, and you *still* have them in your life."

"Esley, you have a family, too. Just because they died doesn't mean they're not your family, and it certainly doesn't have anything to do with your value as a human being. You loved them, you still love them, and I know you miss them. That loss took a piece of your heart, as it should, but never let it define who you are. You are strong and determined and focused. Each one of those traits makes you beautiful."

Sawyer's phone rang and he quickly kissed her again and stood, lifting the phone to his ear.

"Kingsley."

"You're needed at the station right now." The voice belonged to Captain Amerson and it sounded urgent.

"What's going on?"

"You just need to get here. I think we've had a major break in your cases – both of them."

"On my way."

He turned back to Esley who was smiling up at him. "I've gotta go. We'll talk more over dinner tonight. I'll find a quiet restaurant, something with more ambiance than the diner." He chuckled.

She nodded her head in silent agreement and Sawyer rushed out the door. He went into the hallway and rapped on Esley's apartment door. Grant opened almost before the knock was complete.

"Did you sleep late, Cousin?" he asked Sawyer with a knowing grin.

"No, but I did just get a call from the captain. We're needed at the station. He says they may have a break in our investigations."

"Well, let us hustle then." Grant glanced at the rumpled clothes Sawyer wore. "You might want to change out of yesterdays clothing, yes?"

Sawyer laughed softly. "Good point. Come over to my place while I change…and since when do you hustle anywhere? You don't even *say* it fast."

Grant grinned and said quietly, "I can when I have to."

Sawyer changed quickly and soon they were on the way to the station. Grant seemed quiet and pensive.

"What are you thinking so hard about this morning?" asked Sawyer.

"I am thinking about the woman in your apartment," replied Grant. "I am thinking she is a bird…delicate and fragile, yet strong and determined. If you do not let her fly, you may lose her."

"Well, aren't you just the philosopher?" teased Sawyer.

Grant analyzed his cousin as if he were dissecting a fly, his face serious and unmoving. "I speak the truth. You must know when to let her fly and when to hold her close. This is important to her."

The smile faded slowly from Sawyer's face. "You really mean this, don't you?"

"Yes," came the satisfied reply. "I really do."

Once in the captain's office, Amerson motioned for them to follow him.

"This car was stopped for a broken tail light," he said as he opened the door into the garage. "It's over here."

The trunk was open on the vehicle. Sawyer and Grant stepped up to the car and gazed at the items tossed haphazardly inside. Both men struggled into exam gloves and gingerly moved the belongings.

"This guy obviously took at least some of these things from the Franz home," said Captain Amerson. "We would never have known any of it was from their home if he'd not been stupid enough to take a trophy belonging to the Franz boy. Has his name right on it."

Sawyer stepped back and scanned the exterior of the car. He walked around it, scrutinizing every inch.

"What are you looking for? The trunk is the only thing of interest." Captain Amerson sounded impatient. "Forensics has already searched the car. They're running fingerprints now. Other than the trunk, the car was completely empty."

Sawyer looked up and returned to the back of the vehicle. "I wanted to see if the car had recently been painted, but it doesn't appear to have been."

"Why would that be important?" asked Amerson.

"The car that shot up the diner a couple months ago was maroon or some shade of dark red. This one's white." Sawyer stopped for a moment and began again. "Captain, you know this killer plants evidence at every turn. He's been messing with us from the beginning of the investigation, at least since Jack's death. He's far too clever to be caught with a trunk full of belongings from a crime scene. Let me talk to the driver, I can tell you more then."

"I know, I know...but couldn't help hoping we'd finally got our guy. Let me know what you find after the interview." The captain's disappointment was clear. Sawyer nodded his agreement and turned to go. The captain called to him. "Hold on a minute, before you go, there's one other thing."

Sawyer stopped and turned back to the captain, watching Amerson's face expectantly.

"There was blood work done on Clay Carson while he was in the hospital. You need to know that he was drugged. Seriously drugged."

"What does 'seriously drugged' mean?"

"He was given a very high dose of LSD. Clay remembers none of it, and regular drug screenings we do at the station have never shown him to be a drug user."

"People change, Captain." Sawyer's eyes were venomous.

"I'm telling you this because you're heading this investigation, Sawyer. When Clay is up to it, you are more than welcome to interview him. I've spoken with him and he said he would be happy to speak with you. But I want to be there when you do."

Sawyer nodded and motioned for Grant to follow him.

"Breathe, cousin," said Grant, walking beside Sawyer. "Breathe, and let the anger in you dissolve."

"I don't want it to dissolve. I want to use it to find this killer. I need my anger to keep me strong."

Grant stopped. They were in the hallway that led to interrogation. Sawyer turned to face him. Grant's face was soft, pensive, as he spoke. "Anger is not useful in these situations. We only *think* it is useful. Anger protects us from feelings we are not ready to acknowledge. You are part Native, cousin, and if you want to find this killer, find the Native inside you and let him lead you to your answers."

"And just how am I supposed to do that?"

"You already know how to do that. You do not need me to tell you."

Sawyer remembered his anger at the loss of Jack. He'd always thought it was that anger that would lead him and help him. But, looking back, the only thing the anger had led him to was the bottle. And his drinking had paralyzed him. Grant was right. Anger would get him nowhere.

Grant motioned for Sawyer to lead the way and they continued on to interrogation. They stopped at the desk and picked up the file on the man they were about to interview. It felt empty, which meant the man had no priors and no history with the station.

The captain had phoned from the garage when the two men left to have the suspect brought to interrogation.

When they opened the door to the room, a very terrified, middle-aged man sat cuffed to the chair. With sandy hair and blue eyes, he couldn't have been more than five feet five inches tall. Sawyer knew immediately this man definitely didn't have the constitution to pull off the killing of a family, let alone a seasoned police detective. When the two men entered the room, he looked like he was going to lose whatever food he had in his stomach. Sawyer knew this wasn't their killer.

Grant tugged at Sawyer's sleeve, pulled him back toward the door and whispered, "This isn't our man."

"I know," replied Sawyer, also in a near whisper. "He's a mouse in a cage."

Sawyer proceeded to the table and sat down, smiling congenially at the suspect. He set the file gently on the table and folded his hands over it. Grant stayed by the door with his arms crossed, leaning against the wall.

"Why…why am I here?" the man began, his voice shaking. "They…they said I had someone else's stuff in my trunk. I never look in my trunk. I put my groceries in the backseat. I don't know whose stuff that is; I swear it. I didn't put it in there. I didn't!"

"Mr.--" Sawyer opened the file and read the name of the suspect on the single page inside, "Gilkins, is it?"

"Yes, yes, Zacharias Gilkins."

"Mr. Gilkins," began Sawyer, "are you married?"

"No, never married."

"What do you do for a living?"

"I...I'm an accountant. With Simpson and Cutter in town."

Sawyer acknowledged his response with a small smile. "Tell me, have you loaned your car out to anyone in the last few days?"

"No...no one." Mr. Gilkins began to look as though he didn't have a chance of getting out of there without a jail sentence.

"Have you noticed if your car was broken into recently?"

"That I would notice, I'm sure. But, no, not broken into. No broken windows; no jimmied locks. The trunk has to be opened with the key, so I can't figure out how those things could have gotten in there."

Sawyer continued. "You didn't notice suddenly having less gas than you remembered? Or having more miles on your odometer than you remembered?"

The man's eyes widened. "No, I never look at my odometer. The car is so old the odometer doesn't work anymore. However..." he slowed as if remembering something. "About two days, ago I noticed on my way to work one morning that my tank was full. I was fairly certain I'd had three-quarters of a tank the night before, but shrugged it off as forgetfulness. That's the *only* thing I noticed. But until now, I thought I just didn't remember how much gas I actually had."

Sawyer rose and scooped the file off the table. "Mr. Gilkins, we'll have you out of lockup in the next few hours. It can take a while to complete all the paperwork, but we'll get it done. We will need to keep your car for a few days to process it, as the contents came from a crime scene. We'll get it back to you as quickly as we can. Do you understand?"

"You...you're letting me go?"

"Yes, as soon as the paperwork is done."

Gilkins' shoulders slumped with relief. "Thank you," he whispered. "Thank you."

"You're very welcome, and thank you for being so forthcoming. That makes our job a lot easier. You take care."

Sawyer and Grant stopped to report their findings to Amerson on their way out to the car. "You may as well cut him loose," Sawyer said, standing before Captain Amerson's desk. "He's not our man."

"You're sure on that?"

"We're both sure. He's not the killer."

"Okay. Keep me posted on your findings and let me know when you want to visit with Carson. I'll make the appointment."

"Will do," smiled Sawyer as he and Grant exited the office.

As the men continued to the car, Sawyer noticed Grant was especially quiet. He waited until they were in the car before breaking the silence.

"What are you thinking?" asked Sawyer.

Grant sat back in his seat. "We need to take a trip to Smithville. Maybe we could find someone who knew the Martin family. It may take most of the day to get there and then conduct interviews. What do you think?"

"You read my mind. They were longtime residents of the town. There have to be people who knew them for most, if not all of that time."

Sawyer stuck the key in the ignition and they pulled out of the station parking lot. "I'm hungry. You need some breakfast?"

"I could eat."

They stopped at a fast food drive-through and ordered breakfast for the road. As the miles sped by, they ate and discussed the Martins.

"There has to be some link between the Martin family and the Franz family *and* the killer." Grant's eyes were far away as he spoke. "And I also need to talk with this Sergeant Carson."

"I suppose that's needed, but I'm afraid of what I'll do if I walk into the same room he's in."

"He is a large part of this investigation. He may have been coerced, and the drugs have certainly affected his memory, but his injuries, and the timing of them, are too perfect a match to the time of Esley's beating to not be connected somehow. There is no such thing as coincidence. Not in a murder investigation."

"I'll talk to Captain Amerson when we get back about an appointment with Carson. We'll see what he has to say."

The two men arrived in Smithville and decided to begin their search in the local coffee shop. If there was gossip to be had, it was usually at a coffee shop.

They asked around amongst the customers, telling them who they were and that they were investigating the murder. Several people knew the

Martins, but three of the people they interviewed gave them the name of Mrs. Martin's best friend from high school, telling them, if anyone knew the family it was Fancy Ilkton. Fancy and Sylvia were apparently 'thick as thieves' in school.

They stepped up onto the old porch of the Ilkton home. The white paint was peeling from the sides of the house, and the porch slanted down so much it felt like they were walking uphill just to get to the front door. Sawyer rang the doorbell.

There was a slow shuffling inside and the chained door opened just a crack. "What do you want?"

"Ms. Ilkton, my name is Detective Sawyer Kingsley and this is my associate, Grant Mulvane. We'd like to talk to you about your friend Sylvia Martin. We understand you were close."

The door opened to suspicious blue eyes. Fancy was in an old housecoat and slippers. She was barely five feet tall with white hair and a sad, downturned mouth.

"Please, come in," she said softly. She motioned for them to take a seat on the couch and she sat down in the easy chair across from them. "How can I help?"

Sawyer conducted the interview while Grant studied the house and the person that went with it. "You went to school with Sylvia, is that correct?"

A mischievous smile gradually made its way across her face. "Yes I did. We got into a lot of trouble back in those days. I fear we were way ahead of our time. We should've been born in the sixties."

"How so?" asked Sawyer, inviting Fancy to fill in the details.

"Oh, you know, we ran with the wild boys who drove the fast cars. Course, they didn't go as fast then as they do now, but they were plenty fast for the day." Her giggle cracked with the age.

"What kind of trouble did you get yourselves into?" he prodded.

"Oh, the usual; cigarettes, boys, skipping school, that kind of thing. Her parents would be so mad at her when they heard of some of the things we were doing. They forbid us to be friends for a while, but that didn't stop us." Fancy stared into the distance as she remembered the days of her youth spent with her good friend. "Truth was, it was Sylvia that got us in trouble for the most part. I was the 'good' girl of the two of us. But that Sylvia, she was a wild child."

"What was her most wild behavior, that you recall?" asked Sawyer, smoothly guiding her on.

"Oh, it was probably the baby she had."

"She had a baby? Out of wedlock?"

"She sure did, and as soon as her parents found out she was pregnant, they sent her to the other side of the state to live with her aunt and uncle. Who knows if she was really with family, or if she stayed at a home for unwed mothers. They had those back then, you know. She refused to ever talk about it, and forbade me to tell anyone her secret." Fancy frowned. "This is the first I've spoken of it to anyone. She was my dearest and best friend, and I swore to her I would never tell a soul. But, I don't suppose it matters who knows now." She shook her head, taking a deep breath before finishing. "Yes, Sylvia had a baby."

"Do you know if it was a boy or a girl?"

"No, I don't, she never spoke of the child. But, I do recall one day that she slipped and referred to the baby as 'he'." There was another pause. "I never pushed her for more information, never asked her to clarify. She was shocked the word had escaped her lips. I could tell by the look on her face."

"You've been very helpful, Fancy. Thank you so much for talking with us."

Fancy never looked at them again, but sat in her chair as if lost in the memory of her dear friend.

"We'll…see ourselves out."

She didn't move and Sawyer and Grant exited the home.

"Well, that was interesting," said Sawyer as they walked down the path toward his car.

"We need to find out where they sent Sylvia. We need to know what happened to that baby."

"I guess we'll need to figure out who to talk to about that." Sawyer studied his cousin.

They got in the car and as Grant was fastening his seatbelt he said, "Where are your state offices?"

Chapter Twenty-Five

"You mean here or back in Blakely?" Sawyer was beginning to think like Grant. He understood exactly why he wanted the state offices.

"The sooner the better. We're here, let's check here and find adoption services. It would be good to know who adopted that baby and who he grew up to be."

Grant fell quiet while Sawyer scouted out where they would go for the information they needed. After finding out who it was they needed to talk with, Sawyer placed a call to the station in Blakely. The receptionist there, Evelyn, was very helpful in connecting him with the department he needed. In a matter of minutes, he'd made an appointment with an adoption specialist and they were on their way.

Sawyer glanced at Grant. "Seemed like no one had a minute of time to talk to us until I said 'murder investigation,' and then they were all ears. I was suddenly fit in to any number of appointments during the day. All I had to do was pick my time."

They pulled into the parking lot of the Iowa State offices and proceeded through the door and to the information desk.

"We have an appointment with Shannon Norton," said Sawyer. "Could you direct me to her office, please?"

The woman at the desk gave them the room number, the floor, and the best elevator to use to get to that floor. They thanked her and headed to the appropriate elevator.

They entered the office where a beautiful woman worked at the desk. She had jet black hair as long as Grant's and skin the color of warm caramel. She looked up and stood as the men entered. Sawyer began the formal introductions.

"Hello, Ms. Norton. My name is Sawyer Kingsley and this is my associate, Grant Mulvane." He motioned toward Grant as he spoke.

Reaching over her desk, she shook both their hands and cast a careful look at Grant. Sawyer wondered if it was Grant's waist length hair, but said nothing.

"I understand you need access to a sealed adoption file," Ms. Norton began, "and call me Shannon...please."

"Thank you, Shannon," said Sawyer. "Yes, we are investigating a string of murders and we have reason to believe this adoption is pivotal to our investigation." He couldn't help but notice how neither Shannon nor Grant would look at each other.

"In what way?"

"I really can't say at this time, we need more information before we go any further. If we find the information isn't what we believe it to be, we will go no further. However, at this point, we need to see those files."

"I see," she began. "I'm afraid I'm going to need more information than that. I assure you, anything you say will be kept in the strictest confidence. Surely, you understand I can't be handing these sealed files over on a whim." There was a quick glance in Grant's direction, almost unnoticed.

"Yes, I do understand that, but it's not a 'whim' that brings us to your office." Sawyer saw he was going to have to give her at least the basic information or they wouldn't get the needed files. "We have good cause to suspect something in that file will allow us to solve a string of three murders. One of the murders involves a family of five people, mother, father and three children. One is the murder of a police officer and the other, an older couple from here in Smithville, the Martins. Maybe you're familiar with that case."

"I remember that. Yes, it was terrible." Her hands were folded on the desk in front of her and her eyes traveled purposefully between her hands and Sawyer's face. "Could you give me a couple hours to speak with my superiors? I need some direction on this. Support and guidance from the 'chain of command' would be especially helpful. Adoption laws have changed in recent years, and I just want to make sure I'm correct in my thinking."

"We'll get some lunch," said Sawyer, handing her his business card. "If you need to call my captain, his name is Chase Amerson; the station number is on my card. My cell number is also there. Just call the cell when you've come to a decision."

Sawyer and Grant stood and shook her hand. Grant raised his eyes and finally allowed himself to stare into hers.

"You are Native Alaskan, yes?" she asked, raising one eyebrow.

"Yes, I am. It would appear you are as well."

"Yes," she said, picking up the folder. "I am that." Nothing more was said and the men left her office, with Grant walking a little faster than usual.

In the elevator Sawyer rubbed his upper lip with his pointer finger in an effort to mask the smirk on his face.

"You find something funny, Cousin?"

"Well, I was just thinking," said Sawyer as a giggle escaped his lips. "Here I thought you'd found your princess in a mare with dark eyes and a long mane. I'm thinking I could have been wrong."

Grant eyed his companion. "I do not believe in violence. Therefore, I refuse to respond to such ludicrous thinking." The smirk on Grant's face didn't match his words.

"I see," teased Sawyer. "Afraid we might end this in fisticuffs?"

"So old school, cousin. I am surprised you could put a sentence together in that rigid a structure."

Sawyer laughed at the jab. "Hey, I used to watch a lot of those old black and white medieval movies on television when I was a kid."

The elevator doors opened and they headed to the car with Sawyer still trying to hide his mirth. As he slid into the driver's seat, he watched Grant get in and close the door.

"What is it you continue to stare at?" asked Grant, his face blank. He now had his emotions completely back under control, or so he thought. Sawyer on the other hand couldn't contain it any longer and burst into laughter.

"Is this how members of your tribe ask for a date? You just identify each other's tribe and walk away? What does that *mean*?"

Grant was shaking his head, trying once again to refrain from laughing. "Clan. We are clans in our culture, and she could have been married, you know. And I have to ask, married or not, what is she doing so far away from her people?"

"And you didn't ask her this because…" Sawyer's voice trailed off.

"Her personal life is none of my business."

"She wasn't wearing a ring you know."

"I know."

His answer threw Sawyer into another round of laughter.

"You were *checking her out*!" he roared. "My staid, composed cousin was checking out a woman! And a pretty hot woman, at that."

Grant just shook his head with the silly smirk still on his face. There was a bit of blush to his cheeks Sawyer had not seen before.

"I'm surprised your people ever get close enough to make babies."

"I would say it is a good thing for you and I that they do, yes?"

Sawyer chuckled and decided to give the poor man a break.

"Let's go eat some lunch."

"Good idea."

They pulled into a parking place in front of a small restaurant. Sawyer turned off the car the two men strode into the diner, taking a booth seat. While they ate their lunch, Sawyer asked Grant more about how he grew up and what it was like living in Alaska.

"You've never told me what growing up was like for you, Grant. We lost contact when we were, what, ten years old? Eleven?"

"Somewhere in there. It seemed the years flew by before I realized how long it had been since I last saw you. I often wondered where you went and what you were doing."

"Same here," responded Sawyer, his dark eyes studying Grant. "We kind of look alike, don't we?"

"Fancy that," smirked Grant, chidingly. "Cousins that resemble one another. Go figure."

"Very funny," chuckled Sawyer. "You're just mad 'cause I know about your love interest."

"Do not even go there," said Grant with a warning look.

His hair was pulled back into its signature long ponytail, held in place by a band at the nape of his neck. His dark skin and dark eyes, together with the black hair made him an obvious Native. Sawyer felt a tinge of envy the more he became reacquainted with his childhood playmate. He was private, but humble about it, strong and confident, yet completely unassuming. What had his life been like? A life that had molded him into the simple, but unique person he'd grown to be.

"How did the two of you know you were both of the same tribe?" Sawyer suddenly had a desire to learn about this part of his family.

"There are…characteristics unique to Native Alaskan people. It is hard to explain. It is, almost more of a 'knowing' than anything we see. The blood is thick in our people and our way of life is very telling. However, I felt like our ways have been severed in her heart. I am interested to know why."

The waitress came to the table and wrote down their lunch selections. Sawyer watched her scan Grant, taking in his dark eyes, warm toned skin, and long black hair in what seemed like one quick second. She smiled and turned away to place the order.

Sawyer looked at his own skin. He'd never noticed how dark his skin was, not as dark as Grant's, but not white either. He couldn't remember ever thinking about his heritage or his ancestors. Grant seemed to hold both of those things in such high esteem. Sawyer wondered why his own family didn't.

"You know," Sawyer began, "it's not so much that I don't know my family tree, but it doesn't feel like it's as important to me as it is to you. I want to feel the way you do about family."

"You already do," smiled Grant, leaning his elbows on the table between them. "It was our bloodline that prompted that call to me."

"In all honesty, it was more desperation than bloodline, I think."

"You underestimate yourself, Cousin. It was the family connection that made you think of me. The truth is, what I do for a living was simply the catalyst that helped you make the call."

"Yeah, I guess you're right."

The waitress brought their lunch and they began eating. Swallowing his first mouthful, Sawyer wiped his face with his napkin and laid the napkin back down on the table. "I don't remember your mom and dad. Are they still living?"

"Oh, yes, they certainly are." Grant smiled and set down his burger, wiping his hands on his napkin. "It will bring them great joy to hear about you and your family and what everyone's doing now."

"I would really love to hear about your growing up and what it was like, you know, being a Native Alaskan and growing up in the clan."

"That would take days," he smiled. "Maybe one day, when all this ugliness is behind us, I will share with you my youth, assuming of course you will do the same."

"Definitely, although I can't help but believe yours is going to be a whole lot more interesting than mine."

They finished their meals and Sawyer pulled out his wallet to pay. Grant stopped him.

"It is my turn to pay for the meal. You have done enough for me already."

Sawyer looked at him like his nose had suddenly changed shape. "You're spending all this time helping me, you paid for your flight down and back, you refuse payment for your services and *I* have done enough for *you*? Right. Besides, I can turn in my receipts for reimbursement by the department. This was a *work* lunch, was it not?"

Grant smiled his gentle smile and allowed Sawyer to pay.

The two men left the restaurant discussing what their next course of action would be. Certain Shannon would be getting back to them soon, they decided to return to the Adoption Services office building and wait there. As it turned out, they wouldn't have to wait long. Sawyer's phone began ringing as they pulled into the parking lot.

"Kingsley."

"Hello Sawyer, this is Shannon. Are you close to my office?" Her voice was pleasant and professional.

"We're actually in the parking lot. We'll be right up."

Thinking the timing couldn't be more perfect. Sawyer and Grant hurried to Shannon's office and found her, once again, at her desk. A copy of the requested file lay in front of her. Before handing it to them, she studied both men. Her eyes lingered a brief moment longer on Grant.

"These documents are not given lightly," she began. "We take our work here at Adoption Services very seriously. It has been brought to our attention this adoptee and his adoptive parents are deceased, making our decision to release the documents a little easier. We ask that you keep these documents private, and return them to us when you are finished with them. Not by fax or mail, but please deliver them back to us in person. Are you agreeable to that?"

"Yes, we can do that," replied Sawyer. He couldn't help but wonder if this was more personal than professional. Did she just want to see Grant again? Having never done this type of investigation before, Sawyer wasn't sure if this was procedure or a juvenile attempt at further contact between Shannon and Grant. Deciding he was probably the only one in the room thinking like a juvenile, Sawyer sheepishly abandoned the line of thinking. However, if that *did* happen to be her plan, then more power to her. He stopped the grin that was trying to make its way across his face.

They rose to go and for an instant, it almost seemed like Grant was going to say something to her, but the moment was so brief Sawyer wasn't sure he'd seen anything at all. There were no looks between the two of them this time, no tension or discomfort. They were just *there*.

As they left Shannon's office, Sawyer's phone rang.

"Kingsley."

"It's Amerson. Are you in Smithville now?"

"Yeah, what's up?"

"The DNA results came back on the evidence you brought in from the barn. When you get back into town, we need to meet. It looks like we have another body to find."

They ended the conversation and Sawyer relayed the information to Grant. Since they had an hour before they'd reach Blakely, Grant reviewed the adoption file while Sawyer drove. Marston Finch's adoptive family actually lived in Blakely, not far from downtown.

"They live in *Blakely*?" The questions ran through Sawyers mind like a wild fire. "Then why was he buried in Thornton? Does it say they ever lived in Thornton? Does it say anything about the biological mother?"

"Yes, the biological mother is just as we thought. Sylvia Martin. Which means his sister was Marylisa Franz. But it looks like he grew up in Blakely."

"There's our link, but…are you telling me his family could have been interviewed when we first figured out who he was? We only had to look up Finch family names in the Blakely phone book and call until we found his parents?" Sawyer sighed and shook his head. "Maybe we could have found him before he went after Esley."

"Sawyer, first of all, you had no idea that family was in Blakely. You may as well have looked up every family in Iowa with the Finch name. And consider this: had you gone that route, you may never have discovered the link between the Franz and Martin families. That is an important link to solving the Martin murders. The search turned out exactly the way it was meant to. Events happen for a reason, and in the order they happen, as well. Do not place blame on yourself for this. That is a pointless pursuit."

"I suppose you're right," conceded Sawyer. "This whole case makes me feel like a rat in a maze, like I'm running back and forth between points trying to solve it and only wearing myself out. At least now I feel like I can crawl out of the maze and make some headway, even if I do still feel like a rat."

"You are not a rat, Cousin. You are an investigator, and sometimes investigating leads you back and forth, but eventually you progress if you are determined. And *you* are determined. Stop hammering yourself about this and allow us to complete the investigation, yes?"

"Very true. I agree…let's finish this." Sawyer stared at the road ahead.

Grant continued reading the file. "Apparently, the adoptive family had some concerns about Marston when he turned five. He manifested anti-social behavior and acted out violently with other children. Mrs. Finch had to quit work and stay home with him because he could not be trusted in daycare. He sent two children to the hospital with concussions. When he became angry, his adrenaline would kick into overdrive and he would become very destructive, whether with people or with objects, it seemed to make no difference. The Finches made several appeals to Adoption Services, but were told they could not help them."

"Sounds like the Finch family got far more than they bargained for." Sawyer shook his head, sad for the family who'd only wanted to love a child.

"That is where the file ends, but I am certain, if we checked with the police department we would find a significant rap sheet for Marston." Grant closed the file.

"Once we're done at the station, let's see if we can talk with the Finch's."

The men pulled into the Blakely police department and hurried to the captain's office.

"This latest victim is definitely tied to the Franz murders. His name is Justin McAdam, the boy who was hired by Victor Franz to help on the farm." Captain Amerson leaned back in his chair, his hands interlocked and resting on his graying head of once black hair. His intense eyes focused on the men across from him.

"At least now we know what happened to him. No one ever saw him to give us a decent description. We had his name, but no idea where he'd come from. "

Captain Amerson released his hands and leaned forward, picking up a file from his desk. Someone is going to need to tell his family. There is a missing persons file for him, but somehow that file never made its way to our police department. I'm not sure how that can happen, but it did."

"Who's going to talk to the family?"

"I will go see them and find out when they last saw Justin," Captain Amerson tapped his finger on the desk. "If I find out anything we don't already know, I'll give you a call."

"We'll start searching the farm first thing in the morning," said Sawyer. "There's not enough daylight left to do anything today." Sawyer hated the thought of another killing, of hunting for the body of a kid whose only crime was being in the wrong place at the wrong time.

"Agreed. Choose your search team and let them know to meet you at the Franz farm in the morning." Distaste clouded Amerson's normally amicable eyes.

The mood was somber as they left the captain's office. Sawyer notified the officers he'd chosen for the search and he and Grant headed home. Tomorrow would be another tough day. The whole team knew it, and they all felt it.

Chapter Twenty-Six

Before they headed for home, Sawyer wanted to stop by the Finch home for a visit. They rang the doorbell and waited. It was several minutes before the door opened and a kindly man greeted them.

"Mr. Finch?" asked Sawyer.

"That's right."

"My name is Sawyer Kingsley, I'm a detective with the Blakely Police Department. This is my associate, Grant Mulvane. May we speak with you?"

"Certainly," he said, waving them inside. "How can I help you boys?"

Sawyer and Grant sat down on the worn couch. "We'd like to ask you some questions about your son, Marston."

"Oh dear," frowned Mr. Finch. "What has he done now? And, please, call me Charles."

Sawyer cast a nervous glance at Grant. "Charles, how long has it been since you've spoken with your son?"

"He was seventeen when he walked through that door and he never came back." Said the old man, shaking his head and pointing to the front door. "It killed his mother. She died several months later of a broken heart, I'm sure. She always thought he would straighten up and make something of himself. I don't suppose he's cleaned up his act any though, eh?"

Sawyer shifted in his seat and leaned forward. Gazing into the tortured eyes of a father left alone without his wife or son, it tore Sawyer's heart out to have to tell him all his son had done. But it would be in the paper and on the news once the investigation was complete, and the man needed closure. Good or bad, he needed closure.

"Charles, from what we have been able to ascertain, your son faked his own death fifteen years ago. We are investigating several homicides that may be linked to Marston. We believe he has changed his appearance and we wanted to know if he'd checked in with you recently. Obviously he has not."

A single tear rolled slowly down the wrinkled cheek. "I can only be thankful that we were not the ones to bring this child into the world. I am, however, thankful for the opportunity of at least *attempting* to give him a good life. I'm old enough to know now that we did what we could. But a broken heart will always be a broken heart."

When Sawyer and Grant left the Finch home, there was only silence between them. They climbed into the car and sat in silence. After a few minutes, Sawyer put the key in the ignition and started the car. It took every ounce of strength he had to drive home.

When Sawyer walked through his apartment door that night, Esley was dressed and ready to go. He'd completely forgotten about their dinner date, but fortunately they still had time to make the reservation.

Hopefully, she'd not noticed his panicked expression when he saw her there.

"You look...beautiful," he stammered. "I'll just go change my clothes."

Esley smiled at him. She rose from the chair with difficulty, but definitely not as much difficulty as he'd seen before. His surprise was obvious.

"Look at you! You must be feeling better, at least a little, eh?"

"I *am* feeling better. I can't wait to get out of these four walls."

"I'll hurry. Don't leave without me," he teased.

They left the apartment and Sawyer eased Esley gently into the car. He could feel his blood moving through him, his heart beating faster as she cast a thankful glance up at him. It felt as if her large, dark eyes opened his soul. He knew at that moment he would give this woman anything she asked for. *This could be bad*, he thought to himself. But in his heart, he knew it wasn't going to be.

While they waited for their dinners, Sawyer filled Esley in on where the investigation had taken them so far. "Our next step is going to be back at the Franz farm, looking for the body of the young man hired by Mr. Franz. We spoke with Marston Finch's father. His mother had passed, and Mr. Finch is alone. It was probably the hardest conversation I've ever had."

"I'm sure you handled it well. Sometimes there's nothing you can say that will change a circumstance. It's just going to be hard. I'm sorry you had to bear that message to him. I'm sorry he had to hear it."

As sad as the topic of conversation had been, Sawyer smiled across the table, drinking in Esley's beauty like a fine wine. The sadness he felt began to lift and he knew he was lucky, more than lucky. He was blessed, and he'd never felt like that before. Not just beautiful, Esley was compassionate. She cared about people, about their hardship, and that caring came from a place inside she was far too familiar with. A place of loss and incredible pain, and she used her experience to make others feel stronger, better, even in the most difficult of times.

"What are you staring at?" she giggled. Her full lips broke into a shy, intoxicating smile. Her hair fell softly around her face, cascading over her shoulders. The word stunning came to his mind, but it just wasn't enough to aptly describe the woman now seated across from him.

Sawyer cleared his throat. "I was just thinking how lucky it is for you that you are incapacitated right now." His eyes took on a devilish look, warm and inviting.

"So you say," she said, resting her elbow on the table and placing her chin on her fist. "What kind of a girl do you think I am?"

Sawyer sat back in his seat, absorbing her every nuance. "I think you're my kind of girl."

Esley giggled softly, never taking her eyes from his. "Then I suppose it *is* a good thing I'm incapacitated."

The waitress arrived with their meals and the conversation made its way back to the investigations. Still, even as Esley spoke, becoming the sharp, capable professional woman, Sawyer's brain had a difficult time separating the polished detective from the soft beauty he'd just experienced.

He was reminded of Grant's words to him that first morning after arriving in Blakely when he'd stayed in her apartment. He'd said Sawyer would lose her if he couldn't let her fly. Sawyer interpreted that to mean respect. He wanted to respect her, to allow her the freedom to be both who and what she was. As she listed the facts in the cases, her eyes took on the look of a woman who was good at what she did. She needed the respect that came with that knowledge, and he would give her that respect everyday, for as long as he lived.

They returned to the apartment after their 'date.' He gently held her, careful of the broken ribs while silently cursing the killer for even touching her. He kissed her softly, feeling the warmth of her body against him, the gentle sweetness of her lips on his. He never wanted to release her, never wanted to ever allow her to leave his arms again. However, there was a part of him that wondered about the timing of their relationship.

Would he have known about her need to 'fly' without the help of his cousin? Would Grant ever have gotten involved without the attack on Esley? Would he have figured out her need for independence on his own? He had to answer 'probably not' on that one and couldn't help but be thankful for that 'timing' thing.

Esley slowly opened her eyes from the kiss, as if her eyelids were too heavy to lift. She inspected every inch of his face, the outline of his lips, the curve of his jaw, his cheekbones, until her gaze finally met his.

"Tell me something," she whispered into his ear, her breath hot and sensual.

"Anything."

"Are you for real, Sawyer Kingsley?"

He chuckled softly and kissed her again. "I'm as real as they come," he said. "Now go to bed,

Beautiful, before I forget you're incapacitated." Sawyer gave her a devilish grin before gently pushing her toward the bedroom door. "Goodnight, Esley."

She stepped back and closed the bedroom door with the heat still in her eyes. Sawyer thought it must be contagious because he could feel that same heat even with the door closed.

He strolled lazily to the couch and lay down, fully dressed. He wasn't sure if it was the exhaustion of an emotional day or the stimulation of an emotional evening, but either way, his eyes closed and he slept.

When Sawyer opened his eyes the next morning he could hear pots banging in the kitchen as the home health nurse prepared Esley's breakfast. Grant was standing over him like a cat ready to pounce on a mouse.

"Late night?" teased Grant with a sly smile.

Sawyer stretched and stood up, realizing he was still in his clothes. "Not so much," he said, ignoring the inference. "She needs her rest, you know. She's still healing, so I didn't keep her up late. But it was a busy day yesterday and I think I was exhausted. How did you sleep?"

"I slept well, and soundly. My meditation this morning eased me into the day. I feel rejuvenated."

"I'm going to have to try that, I think."

Sawyer noticed someone in the easy chair and saw Esley was already up as well, sitting with her feet up and a blanket over her.

"How long have you been sitting there, lusting over me?" His mind raced through the conversation he'd just had with Grant, hoping he'd not said something he shouldn't have.

Esley giggled and stayed put. "Long enough to know you snore."

"At least I don't drool," he laughed, stretching again.

Esley's eyebrows transformed her whole face into a playful frown. "I *knew* you had to have seen that. It was the night your house exploded and we were looking at evidence. I fell asleep with my head on the desk and when you said something, I woke up and the desk was wet, as well as the whole side of my face. I *knew* you'd seen that!"

Sawyer poked Grant in the ribs with his elbow. "You had no idea I was such a gentleman, on top of all my other talents, did you?"

Grant shook his head with a smirk. "Perhaps you could remind me what those other talents are."

Esley laughed, hard enough to hold her ribcage and wince. The laugh didn't last long. Sawyer moved around the couch and made his way to the bedroom.

"You're both just jealous," he said as he shut the door.

When Sawyer emerged from his bedroom thirty minutes later, he was clean-shaven, showered, and dressed for the day.

"We were supposed to be out at the Franz farm forty-five minutes ago to meet your team." Grant was looking at his watch.

"Then we better get moving," said Sawyer. "What's keeping you?"

"You are," said Grant, returning the tease.

Sawyer hurried to the door after kissing Esley on the forehead. "Be safe," she said as he closed the door.

The car was silent until Grant queried a question. "Which part of yesterday was so exhausting?"

Sawyer sighed and a look of frustration swept across his face. "Have you ever really cared about someone and couldn't do anything about it?"

"You mean, like your mother?" Grant couldn't help the chuckle that escaped his lips.

"Yes, that's exactly what I mean," he said, giving Grant a flat stare. "No, not your *mother*. A woman."

"Your mother is not a woman? Mine is."

"Very funny. You know what I mean. I have to be so careful around Esley, she's still hurting a lot."

"So what is your point? That her pain is in the way of loving her? That is ridiculous. Love is a connection between two people, which then *promotes* the act of lovemaking. Love is not just the *making* of love; it is more the awakening of the senses. People jump into bed too quickly. When they do this, the whole purpose of loving is ignored. They forget to enjoy the experience of feeling a strong kinship with another human being, of reveling in all of the different ways one can show they care. It is learning to care about another person, and understanding how to hold that person's needs above their own."

Sawyer was silent as Grant continued. "There is a large difference between having sex and making love. If two people skip the part of loving where they get to know one another, where they pay attention to whether a person's character is congruent with what they believe and hold sacred, they miss the whole point of what love is. Those who remember these things and practice them will experience love and this love will last a very long time. When only one, or neither, practice these ideals, love can never be, and what was thought to be love, dies of starvation."

"Well aren't you just the philosopher," said Sawyer, then, surprised, he added, "That actually made sense to me, though."

"When I turned thirteen, my father explained that to me. Once. That was all it took."

"Are you telling me, you've *never* had sex?"

"I am not telling you anything. I am only telling you what my father told me."

Sawyer grinned and shifted in the driver's seat. "You've never had sex," he said with a giggle in his voice.

"I see you are not going to let this go, so I will tell you that you are correct, Cousin. But I feel differently about it than you do. For me, it is something I'm very proud of, but also something incredibly personal and profoundly spiritual. I will say this: when I meet my future mate, I will give her a part of my soul no one else has ever touched. It will be my gift to her."

"You're totally serious about this, aren't you?" Sawyer stared at his cousin with a look of shock.

"I am absolutely serious."

"Well, great," said Sawyer, turning into the gravel drive of the Franz home and parking the car. He pulled the keys from the ignition and turned to Grant with a twinkle in his eye. "Thanks for making me feel like I've got nothing special to offer someone."

"Oh, I would not say that," said Grant, looking amused. "You do have all those *other* talents you mentioned this morning."

Sawyer snickered as he exited the car. He stared over the roof of the vehicle at Grant, shaking his head. "You really know how to make a guy feel important, you know?"

"I do what I can."

One of his team members, Officer Barrow, approached the car. "I think we've found what you're looking for."

The mirth was gone as Sawyer and Grant followed the officer to the forested area in the back of the property, about fifty yards from the barn. The air was cold and seemed to be getting colder by the minute. Forensics was already there and Sam Golding, CSI team lead, approached Sawyer.

"I'm not sure we'd have found this victim if we hadn't had the rain we've had this month. It melted the snow and made the grave more visible. The victim is a young man, in his late teens to early twenties. I would say he's been dead about four to six months. I'm not certain how he died, but he has marks all over his body. It's like he was trampled to death and buried here. I can give you a more exact time of death when I get the body back to the lab."

"Thanks, Sam. Is it safe to have a look?"

"Sure."

Sawyer strode to the makeshift grave with Grant following reverently behind. Sawyer crouched down and leaned over the corpse, examining the massive damage that had killed him. The body *had* been trampled, most probably by the horse, but for what purpose? With gloves and tweezers, Sawyer pulled a small wallet from the shirt pocket of the deceased. The driver's license belonged to Justin McAdam. He was twenty-two years old. Sawyer stood and showed the contents of the wallet to Grant.

Grant turned away, shaking his head, and began to examine the ground between the barn and the burial site. He walked slowly, often bending over to examine the grass, or the spots of mud. Occasionally he would stand, lift his face to the sky, and then return to examining the ground.

Sawyer watched him as he proceeded to the barn and went inside. He hurried after Grant.

"What have you found?" Sawyer spoke quietly, unwilling to disturb Grant's search.

"The same man who was in this barn buried Justin McAdam."

Chapter Twenty-Seven

Grant walked to the backdoor of the barn and removed a pair of exam gloves from his pocket. Putting them on, he leaned over a shovel propped against the wall next to the wide door and studied it. Once the gloves were on, he picked it up and inspected the handle and the scoop. "That same man used this shovel."

Sawyer went outside the barn and whistled to get the attention of the team. "Wheatle, come in here, and bring some tags." A tall, lanky officer nodded and proceeded to the barn. "Tag that shovel and put it with the evidence from the scene."

"Yes, sir."

Grant returned to the mare's stall where the DNA evidence was found. She nickered softly, deep in her throat and greeted him as she nuzzled his chin and neck.

"Good girl. Will you allow me to invade your space once again?"

He opened the gate and stepped through, stroking the mare's neck and speaking low and soft.

His hand traveled down her neck to her chest. He moved his hand slowly across the chest area and found what he'd missed during their first meeting. Small burn marks were spaced sporadically across her chest. Grant growled low in his throat and put both arms around the mare's neck. "I am sorry, my friend. I am so sorry."

"What?" asked Sawyer. "What did you find?"

Grant bowed his head until it rested on the mare's nose. "This horse was tortured; she fought her attacker, and in so doing, she trampled a man lying on the floor of her stall. That was the plan, for her to trample the victim. She had no choice but to protect herself."

***

The McAdams were an older couple who lived about forty-five minutes north of Blakely. They were a farming couple, their children all grown and gone. Mr. McAdams was a tall, gray-haired man, barrel chested, with strong arms and a trim waist. He looked young for his age, as did his petite wife, also gray-haired. She had sad eyes and her mouth turned down slightly at the sight of Sawyer and Grant on her doorstep. Sawyer hated these meetings.

"Please come in," she said as she motioned them into the living room. "You've come about our Justin, haven't you." It was a statement, not a question.

"Yes, ma'am," replied Sawyer quietly. "I'm afraid we have."

"Please…" Mrs. McAdams directed them to the couch. Mr. McAdams sat opposite them on another couch and she sat down beside him with a heavy sigh. A coffee table separated the two sofas.

"Mr. and Mrs. McAdams," began Sawyer. "We've--"

The deep voice of Mr. McAdams stopped him. "Just tell us how he died."

Sawyer wasn't any more comfortable explaining that than he was with bringing them word of his death. Sensing Sawyer's unease, Grant took over the conversation.

"Your son was the victim of a serial killer, Mr. and Mrs. McAdams." There was a gentle reverence to his words, a *feeling* in the room that permeated the awful news and softened the blow. "I believe he was rendered unconscious and placed in a stall with a horse. The mare was then tortured with some kind of electric shock instrument. In fighting off her attacker, she trampled your son to death. She would never have hurt him if she hadn't been in a battle for her life."

Mr. McAdam took a deep breath, his eyes boring into Grant's. "Perhaps you could explain to me how you know what this horse would or would not have done."

"The mare's soul is good. She is a gentle creature and the death of your son has affected her in ways that cannot be measured with words." Grant returned the stare with equal intensity.

"You know horses," replied Mr. McAdam.

"That I do."

"We raise horses on this farm, it's how we make our living. I know you are speaking the truth because our boy would never have stepped into a stall with a horse if he thought the horse would be uncomfortable or frightened. He'd never do that to an animal. He would have to have been unable to prevent it. The *only* way this could have happened is if he were unable to prevent it. He knew better."

"I am sorry you have lost your son to this world," said Grant. "I will pray that his soul is delivered safely to the other side."

"You honor us with your prayer."

Mrs. McAdams could hold her pain in no longer. The tears came in great wracking sobs as she held her face in her hands. In an instant, her husband's arm was around her, comforting her, holding her against him.

"We should go," said Sawyer, his eyes apologizing for not just the intrusion into their pain, but for the delivery of the sad news.

"No," said Mrs. McAdams, pulling her heart together. "No, please don't go. You must hear about our boy."

Sawyer and Grant sat back on the sofa. "We would love to hear about your son," said Sawyer. "In fact, anything you could tell us would be most helpful. We want to stop the man who did this to him."

"Justin was as good a son as any mother could ask for," she said, determination replacing heartbreak. "He did what he was told, when he was told to do it. He loved horses, and when he found the Franz family, he thought he'd found the ideal job. He'd come home from work with the greatest stories about how nice the family was and how beautiful that mare was. He loved that horse, and hoped to buy her one day."

"I can understand why," smiled Grant. "I have fallen for her myself."

Mrs. McAdams' face was tender as she gazed at Grant. "Our Justin would have liked you, Mr. Mulvane. You have the same love of horses that we have always had in our family."

"Just Grant, ma'am. Please call me Grant." He continued. "Truthfully, ma'am, I love all animals, but there is a very special place in my heart for horses. They are magnificent."

Mr. McAdams spoke softly, looking at the coffee table before him, then raising his eyes to Grant. "Grant, should you ever need work, you'll always have a place at our ranch, and at our table. We are grateful you came."

Grant and Sawyer turned to go. "I thank you for that. I will remember you, and I will remember your son."

The two men were led to the door without further conversation. They stepped onto the porch into softly swirling snow as the door closed behind them.

"Someday I want you to show me how you do that."

"How I do what?" Grant eyed Sawyer curiously.

"How you can take bad news, even horrible news, and turn it into a gift."

"Our life is a gift, and as is our death. If we have lived a good life, as Justin obviously did, it is a gift to return from whence we came."

"Yeah, well, I don't know about all of that, I guess." Sawyer shrugged his shoulders against the cold air.

"I do," said Grant, softly. "I do."

Arrangements had been made to meet at Clay Carson's home, where he was recovering from his injuries. Sawyer had finally come to terms with the fact that Sergeant Carson wasn't the killer they were looking for, but it was still hard to dismiss him as Esley's assailant.

When they arrived at the home, Captain Amerson was already there. Clay was in a recliner and tried to sit up, but winced and stayed put. He was obviously in worse condition than Esley had been.

"One of my broken ribs punctured a lung. I'm still having a hard time breathing, but it's getting better. I apologize for not greeting you."

The mood in the room was somber as Clay motioned for Sawyer and Grant to sit on the couch. Captain Amerson stood by the fireplace, warming himself.

"Sergeant, do you remember how you got your injuries?" Sawyer was doing his best to keep his voice pleasant, but it was difficult.

"I don't. I only remember waking up in my car in a ditch, in the middle of a snowstorm. When I got home, all my power was off, and I assumed it was from the storm. I only just found out yesterday that the main power to my home had been turned off…at the city. I don't know how that happened; my bill is always paid on time. When they checked, they apologized profusely."

"Do you know how long you were unconscious?" asked Sawyer.

"No, I don't even remember leaving my home. I don't remember the whole day prior to the accident. It's completely gone. The doc said I'd been drugged. But why would anyone do that? I work in evidence. I don't have knowledge regarding any cases in those boxes. I just log in boxes and check them out."

"I understand," said Sawyer. He smiled, trying to be cordial. "Tell me, Sergeant, how did you get home from the accident?"

"I…I don't know. I was in my car…" Clay was forcing his mind to work for him, but it wasn't happening. "…and then I was in my house. Somehow I knew I'd been in a car accident and needed an ambulance. I was having a very hard time breathing. My cell phone was dead…and then suddenly it wasn't, and so I called 911. I don't understand. It's all so...so disjointed."

"That is probably from the drug you were given," said Sawyer. He was beginning to feel very sorry for Sergeant Carson. Someone had used him and doped him with enough LSD to cause giant holes in his memory.

"Do you remember seeing anyone? Did anyone help you once you were home?"

"N...no. Yes...yes, but...no. I mean, I feel like someone was there, but when I try to see the person's face, there are only blurred images. I can't see anything, but I can *feel* someone in the room with me. I can't even tell for sure if it's a man or a woman. Somewhere in my mind there is a woman, I think...and a man, or maybe one or the other, or maybe no one at all. I just don't remember."

Sergeant Carson's frustration level was rising, and with his elevated frustration came difficulty breathing.

"We should go, Sarge. You've been very helpful, but you need to rest. We'll come and talk some more when you're better. Until then, if you need anything, please call us. We're a team at our station, you know."

"Thank...you," he said forcing a smile and struggling to breath. "Wait..." The word was nearly a whisper. "Please, I...I need to tell someone."

Sawyer and Grant stopped and turned to face Sergeant Carson. They stepped a little closer so they could hear him.

"I...I think I hurt someone, a woman. I have such awful dreams and when I wake up I'm covered with sweat and I can't breathe. In my dreams I hear voices screaming at me to hurt her, to kill her, and somehow I land on the floor, hoping against hope that I wasn't successful. Please, if I hurt someone, anyone, please, tell them I'm sorry. Tell them I didn't know what I was doing." A tear trickled down his face and his eyes closed, as if unable to face the men.

Sawyer spoke. "Clay, you are going to be just fine. Ignore those dreams, they mean nothing. They're just remnants of the drug you were given."

The whisper was nearly inaudible as the Clay drifted off to sleep. "Thank you. Thank you."

Captain Amerson stayed at the fireplace, and nodded his acknowledgement to Grant and Sawyer of the kindness extended to the Sergeant. The two men left, closing the door firmly behind them. The wind was picking up, and the snow was falling harder. Sawyer pulled his collar up over his neck and jogged to the car with Grant close behind.

Grant and Sawyer jumped quickly into the car and shut the doors, shaking the snow from their coats and brushing it out of their hair.

"That was a very kind thing for you to do in there," said Grant, placing his hand on Sawyer's shoulder. "It couldn't have been easy."

"I've known Clay Carson since I started with the department. He's in evidence storage because he couldn't hurt a fly. He wanted to work on the force, but he would never have been able to actually hurt anyone, even in self-defense. When I realized that, it wasn't hard to do at all. He may have been Esley's attacker, but like that mare out at the Franz farm, Carson would have to have been forced into it by extreme measures."

Grant nodded and Sawyer started the car. "This storm could turn kind of nasty," he said, clearing the powdery flakes from the windshield with his wipers.

"It won't," said Grant, holding back a shiver.

"Okay," replied Sawyer, doubtful. "Whatever you say."

They started home and as they drove, the snow lessened until by the time they pulled into the apartment complex, it had stopped completely. The wind was blowing cold and hard as they hurried to their apartment doors. A sly smile slid across Grant's face.

"Told you," he chuckled, as he slid into Esley's apartment and quickly shut the door.

"Pathetic," muttered Sawyer to himself. He opened the door to his apartment, surprised to find the lights out and an eerie silence in the room. In the split second it took him to turn on the lights he figured Esley has sent the nurse home and was sleeping in the bedroom. As the room filled with light, Sawyers stomach lurched. His apartment was completely destroyed. Furniture was overturned and in pieces, dishes from the kitchen were in shards all over the floor. The living room curtains were shredded, lying in pieces throughout the room. Panicked, his eyes scanned the room, desperately searching for signs of life.

Where was the nurse? Striding quickly into the kitchen, Sawyer nearly tripped over the body of Esley's nurse. A cold, blank stare was etched on her face; a single bullet hole in her forehead. Sawyer didn't have to check her. The nurse was dead. His eyes widened as he screamed for Esley.

"Esley! ESLEY!!"

"Here," came a reply that was almost a whisper. "I'm here."

Chapter Twenty-Eight

Sawyer sprinted to the bedroom but couldn't find Esley. "Where?" he called in a panic. "Where is 'here'?"

"Bathroom."

Sawyer ran to the master bathroom, but she wasn't there. He turned and ran down the hall, phone to his ear, calling 911. He found her in the hallway bathroom, bleeding badly from a cut on her face and holding her ribcage. There was a gash on her leg and another on her arm, both bleeding. There was a lot of blood on the floor; Sawyer knew he had to get her to the hospital quickly.

"911. What is your emergency?"

"Ambulance! I need an ambulance! And police. This is Detective Sawyer Kingsley. I need an ambulance and police at my apartment. NOW!!" He shouted the address into the phone, and for the first time heard pounding and yelling at the door.

"Lie still, Esley. I'm not going to leave you, I'll be right back."

He ran to the front door, only just remembering the officers guarding the door hadn't been there. How could he not have noticed they were missing? Sawyer heard Grant's voice and opened the door. Grant stood breathless before him.

"The officers are dead. The undercover detectives are dead as well."

Sawyer had no idea how long Grant had been standing at the door pounding to get his attention.

"It's Esley. I have to help her. I've called 911."

The two men hurried back to the bathroom, hesitant to move her. Grant went back out to the living room to wait for the paramedics and police to arrive.

"Esley, I'm here. I'm here." With difficulty, he kept his own fears inside, forcing himself to speak calmly and slowly. He needed her to know she was safe now.

The whispered words came in short bursts and with great difficulty breathing. "Bedroom. Heard…gunshot…Didn't…see him. Moved so…fast. Kicked…gun from…his…hand. We…fought…he…ran."

Esley's face was swelling as she spoke. "Shh," he said, "don't try to talk. I'm going to stay with you. We'll have plenty of time to talk when we get you to the hospital. Just lay still and don't talk." Sawyer stroked her hair, touched her face. He needed her to know he was there, next to her.

Esley closed her eyes and Sawyer panicked, thinking he was losing her. He watched her chest for signs she was still breathing and checked her pulse. It was weak and her breathing shallow, but they were there, she was only unconscious.

Where is that ambulance? Where are the paramedics. Please, let them hurry. I can't lose her now. I can't lose her. I love her."

"Grant!" Sawyer called down the hall. "Search the living room for a gun. Esley says she kicked the gun out of his hand and he ran."

The words had barely escaped his mouth when Grant came down the hallway with the gun hanging from a pen.

"I have evidence bags in my desk in the living room."

Grant returned to the living room. Sawyer heard drawers open and shut, until one opened and stayed opened. The sound of footsteps running outside his apartment echoed down the outside hallway. Grant opened the door and two paramedics ran inside with a gurney between them. He directed them down the hallway and to the bathroom. Sawyer stepped quickly aside and watched from the door as the paramedics tended to Esley.

How much more of this can she stand?

***

Sawyer woke the next morning with a start. His head had been resting on Esley's hospital bed and he nearly snapped his neck when he sat up. Esley was sleeping peacefully; Grant was meditating on the floor in the corner of the room.

Sawyer shook his head and stood to stretch. The room was still fairly dark with only a small bit of light coming through the window. Grant stirred and opened his eyes.

"Ah, you're awake," teased Sawyer.

"Funny."

"Grant, I need to review what we know about this case. It all feels so disjointed and unclear. Will you do that with me?"

"Certainly."

"We know the Franz family and the Martin family are related through Marylisa Franz. We know Sylvia Martin gave birth to a baby boy and put him up for adoption. That baby was Marston Finch. We know DNA belonging to Marston Finch was found at the Franz farm. But what's the link to Jack?"

Grant rose from the corner and placed his hands in his pockets. He walked slowly to the other side of Esley's bed and gazed down at her sleeping figure. His eyes rose and met Sawyer's. "You are the link, Cousin. You are."

Sawyer could feel raw bile rising in his throat and with it, anger, hot and furious. "My partner, who was like a brother to me, was killed because of *me?*"

Grant's look softened and he studied Sawyer's face. "You have known from the day of Esley's abduction the killer was jealous of the Kingsley and Baker duo. You have not spoken of this, Sawyer, but you know it is true. *Know this*," Grant stared with deep conviction into Sawyer's eyes. "Your partner was killed because an evil man killed him, because this killer is not just evil, he is sick. He is rotting from the inside out, like a spawning salmon. There is nothing good remaining in him, only killing and vengeance."

He stopped for a moment to allow Sawyer time to process what he'd said before continuing. "Remember how you said to me on my first day here that this killer had wiped out a whole family line? Think of what we have learned about the killer recently."

"I'm not following you."

"Yes you are. You had the key to this whole investigation in your head from that day. He killed a whole family line. Whose family line was that?"

Sawyer's eyes widened. "That was *his* family line, his own family." As the thought cemented itself in his brain, he spoke faster and faster. "Marylisa Franz was his *sister*, the Martins were his *parents*! He was…" his voice turned in on itself, as the thought finally came to life, and he whispered, "…could it be that simple?"

"Keep going, Cousin. Finish that thought."

"He killed them out of jealousy. Esley told me that when she was in the hospital. She said she thought the killer was jealous. He was jealous that they were an intact family, and he was given away. Even though he had a family that loved him, he couldn't see them for what they were…loving, kind people who wanted to give him a good life. He could only see there was a family out there who gave him away, and that made him angry."

"Yes, exactly. Now, why Jack? Why do you think he killed your partner?"

Sawyer dropped his eyes to stare at Esley. "Esley told me there were newspaper clippings on the wall where she was being held after her abduction. She said she could barely make out the words over the pictures, but that they were all about Jack and me. She said there were red marks on the pictures, and I'll bet that was crossing Jack out because he'd killed him. This guy is driven by jealousy. Jack and I had nothing to do with his family, but our success fed into his issue of jealousy!"

Grant smiled. "Yes. That is it. Now, think about this. Why would an average citizen have jealousy issues with the success of police detectives?"

"*He's not an average citizen! He's a cop!*" The thought had been presented to Sawyer several times but he'd dismissed it immediately as impossible. The concept of a cop doing what was done to Jack made his stomach want to lose its contents. His voice seethed with a slow burning fury. "Jack was killed by one of our own."

"Before you go down that road, Cousin, I want to clarify something." Grant waited until he had Sawyer's attention. "You need to hear what I'm saying. This killer is *masquerading* as a cop. He is *not* a policeman. Somehow, he's managed to find a way to mask his fingerprints, but his DNA would give him away. We need to get DNA samples from every person in your department. This man is the leak and that is why the killer has stayed one step ahead of us at every turn. Now, we know that he has been injured and that it was not Carson. The question remains, *who* is he?"

"We need fresh DNA samples, and we need them on each employee," Sawyer's mind was racing. "It's going to have to be done covertly, so whoever our imposter is won't know what we're doing."

"It may be easier than that. We need to ask your captain who has called in sick or not shown up for work. Then we can check *their* DNA."

Sawyer was on the phone before Grant even finished his sentence.

"Amerson."

"Captain, who called in sick today? Anyone?"

"No. I'll check, but to my knowledge everyone is here who should be here."

"Anyone bandaged or look like they were in a tussle?"

"No, not that I've seen, but I'll do a check to be sure. Why?"

"Because our killer is a cop. He's not one of us, he's an imposter, but Grant and I believe he's somehow managed to mask his fingerprints. We need DNA on everyone in the department. Then we need to match that DNA to that of Marston Finch. When we get a match, we've got our killer. Also, make sure CSI goes over my apartment thoroughly. He may have left some blood behind, or a hair or…or…anything. Just have them check it and recheck it."

"I will, Kingsley. You take care of Esley and we'll do our jobs on this end. We'll get this guy. You can count on it."

Esley stirred and her eyes opened slowly. She tried to move and moaned softly.

"Stay still Esley," Sawyer warned. "You've reinjured those ribs, I'm afraid."

"Oh yeah?" she teased, her voice a low murmur. "Who told you that?" There was a brief smile and then a wince.

"See? It hurts to disrespect the one you love." He chuckled softly.

"Who said…anything…about love?"

"You did, with your eyes," replied Sawyer, sitting down in the chair beside her bed. "The eyes never lie."

Heavily drugged with pain meds, Esley closed her eyes and was asleep once more.

"I can't leave her, Grant," Sawyer ran his hand through his hair. "I feel like I need to be at the station and beside her at the same time, but I can't leave her. Even with guards posted at her door. He got to her with guards and undercover detectives and I can't take the chance of him doing that again. How many would he kill in this hospital to get to her?"

"What did the captain say?"

Sawyer forgot he'd not told Grant of the conversation. "Oh, yeah, he said they'd get the needed DNA. He also said no one has called in sick or not shown for their shift."

"Interesting. It could be possible that the damage she inflicted on her assailant was not something anyone could see. Give me the car keys."

"That's a new car, you know."

"Yeah, because your old car blew up with your house. Now, really, who has the better track record with cars here?" Grant smiled and held out his hand.

"I see your logic. What are you going to do?"

"I am going to the station. I need to have a chat with Officer Tarynton."

"Why? What is your thinking?"

"I think he smells bad."

With that, Grant strode out of the room and down the hall to the elevators. Sawyer watched him go, shaking his head. Grant Mulvane was a good man. A little weird…but a good man.

Chapter Twenty-Nine

Grant pushed open the stations large glass door and proceeded upstairs to Captain Amerson's office.

"It's good to see you, Grant," said Amerson. "How is Esley doing?"

"She's awake. Sawyer is staying with her." Grant stood quietly in front of Amerson's desk. "If you do not mind, Captain Amerson, I need you to come with me."

The captain raised his eyebrows and stood up. "What's going on?"

"I need you to come with me to the evidence lockup. Do you have time to do that?"

"Certainly."

"I also need you to bring your gun, and maybe a couple other officers, if that would be acceptable."

"What's this about, Grant?"

"I believe I know who your killer is, Captain Amerson. I do not use guns, myself, so I would prefer to have someone with me who does."

"And the killer is in evidence lockup?"

"I believe he is."

"That's good enough for me."

Amerson exited his office with Grant close behind him. "Hammond, Standing, follow me. Lead the way, Grant."

"Yes, sir." Grant led the group down to evidence and walked through the door. Sergeant Tarynton stood at the desk reviewing the log and making notes on the pages. He looked up casually as Grant and the group came through the door.

"Mr. Mulvane," he said with a smile. "How can I help you?"

"Would you please take a seat at the desk, Sergeant?" Grant's voice was quiet, but firm.

"I'm afraid I've hurt my back and sitting is a bit painful. I'd prefer to stand." He smiled genuinely and waited at the counter.

"How did you hurt your back, Sergeant?" Grant looked him in the eye and Tarynton looked down nervously at the logbook.

"I…I was shoveling snow from my drive. 'Tis the season, or so they say."

Grant approached the counter. "So they say, Mr. Finch. It is Finch, is it not? You are Marston Finch and I'm willing to bet it is your ribcage that is troubling you, not your back. You had a run in with Detective Rider after you murdered four members of this station. You are a very angry man, Mr. Finch. You have done some very bad things."

Finch stepped back, pulling his gun quickly from its holster.

The captain and his officers drew theirs as well; all three were aimed at Tarynton.

The captain spoke. "You might have time to hit one of us, but that would leave two guns to take you down. Is it worth it?"

"I have no intention of shooting anyone. You're all just going to back away slowly against the wall and I'm going to walk out of here.

Captain Amerson planted his feet. "Not gonna happen."

Finch quickly shifted the aim of his gun and pointed it at Grant. "I'll kill one unarmed man before you bring me down. I really must ask *you*…is it worth it?"

Before another word could be spoken, Grant reached over the counter in one smooth, fluid movement, grabbing Finch's wrist with such speed, it was hard to believe he'd moved at all. He twisted Finch's arm and the man cried out in pain, dropping the gun onto the counter. Grant grabbed the gun with one hand and tossed it to the captain. He slammed Finch's twisted arm, elbow up, onto on the counter and brought the side of his other hand down on Finch's elbow. The man screamed in pain as the bones in his elbow cracked.

With no visible strain in his breathing or his speech, Grant spoke in quiet tones, each word released firmly, yet calmly. "I really do not like it very much when someone points a gun at me. It makes me nervous, and when I am nervous I can become quite unkind. Unkindness is not my way. Now I will have to spend extra time in meditation to remove your taint." Grant still had Finch's broken arm against the table. Finch was beginning to sweat from the pain. "But rest assured, Mr. Finch. I will remove your taint from my mind and from my body, and as soon as I do, I will forget you ever existed."

Captain Amerson came around the end of the counter and Grant gladly released his grip on Finch's wrist. Amerson grabbed Finch by the shoulders, whipping him around to face him. Finch cried out in pain as Amerson open his uniform and found the bandaged ribcage. "Get him out of my sight," he spat. The officers took Finch from their captain. When the men had left, Amerson chuckled. "That was impressive for a man who shuns violence."

Grant turned and saw the men hurrying their prisoner down the hallway. He sighed softly. "I have never said I will not protect myself. I just do not participate in violent exchanges that begin in anger. I wasn't angry. I would even go so far as to say that was really quite exhilarating. I have much meditating to do."

Grant started for the door and Captain Amerson's grin split his face. It was hard to wipe off, even though he knew how serious this man was about his 'repentance.' Amerson wasn't quite sure why Grant felt he had to meditate for his actions. He brought down a serial killer responsible for the murders of twelve people and two separate beatings of Esley Rider. In the captain's estimation, that was a hero, not a sinner.

***

Sawyer was called as soon as Finch was in custody. Sawyer told Esley the good news, before hurrying to the station. He left the guards at her door, just in case.

When Sawyer arrived at the station, Amerson informed him he wouldn't be involved in the interrogation, for obvious reasons, and Sawyer was more than happy to watch from observation. He could already feel how hard it would be to keep his emotions in check. Amerson would be conducting this interrogation himself.

"Mr. Finch," he began, "why did you kill your birth mother?"

"You have no evidence to that accusation."

"Well then, maybe you could tell me why you killed your sister and her family."

Finch's venom was rising and he eyes glared at the captain.

"You have no evidence against me for that crime either." The words flew from his mouth like poisonous darts.

"Don't I?" A smile slid smoothly across Amerson's face. "How does DNA evidence sound?"

"You don't have any DNA evidence."

"Mr. Finch," began Amerson, speaking very slowly to make sure the man understood what he was saying, "how do you suppose we found out who you are?"

Finch's eyes widened, as if the thought of them calling him 'Finch' had never fully registered in his brain.

"That's right, Marston, you left us some DNA, which I personally feel was very thoughtful of you."

"I never leave DNA! I clean up my kills! You have no evidence against me! Admit it!"

Captain Amerson remained calm as a small grin creased his lips. "And just how many kills have you cleaned up, Marston?"

"Don't call me that." Finch was breathing heavily, but working very hard to regain control of his emotions, obviously not used to losing that control.

"But it's your name, Marston. You can disguise or erase fingerprints easy enough, but you cannot alter your DNA. Tough luck, that."

In spite of his best efforts at controlling himself, Marston Finch looked as though he was about to pop an artery. His eyes were huge and protruding from their sockets. His face was deep red, and the veins in his neck bulged. His shoulders were stiff as he pulled at the chair he was chained to, attempting to stand, but gravity yanked him back down with each attempt.

"Now, Marston. You really need to calm down. We're going to leave now and give you an opportunity to collect yourself. It would be in your best interest if you relaxed a little. Let's go, Grant."

The two men left the room followed by the sounds of their prisoner bellowing and shrieking mostly unrecognizable words. A few obscenities and threats made their way through a voice box knotted and twisted in rage and fury. Mucus dripped from his mouth and ran down his chin. He shrieked and fought at his bindings until his body collapsed in exhaustion.

Sawyer watched every minute of his tantrum, and relished in how good it felt. Finch lost all the control he'd stolen from the people he'd killed or harmed. Sawyer could feel a sense of control and calm he'd not felt since Jack's death.

"This one's for you, Jack," said Sawyer. "I know it took a while for me to pull my head out of my butt, and that had to be frustrating for you. I did, eventually, though. Now, in the same interrogation room we used so often, is the man who took your life, and for no other reason, than jealousy of our success. A small-minded man who had no idea who he was dealing with. Maybe I should say, no idea whose *cousin* he was dealing with. And thanks for saving Esley. I know it was you, Jack. I know it was. Thanks."

Sawyer turned and left observation with a sense of satisfaction and thankfulness. He found Grant and the captain in the hallway outside interrogation waiting for Finch to calm down.

"How did you know, Grant?" Sawyer stood next to his cousin and leaned against the wall.

"I thought I knew the first time you took me into the evidence lockup," said Grant. "The room smelled *wrong*. Truthfully, when you told me Tarynton was taking over for Carson, I was not sure which one was the killer. I could not distinguish if the stench was from the current resident of the room or someone prior to him. Then when we interviewed Carson I knew he was not the killer. There was no wrong smell to him. But, at that point, I did not have enough evidence to approach Tarynton."

Amerson was listening intently. "So what changed? We still didn't have any hard evidence against him."

"No, we did not," said Grant leaning into the wall, "until Esley gave us what we needed. She said she felt his ribs crack when she kicked him. It is easy to hide injured ribs, especially if they are only cracked. If you are determined, you can hide the pain. I thought if I could get close enough to Tarynton, I would be able to get him to expose the pain he felt and that would be our evidence."

"Well, you did a great job of that. Have you ever thought of going into law enforcement fulltime? Any agency would be lucky to have you." Captain Amerson studied Grant's face.

"I help as I can," said Grant, his face a mask of calm confidence. "My work in Alaska gives me ample opportunity to share what I can with others. I am pleased my cousin thought to ask for my help with this case."

"Well, when you've got a relative that's larger than life, it's kind of hard to ignore it. Sort of like a hangnail on your big toe." Sawyer studied his cousin proudly.

"Oh, nice," laughed Grant. "That is a very nice comparison. I will have to remember that."

Sawyer didn't care to watch the remainder of the interrogation of Marston Finch. He'd seen what he wanted to see, an evil man who was no longer free to impose his will on innocent people. He waited at his desk in the bullpen for Grant and Captain Amerson to complete the interrogation, filling out the paperwork that would end this nightmare once and for all.

Paperwork. He'd always hated that part of his job, but today, right now, it was hard not to completely enjoy the experience. Even the feel of the pen in his hand as the ink flowed onto the paper exactly where he wanted it to…everything about the paperwork felt good and right. For a moment, he had a brief sense that it even *smelled* right. *Impossible. Now you're just getting too full of yourself. Finish your paperwork.*

Staring down at the page in front of him, he wrote the name of Jack Baker on the line for the victim, along with the names of Victor, Marylisa, Jansen, Skylar and Samantha Franz, then ended with Justin McAdam. He sat back in his chair and wondered about the Franz family. *What would the children have grown up to be? Would any of them have stayed on the ranch and worked the land like their parents had? They should have had the opportunity to make those decisions, and now they never would.* He thought about Justin McAdam, the young man who was so happy to have found a nice family to work for, and loved his new job. *Would he have saved and earned enough money to one day purchase a farm of his own?*

Did he really love his job that much? Last of all, he thought of his partner and best friend. How could he reconcile that death? *Oh, Jack, I was not there to save you, and I should've been. I'm sorry, Jack, I will always be sorry.*

He sighed and picked up the form, leaning back in his chair. Jack was like a brother to him, almost an appendage. He remembered the feelings he'd had that drove him to alcohol, a pain so intense he couldn't bear it. Sawyer needed something that would deaden that pain, something that would allow him to not have to feel the loss so keenly. Even now, he could close his eyes and relive that awful night. The blood smeared on the bathroom floor, the sense of hopelessness when he called Jack's name and heard nothing in return, the despair of finding his friend tossed in the alley, blank eyes staring up at a dark sky. He couldn't handle the constant reminder of the sick, twisted way Jack was killed. Not even alcohol would lessen the pain enough to allow him to live.

What did help, what *did* give him the reconciliation he needed was watching that interrogation and seeing how little, how insignificant this killer really was. He was only a small, emotionally stunted child inside a man's body, unable to function as an adult. That was the closure Sawyer needed. It was *all* he needed.

Grant stepped through the entry into the bullpen searching for Sawyer. Finding him, he made his way to Sawyer's desk.

"Well, Cousin, it looks like you are done with me."

"You in a hurry to get home or something?" chuckled Sawyer.

"I just got a text from Greyson, the ranger I work for," he said. "It would appear we have another case to work. I am sorry to leave so quickly, but I must make arrangements for the transport of the mare as soon as it is legally possible to do so. Can I count on you to see that she is made ready when the time comes?"

"Absolutely," replied Sawyer. "As for that *other* princess…"

"She has my card."

Sawyer tossed the paperwork in his hand onto the desk. "She *what*?" He couldn't mask the incredulous tone in his voice. "You gave her your *card*? When did you have time to do that? How could I have not seen that?"

"It is none of your concern."

Grant turned and headed for the exit. "Are you coming? I hear flies can enter mouths that hang open. You might want to close that." He laughed out loud as he walked down the stairs.

Sawyer hurried after him, running through each of their encounters with Shannon in his mind, trying to find a time when Grant could have had even a minute to toss a card on her desk. It was impossible! There was *no* way he'd have missed that. And yet, he hadn't seen it. He shook his head, as he hurried down the stairs.

Chapter Thirty

Sawyer sat beside Esley's hospital bed, deep in thought. He had a question for Esley, an important question and he wondered what would be the best way to ask it. He needed her answer, because her answer would determine their future.

He'd been holding her hand, rubbing the back of it with his thumb while he mulled over what he wanted to say.

"I don't think I've ever seen you so introspective," she said with a smile. "Where are you?"

"Hmmm? Me?" Sawyer was yanked from his thoughts. "Oh, I was just thinking how anyone could want to bring children into a world like this."

There it was. Laying out on the blanket in front of him. Not exactly how he'd planned it to come out, but…yeah. There it was.

"I'd come back with a smart reply to that, but it hurts when I laugh." She smiled at him. "I don't know how I feel about that, really. I think of my life, how my whole family died and I fill with anxiety when

I think about bringing little ones into this world and having that possibly happen to them. It terrifies me. But I can't imagine a life without children in it, you know?"

A huge grin split Sawyer's face nearly in half. "You mean it? You would want children after all we've seen on this case alone?"

"Yeah, I believe I would."

Sawyer stood and bent over, kissing Esley on the forehead. "I've got to run some errands, I'll be right back."

He left the room feeling like someone had just lifted a thousand pound weight from his shoulders. That was the right answer. It was exactly what he'd hoped to hear.

He'd dropped Grant at the airport earlier that morning. It was hard to believe he'd been in Blakely nearly a month. Sawyer missed his cousin, missed the confident peace he carried with him everywhere he went. His soft-spoken way, his quirky sense of humor, pretty much everything about him...Sawyer missed it all. He'd have to make sure another fifteen years didn't go by before they met up again. He had a profound respect for Grant, and in working with the man, found a bond that went far beyond cousins.

Sawyer smiled as he hurried down the hallway to the elevator. He reviewed the events at the airport in his mind, when he'd dropped Grant at the curbside for check in.

"Do not let her get away," Grant cautioned. He set down his bag and wrapped both arms around his cousin in a huge bear hug. "Your souls belong together. You know this."

"Yeah," said Sawyer, as Grant released him. "I believe I do know that."

Grant nodded his head in approval and began walking into the terminal. Before he went too far, he stopped abruptly and turned to face Sawyer one more time. "And don't forget about my mare. I will be expecting her."

Sawyer laughed. "You mean the one in the stall or the princess in the office?"

"You know exactly the one I mean. The company will be there on Saturday to prep her for transport to Alaska. Be safe, Cousin. Let us not stay away for another fifteen years, yes?"

"For sure."

It was nearing one in the afternoon and Sawyer had an appointment with the realtor who'd helped him with the details of the rebuild. She'd found him the perfect architect to draw up the plans for the house and referred him to an excellent builder who'd done a beautiful job. Today would be the final walk through on the finished product, and he couldn't wait to see it.

A short drive from the hospital, Sawyer pulled into the driveway of his new home. What was once an aging rambler built in the sixties was now a modern two-story home with a wide porch and three-car garage. He'd paid a little extra to have the third garage bay and given up a little of his one acre plot, but he was more than happy with the outcome.

The house was a light brown with white trim, four bedrooms, three bathrooms, a large kitchen, and both semi and formal dining rooms. It was everything he'd hoped it would be. He walked through the finished home while his realtor reviewed the amenities of the home, showing him the warranty and instruction information on all the appliances, including the A/C unit outside the back patio doors. She explained how to care for granite countertops and wood floors, citing he was, after all, a bachelor, and would need to know these types of things. The comment made him smile.

Once the realtor was gone and he had the keys in his hand, he put in a call to some of his buddies down at the station. Several of them agreed to help with the move from his apartment to his new home, and planned to be at his apartment bright and early the next morning. There was a large storage unit that would also need to be moved, as not all of his new furniture fit into the apartment. When those arrangements were made, Sawyer drove to a jeweler in downtown Blakely.

With ring in hand, he drove back to the hospital and rode the elevator to the third floor, his heart pounding in his chest. Now for the *next* question.

***

Esley lay in bed with a silly smile on her face. Sometimes Sawyer could be so…out there. Children. Why would he be thinking about children now? She thought maybe she understood. He'd lost Jack, who was like a brother to him, he'd seen a whole family slaughtered, including three children, and he'd nearly lost a second partner…twice. At least Esley thought that might be part of his thinking. He was a good man, honest, committed to those things that mattered to him. Progeny would definitely be part of his thinking, not so much in spite of what he'd seen, but *because* of what he'd seen. Having children and keeping them safe would be his answer to the chaos around him, his anchor to the goodness that still existed in the world. She could see that in him.

Esley had to admit, however, the thought of children did make her stomach turn to a pile of knots. She had no clue how to be a mother, her own mother dying when Esley was so young. With the exception of the extended family who took her in, the examples she'd had after that hadn't actually been all that great, which made her think. *If they weren't all that great, what would I do differently to help my own children through life? What is* my *idea of a good mother?*

For one thing, she knew no child would ever come through the door of her home who would not feel like he or she belonged there. Whether they were her children, or friends of her children, she would treat them like her own. That was the bottom line.

Esley knew firsthand what it felt like to be a burden; or at least feel like one. Her experience after the death of her family, however brief, taught her how important family was. Even though her stay with her new family hadn't been a particularly long one, she'd grown to feel like part of the family to them.

Maybe she could be a mother. Between the memories of the family she'd lost and the one she'd gained, maybe she'd been given enough of an example of motherhood that she could be successful at it. She'd never thought about this before, never even considered the possibility. She could blame Sawyer for this line of thinking.

Stretching ever so carefully, Esley whispered to no one, "I really want to go home." She was tired of the hospital; tired of nurses and doctors and the noise and smell of the floor she was on. Not loud noises, just noises that weren't her home.

She heard familiar footsteps in the hallway and knew that Sawyer was coming. The butterflies started just like they did every time he entered her room. His kisses on her forehead made them increase in speed and vibration. When their lips met, the butterflies exploded, leaving her stomach a mess she thought she could never fix, a mess she didn't want to fix. Ever.

***

Sawyer strode confidently into the room. "You're awake," he said, greeting her with the wonderful kiss her on the forehead. "I thought I'd find you asleep."

"I want to go home," she said. "This is only a few broken ribs, why are they keeping me this long?"

"My lady," he said, sitting down in his usual chair beside the bed. "One of those broken rib bones lays very close to your heart. They just want to make sure it's moving into its correct orbit before they release you on the world."

"Release me on the world? That sounds pretty ominous. What is it 'they' think I'm going to do?"

Sawyer laughed and squeezed her hand. "They've seen what you can do even with cracked ribs. No one is taking any chances."

Esley grunted without so much as a wince this time. "See? I'm getting better, what do they want? Complete healing before I go home?"

"You're going home in two days. I'm taking you myself. Be patient and enjoy being waited on hand and foot." Sawyer winked and raised a warning brow. "Just don't get used to it."

"I hate it. I guarantee I won't be getting used to it. You have no idea the joy I will take in walking to *my own* refrigerator, getting *my own* milk and pouring it over *my own* cereal. I wanna go home." Sawyer loved the whine in her voice, and her cute pout. He hid his smile well.

"Two days. I'll get you some groceries so you can do just that. What's your favorite cereal?"

"Lucky Charms. I want some Lucky Charms. My mom used to call them Chucky Larms and it kind of stuck. So, yeah, I want some Chucky Larms."

Sawyer let himself laugh this time. "Then Chucky Larms, it is."

***

Two days later, Esley was in a wheelchair riding not so passively to the curb in front of the hospital, and to Sawyer's waiting car. He came around to the passenger side and helped Esley stand.

"Just smell that fresh air," she said, smiling broadly. "The cold feels so good on my face. I could stand here all day."

"Yeah, well," said Sawyer, ready to get her into the car. "Let's not, and say we did."

She suppressed a giggle and allowed him to help her. He slid her gingerly into the seat and closed her door, hurrying back around to the driver's side. He closed his door and turned to Esley. "You ready to go home then?"

"You have no idea."

Neither do you, he thought to himself with a smile. "Let's go for a ride first. You want the window down?"

Esley's eyes glowed with joy for the first time since her abduction. "Oh, that would be perfect." The 'ninja persona' was gone, and he liked the replacement.

They drove out to the country and through the plowed roads. Esley rolled the window back up after no more than a couple of blocks. The wind was icy, but she'd enjoyed every minute of cold air on her face. The trees, once covered with snow were now bare, with bits of the snow still hanging on the bigger branches. It was only a few days to Thanksgiving.

As if reading her thoughts, Sawyer said, "You have any big plans for Thanksgiving dinner?"

"Oh, yes, I do," she teased. "First I'm going to fix this twenty-pound turkey, stuff it and dress it and stick it in the oven. Then, while that's cooking I'm going to bake a couple pies, and fix my favorite salad...Frogeye salad. Then I'm going to set a beautiful table complete with a candelabra and a place setting for one. It's going to be *fabulous!*"

Esley literally glowed while she planned the meal, then grinned sheepishly. "No, I have no plans, what are you doing?"

"As luck would have it, I have no plans either. What do you say we join forces and work at that Thanksgiving feast together?"

"That sounds nice. I believe I could do that."

Sawyer shot her a warning look. "Be prepared to do nothing. You will be waited on hand and foot for a while yet."

"I was afraid you were going to say that."

They were back into town now and Sawyer was driving through his neighborhood. He pulled into the driveway of his new home.

"This is the home you had *built*? It sure didn't look like this the last time I was here. This is beautiful." The wonder in Esley's eyes took in every inch of the beautiful exterior, from the second floor dormers to the bay windows on the first floor.

"You want to see the inside? We can walk slowly."

"Yes! Yes, I want to see the inside. Are you crazy? *Try* to keep me out here." Esley was already opening her door.

"Whoa there, miss. Let me get that. Just sit tight."

Esley moaned and laid her head against the seat back, trying to be patient. Sawyer could see it was an effort. He had some knots in his stomach he was most anxious to get rid of, so he didn't prolong either of their misery.

He helped her carefully out of the car. Esley even noticed the driveway, not just cleared but dry and ice free. "How do you keep the driveway so clear? It should have ice all over it!"

"I had a driveway heater installed when they laid the concrete. It's safer that way, don't you think? I won't hurt myself shoveling snow."

What Esley didn't know was that the house was all set up, unpacked. Sawyer was completely moved in. Most of the furniture had never been used and still had that new furniture smell to go with the new home smell. All the 'new' smells put together gave the place that 'model home' look. Esley oooh'ed and ahhh'ed her way through the house, and when they finished, they came back out to the living room.

Sawyer sat Esley down on the couch and he knelt before her on one knee, hoping he didn't look too corny. He pulled the small box from his pocket, opened it and displayed the ring for her to see.

"Esley Michelle Rider, would you do me the honor of being my wife and the mother of my children?"

Esley's eyes filled with tears and her hands flew to her mouth. She hated crying, she never cried in front of people, but today all of that was behind her.

"How did you find out my middle name?"

"Really?" asked Sawyer dumbfounded. "That's what you're going to say? How did I know your middle name? Seriously?"

The tears streamed down her face and she laughed gently as they covered her cheeks. Holding out his hands to his sides, he said, "So are you going to marry me or not?"

"I am," she whispered, dropping her hands to her lap. "I am going to marry you."

***

Six months later, Sawyer and Esley were married. Grant came and stood in for the best man, one Jack Baker, whose name was taped to an empty chair on the front row. It was a beautiful ceremony, and the couple became the first husband and wife detective duo in the history of the Blakely Police Department. That partnership didn't last long, however. Within a year, Sawyer and Esley began to enlarge their family, and the famous duo was once again reduced to a single detective with a new partner - a male partner this time. But Sawyer's *real* partner was home, tending a little boy named Jack Baker Kingsley.

The End

Other books by JL Redington

Juvenile Series (8-13):

The Esme Chronicles:

A Cry Out of Time
Pirates of Shadowed Time
A View Through Time
A River In Time

Broken Heart Series:

The Lies That Save Us
Solitary Tears
Veiled Secrets
Softly She Leaves
Loves New Dawning

Passions in the Park:

Love Me Anyway
Cherish Me Always
Embrace Me Forever

Duty and Deception:
Novella Series

Erased
Entangled
Enlightened
Extracted
Eradicated

Come join me on:
Facebook: Author JL Redington
Email: contact@jlredington.com
Twitter: @jlredington

Made in the USA
Charleston, SC
01 May 2016